THE BARON'S WIFE

MAGGI ANDERSEN

First published as Night Garden in 2011 by New Concept Publishing
Copyright © 2017 Maggi Andersen
The moral right of the author has been asserted.
All rights reserved.
All characters and events in this publication, other than those clearly in the public domain, are fictitious and any resemblance to real persons, living or dead, is purely coincidental.

ISBN: 9781521436370

www.maggiandersenauthor.com

DEDICATION

To my mother, who inspired me to write this book.

ACKNOWLEDGMENTS

Editor : Miranda Miller
Cover Artist: Erin Dameron Hill
Cover adapted for print by: Josephine Blake
Cover Model: Jimmy Thomas
Photographer: Bruce Heinsius

Now float above thy darkness, and now rest

Where that or thou art no unbidden guest,

Mont Blanc

Lines Written in the Vale of Chamouni.

PERCY BYSSHE SHELLEY (1792-1822)

CHAPTER ONE

Wimbledon, England, Summer 1899

    Heathcliff, a character from *Wuthering Heights*, came to Laura's mind after a brief glance at the troubled brow of the dark-haired gentleman waiting silently beside her. They'd come from different directions and sought shelter from the rain beneath a building's awning. The late afternoon was gray and dismal, the lowering clouds taking on a set-in appearance. Rain dripped steadily from the rim of the cover overhead. She pulled at her hat, which had turned into a shapeless, soggy mass, and discovered wet tendrils of her hair glued to her cheek.

    He nodded politely, and she noticed how handsome he was, with a strong, clean line to his jaw, his gray eyes rimmed with dark lashes, his firm lips faintly sensual.

    Finally, a hansom appeared, the horse splashing along the thoroughfare. The man beside her stepped out to hail the jarvey with his umbrella.

    When the driver pulled up the horse, he turned back to her. "Allow me to assist you." His beautifully modulated tone heralded a member of the upper class. His fine clothes re-enforced that view.

    She hesitated, then offered him a small smile. "Oh, but you were here first."

    He arched his dark brows. "What sort of gentleman would I be to leave a lady standing here alone?"

A chill wind swirled around her ankles and pulled at the hem of her dress. Lambeth wasn't exactly pleasant, it was true. The hall where she'd attended the meeting was around the corner. It would be empty now, for as soon as it concluded, everyone rushed away to get home before the rain set in.

"Do you want a cab or not?" The jarvey scowled at them from his seat behind the cab.

"Yes, of course I do, my good man." Holding her skirts above the flowing gutter, Laura stepped down from the pavement.

The gentleman moved forward to offer assistance. About to climb into the cramped interior, she turned. "I'm traveling to Wimbledon. Perhaps I can drop you somewhere?"

"I would appreciate it, thank you."

"Wimbledon, cabbie, but first, set me down at the nearest railway station." He joined her inside and, adding his dripping umbrella to hers on the floor, closed the wooden half-doors.

His broad shoulders touched hers as he settled beside her. At a crack of the whip the carriage rolled forward.

"Are you sure a train is the best course? What is your direction?" she asked, aware she sounded inquisitive.

"The city. I'm staying at a hotel."

So, he didn't live in London.

His gray eyes sought hers with a hint of a smile. "What are you doing out on a day like this?"

She flushed. The smell of damp wool, leather, and his expensive cologne filled the small space. "I've just attended a meeting. The Women's Suffrage Movement."

"Ah."

She tried to interpret what lay behind that single utterance. Might he disapprove? Many men did. "And you?"

"A visit to the Lambeth Workhouse."

He didn't look like a doctor. He was altogether too—too elegant. Might he be on the board? Her mother would be appalled to see her sharing a cab with a strange man, well-dressed or not. She was outraged enough that Laura had joined the movement. Mother's notion of a woman's role in life was woefully outdated.

He attempted to stretch his long legs in the confined space. His thigh brushed against hers, warm and hard through her brown wool skirt. She glanced at him. Had he done it on purpose?

"I beg your pardon." He tried to move away, but their shoulders touched again. He half turned in amused apology and offered his hand. "Look, in these close confines, I feel as if I should introduce myself. Lord Lanyon."

Of course. It was written all over him. She shook his big, gloved hand. "Miss Parr."

"Women's suffrage is a worthy cause."

"It would help our cause greatly if more men agreed."

She wondered if he meant it, or was he merely being polite? A hereditary peer would have an old-fashioned view. Women were viewed as wives and mothers, required to provide them with heirs to secure the line. And even though much was changing as the new century approached, some things stayed the same.

"I'd like to learn more, if you'd be so good as to tell me."

She took him at his word and launched into a detailed description of the movement's aspirations. "We are fighting for the right for women to vote and to have the same work opportunities offered to them as men. Why should women not?" Aware of how animated she'd become, she paused.

Interest flickered in his eyes. "I admire your dedication."

"Are you a doctor or an administrator of the workhouse?" she asked, to change the subject.

"No, a political matter, Miss Parr."

"You might know my father, Sir Edmund Parr." She thought it unlikely. Her father was a member of the Commons.

He nodded. "We have met once or twice."

The carriage rocked violently as the horse broke from its trot. "We seem to be traveling very fast," she said with alarm as the houses along the road flashed past.

Lord Lanyon opened the panel to the rear of the roof. "Slow down, driver!"

A loud, rambunctious ditty drifted down.

"Hoy! Slow down, man!" Lord Lanyon yelled, banging on the roof.

A face appeared above them along with the waft of strong spirits. "Right you are, guvnor."

"The fellow is drunk," Lanyon said. He banged on the roof once more, but the horse continued at the same frightening speed, the hansom swaying as they careened along the street. Laura found herself clutching Lord Lanyon's sleeve.

Suddenly, a juddering was accompanied by a loud crash. Laura was thrown forward, banging her knees against the door. Lord Lanyon's hands gripped her waist.

The carriage shuddered to a stop, the horse whinnying and snorting. People crowded around them yelling curses at the driver. He shouted back at them.

Lord Lanyon removed his hands from her waist. "Are you all right?"

Her breathlessness was not entirely due to the accident. "I think so."

"At least the dolt has released the doors."

When Lord Lanyon assisted her down onto the pavement, her knee throbbed and a flash of pain shot through her ankle.

She gasped. "I...I'm afraid I must have wrenched my ankle."

He placed a strong arm around her. There was now a small crowd gathered around the two hansoms which had locked wheels. A bobby in his dark cloak appeared. The drivers' voices were raised in a heated argument, the crowd interjecting with their version of events.

"We'd best leave," Lord Lanyon said. Before she could answer, he'd tossed their umbrellas onto the pavement and had lifted her into his arms.

"Really, I don't think this is necessary..." She lost her breath as he carried her effortlessly across the road, and she a strapping female who prided herself on being athletic and strong. She was placed gently on her feet beside a lamppost.

"Hang on there for a minute." He stepped out into the road and, placing two fingers to his mouth, whistled. Another hansom threaded its way through the bottleneck caused by the accident and pulled up in front of them.

"Allow me to take you home," Lord Lanyon said.

"Really, that's not necessary," Laura said faintly. If her mother found him to be a bachelor, she'd see them married, even if it took the last breath in her body.

"I insist."

Feeling unusually compliant, she allowed him to usher her inside.

He climbed in after her with the umbrellas.

"But Wimbledon is so far out of your way."

He had a lovely smile. "I am returning to an empty hotel room, Miss Parr, where I shall partake of a lonely dinner. I really don't mind."

Laura found herself wondering if there was a Lady Lanyon. "Then you must stay to dinner." It was the least she could do. She would handle her mother.

"That's kind of you, Miss Parr." He laughed. "Did I sound like I needed rescuing?"

She laughed with him. "Only a little." It was nonsense, of course. The broad-shouldered, strapping fellow in his fine wool coat and French kid leather gloves was anything but.

The cab stopped outside her parent's home, Grisewood Hall, newly built in the Queen Anne style with a soaring roof, turrets and bay windows. Shiny carriages lined up along the avenue of dripping beech trees. A pair of gray horses reared nervously as a horseless carriage appeared, belching smoke. The rain had returned, heavier still. Grooms darted about with umbrellas as ladies wearing cloaks over their tea gowns rushed to their carriages with squeals of dismay.

"My parents are hosting a cocktail party. I'd forgotten about it."

"Then I'd best leave you here," Lord Lanyon said.

"Do come in," Laura said. "It will be almost over."

"I'm not dressed." He removed his hat and ran long fingers through his black hair, sending droplets flying.

"As if that matters. You need to dry off or you'll catch pneumonia."

"How is your ankle? Shall I assist you inside?"

"It feels much better," she said hastily, not wishing to be swept inside the house in his arms.

Lord Lanyon paid the driver and followed her to where the butler stood at the open front door.

"Good afternoon, Miss Laura." Barker took their coats and hats.

"Lord Lanyon got caught in the rain, Barker. Could you send a maid for a towel?"

"Certainly." Barker hurried to give the order.

"Are your clothes damp?" Laura asked, resisting the urge to place her hand on the double-breasted tailcoat covering his broad chest. "My father's coats are about the same size, although they would be shorter in the sleeves."

He smiled. "Please don't worry. My overcoat and hat bore the brunt of it."

Lord Lanyon disappeared into the powder room with the towel. He emerged with his hair neatly combed.

She was suddenly aware of her own disarray. "Come and meet

my parents." Tidying her hair with her fingers, she led him down the corridor to the drawing room. Entering, she searched for her mother among the guests. She guided him across the expanse of soft carpet while people greeted her, Lord Lanyon nodding to the inquisitive guests. Ladies in their organdie, taffeta and silk gowns, their hats trimmed with plumes, ribbons and flowers, followed his progress with unbecoming eagerness, it seemed to Laura.

What would such a man make of her parents' home? The drawing room was suddenly revealed in a new light. Everything was so new it squeaked. Mother had ruthlessly decorated the reception rooms in coffee and cream. A pair of chiffoniers displayed an abundance of porcelain and colored glass. Framed prints covered the wallpapered walls. At the windows, white muslin curtains stirred below their scalloped velvet valances, and the smoke from the gentlemen's pipes and cigars in the adjacent smoking room fought with the women's heady perfume.

Laura's mother rose from the cream serpentine-backed upholstered sofa flanking the fireplace to greet them.

"Mother, I'd like to introduce Lord Lanyon. His lordship and I got caught in the rain and shared a cab. I've invited him to dinner."

Her mother's frown of annoyance at the state of Laura's clothes melted away at the mention of his name. She gave him her hand. "How do you do, my lord? You are most welcome."

"I'm sure an extra guest will prove a great nuisance, Lady Parr."

"Not at all. With my husband's work, we always expect an extra guest or two," her mother said briskly. "Sir Edmund will be delighted. Laura, take Lord Lanyon through to the conservatory."

Her father held court among the ferns and orchids with the other smokers exiled from the drawing room. Laura paused at the door. "If you'll excuse me, Lord Lanyon, I must do something with my hair."

His gray eyes studied her auburn locks. "Don't let me keep you." He smiled. "I shouldn't like you to come down with pneumonia either."

She resisted tucking the damp hair which sat heavily against her nape into place. "I'll just introduce you."

After her father greeted Lord Lanyon, Laura left them. Her intention to hurry to her room was halted when a lady approached her. "Hello, Laura."

"Mrs. Courtney-Smith, how nice to see you."

The politician's wife was dressed in a plum silk gown, her pigeon breast adorned with several rows of Venetian glass beads. Her gaze swept over Laura's disordered hair and down to the damp hem of her dress.

Mrs. Courtney-Smith made it her business to know everyone who might be of benefit to her husband. "I don't believe I've met your escort?"

"Lord Lanyon, Mrs. Courtney-Smith." Laura resisted explaining how they'd met. She was already aware of the necessity to avoid facing the lady's censure. One word from her and her mother would clamp down on her activities with the suffrage.

She raised her eyebrows. "The baron? I believe I read about him in the social column of the *Times*. A widower. But not for long I suspect."

He was a widower? Laura wondered what the article had said about him, as Mrs. Courtney-Smith launched into a potted version of her day. As soon as she could extricate herself politely, Laura made for the door. Fortunately, no one else sought to detain her. Her father invited many new acquaintances to their home. He worked hard and was an ambitious member of the government who hoped to become prime minister. Father had always encouraged Laura to pursue her dreams. His support had allowed her to sit in on lectures at the university while accompanied by her maid. But although she finished the degree, she could not claim it as hers.

Laura returned after changing into a cream silk tea gown embellished with opulent lace, a tight corselet at the waist and a low square-cut neckline. She found Lord Lanyon still closeted with her father in the conservatory. They were talking politics, and she would have loved to join them. Annoyed that women were excluded, she returned to the drawing room.

Mother beckoned her from the sofa, a sherry glass in her hand. "Well! That is an improvement, I must say. Did you really have to appear in such a disheveled state?"

"I can't control the weather, Mother."

Her mother was not in the mood to argue. "Lord Lanyon is an interesting man. Where did you meet him?"

"We shared a cab. There was an accident. The driver was drunk."

"Sharing a hansom?" Her mother took a sip from her glass. "Simply not done in my day."

Her mother had a knack for passing over details which did not interest her. Annoyed, Laura resisted mentioning that her mother had never been in a hansom.

Lord Lanyon was not placed near her at the table, and as fashion was discussed on her right, and staffing problems on her left, she found the whole affair quite tedious. When she later saw Lord Lanyon to the door, she offered her hand. "It has been a pleasure to meet you, my lord."

He held her hand in his for a long moment. "I have tickets for a concert at the Royal Opera House on Saturday evening—the pianist, Paderewski. The person accompanying me cannot attend, and I don't wish to go alone. I hope you'll take pity on me once more." He tilted his head with a smile. "These occasions are so much better shared, don't you agree?"

Paderewski! She would love to hear him play. How could she resist? It was only a concert after all. "I'd be pleased to come. Thank you."

He nodded. "I shall telephone and ask your father."

"Yes. Good night."

He opened his umbrella and hurried out to the cab her father had ordered for him. What had she done? Her mother would never give up now until she married the man.

Nathaniel entered his hotel room and sat in an overstuffed chair, gazing out through the window at the blurred row of lights along the Thames. He'd come to town to present a bill to Parliament, and then return to Cornwall. He was not seeking a bride. In fact, he had decided not to marry again.

Laura Parr. What was it about her that drew him? Before going in to dinner, Lady Parr had expressed her frustration at Laura's modern views. "What is happening to young women today?" she'd said with a moue. "Laura is too independent. I am at my wit's end to know what to do with her." She had taken his arm and led him toward the dining room, with Laura and her father following, he hoped out of earshot. "My daughter read far too many radical essays at university," she continued, "and they have filled her head with useless knowledge. Marriage to a strong man will settle her down."

Should she become his wife, Miss Parr would have to be prepared to deal with tenants and villagers, and suffer a dearth of the intellectual conversation she was accustomed to, and he sensed, very much enjoyed. The abbey was miles from a large town. A young lady such as she would find it difficult to accept the way things were at Wolfram. Had he the right to extinguish her youthful romanticism? Was he losing his good sense?

His struggle for peace had been so tenuous, and he suspected she would turn his life upside down and dig into secrets it suited him best to leave buried. But when her eyes had met his in the Parr's entry foyer, he'd have sworn a frisson of excitement, breathtaking with promise, passed between them. His body had leapt to life, as if he'd been in a long sleep. Such a coltish beauty, with her coil of auburn hair baring her long, graceful neck. As he returned in the carriage to the city, he was already confident of Miss Parr's passionate nature. It was evident in the flash of her beautiful green eyes and her willful mouth that he wanted badly to kiss. A serious young woman, she seemed completely unaware of her charm. She had a frankness that he liked.

Damn it. He wanted her. And for a young woman as gently reared as Laura, that could only mean marriage. Her independent spirt and strength of character made him hopeful theirs would be a good future despite everything. A passionate one if he was any judge.

Nathaniel frowned and drummed his fingers on the arms of the chair. He doubted even this fiery beauty could penetrate the thickness of the wall he'd built around himself in the last two years. Would what he offered of himself be enough? Was he mad to think that a wife as engaging as Laura could charm the villagers, quell the gossip and return Wolfram to the home it once was?

He left the room, wondering if he might find Horace Tothill at his club.

"Nathaniel!" Horace rose to shake his hand. "Good to see you in London. A session at the Lords I gather?"

"I've been doing some research for a project I'm considering. A much-needed orphanage for the Southwest."

"A commendable venture, by the sound of it. What news of Wolfram?"

Nathaniel signaled a waiter. "What are you drinking?"

"Whiskey, thanks."

When the waiter scurried off to fill their order, Horace ran a hand through his sandy hair. "You haven't answered my question."

"Wolfram? Not much changes, Horace."

"But it's been two years. I would have thought…"

Nathaniel shook his head, not wishing to discuss it. "Nothing untoward has occurred since, but people have long memories."

"Especially when they're fed a lot of outrageous lies."

Nathaniel accepted his drink from the waiter. He raised his glass to Horace. "I have made a decision, however."

Horace's brown eyes studied him. "Whatever it is pleases you at least."

"I trust that it will. I plan to marry."

"Well, that is one for the books, I must say. Very good news indeed!"

Nathaniel offered him a small smile. "Let us hope so."

CHAPTER TWO

At breakfast the next morning, Laura's mother tackled her in a purposeful manner. "Lord Lanyon sought permission from your father to take you to the opera." She studied Laura. "You've made it plain that you're not ready to give up your freedom, as you put it, to marry. May I ask why you've accepted his invitation?"

Laura finished buttering her toast and reached for the strawberry preserve. "Because I want to hear the pianist, Paderewski. He's brilliant."

Her mother added hot water to the teapot. "Lanyon is a very attractive man, although perhaps a little swarthy for my taste. Your father wasn't the most handsome of men."

"Didn't you marry for love, Mother?"

Lady Parr poured milk into her cup. "What a question. Marriage isn't about love."

"Can't it be?"

"A good marriage isn't based on passion. It's a business partnership, which can, if you choose wisely, become one of mutual satisfaction."

She'd never witnessed real affection between her parents, but she still hoped to one day experience it herself. "Did you never want something more?"

Mother frowned. "I'm not the one we are discussing. You are twenty-two years old. If you manage to lead Lanyon to the altar, the whole of London society will be at your feet." She topped up Laura's teacup from the blue-and-white porcelain teapot. "The barony is an ancient one. It goes without saying that Lanyon is an excellent catch. His country seat is in Cornwall, once an abbey, I believe."

Laura firmed her lips, refusing to revisit the old argument again. She planned to find employment soon and move into lodgings in Bloomsbury with some of the single women from the movement. She pushed away her half-eaten toast and touched a napkin to her lips. "It's only a concert, Mother."

"Must you always make things difficult, Laura? Your sister would have welcomed this," she said with a clash of the silver teaspoon against the dainty floral china. "Eliza would have been pleased."

Laura took a slow, deep breath. "I am not Eliza."

"New shoes are definitely in order." Lady Parr continued, her mind already ticking off an invisible list. "Robb shall drive us into London this afternoon. We'll go to Worth for a pair of French kid opera slippers."

Laura was so tired of her mother comparing her with Eliza she wanted to scream. But she'd learned to hold her tongue. Since her twin sister died of diphtheria, Laura had found it difficult to rise above the sadness that still hung over them like a pall. She seemed unable to assuage her own grief, let alone her mother's. She urgently wanted to break free, to become an independent woman, aware she'd have to fight her parents as well as society's expectations. But if she didn't, she'd sink into abject despair.

"Lord Lanyon is a widower," her mother continued, breaking into Laura's thoughts.

"I know."

"He told you?"

"No. Mrs. Courtney-Smith mentioned it."

"There's not much that lady misses." Her mother's gaze settled on her. "His wife passed away. Two years ago, I believe."

"How did she die?"

"I don't know the circumstances, but she was with child. How the poor man must have suffered."

"Indeed," Laura said softly. Had she caught a glimpse of sadness in his gray eyes? "Which gown should I wear, Mother? The blue?"

"The pale-yellow silk Charmeuse with the sash at the waist." Her mother's tone became brisk like a hound scenting a fox. "And my pearls."

She must keep on her toes. Her mother planned to have her marry this man. A plot to bring it about would already be in place. While Laura hated to be manipulated, she was confident she could enjoy Lanyon without risking her freedom, and looked forward to seeing him again.

On Saturday evening, Lanyon called for her in a smart black carriage, his own this time, with a crest on the door panel, which her mother took note of, a speculative gleam in her eyes. In his superbly cut evening clothes he looked every inch a peer. His black tailcoat fitted his broad shoulders; pearl buttons peeked from his shirtfront above the white silk waistcoat. An elegant stripe ran the length of his trousers, emphasizing long, strong thighs. His black silk top hat and gold-topped cane completed the picture of sartorial elegance.

"My, he looks well tonight," her mother said, as she accompanied Laura to her bedroom to fetch her cape. "Such a fine figure of a man."

Oddly unsettled by his dark good looks, Laura smoothed suede gloves to her elbow. Surely a man such as Lanyon wouldn't be interested in her beyond a mild flirtation. He would marry a debutante from a family as old and noble as his.

"The most important thing is for the two of you to suit," her mother said, her eyebrows forming twin peaks. "And I believe you will."

Laura wasn't sure on what basis her mother formed that opinion. But for once, they agreed on something: he was handsome. Mary settled the waist-length, sable-collared evening cloak over Laura's shoulders, and she tucked a scented lace handkerchief in her beaded reticule.

"Perfect." Her mother tweaked the bow at the back of Laura's gown. "Don't spoil the evening with your foolish ideas of women's independence. I assure you that Lanyon will not find it at all interesting."

"How can you be sure?" A wave of apprehension swept through her. What if she bored him?

"He is thirty-two and needs an heir." Her mother smoothed Laura's fur collar. "His interest in you is not intellectual, but rather in finding a wife, a suitable mother for his children. And after all, that is a woman's role in life. Especially those of the landed gentry."

Laura held her tongue. She studied her appearance in the mirror and had to admit her mother was right about the pastel gown. It did suit her.

On the way to the concert, Lord Lanyon's dark gaze studied her in the gloom of the carriage lights. "You look like an angel."

"How deceptive of me. I am far from angelic."

"Such a heated retort." He smiled. "Perhaps I was clumsy. A lady might wish for a more elegant homage to her charms."

"I don't wish for flowery compliments, my lord." She chewed her bottom lip. She'd been ungracious. She still seethed from her mother's interference. "I'm sorry. I'm annoyed with my mother. Please forgive me."

"You and your mother are at odds?"

"We don't see eye to eye on some things. The world is changing rapidly, but Mother hangs onto a past where women could do little more than be an adjunct to a man. Merely there to give him children."

"Children are important though, are they not?"

"Well, of course." And to someone like him especially. She took a deep breath, determined to get her point across. "But there are other roles for women besides childbearing. A woman could juggle more than one, I feel sure. I know I could."

"Perhaps you would like to follow your father into politics."

"If it was possible, but it isn't."

"I can understand your frustration, my dear."

Did he mean it? She stared at his handsome face, searching for a sign that he merely patronized her. "Women do achieve great things. But they have to fight every step of the way."

"A wife of mine would need the skills of a politician. There's a lot she must deal with."

"What, for instance?"

"A large staff, tenants, those who look to the baroness to become involved in village affairs. Raising my children, but that goes without saying." He eyed her carefully. "My wife would be my partner in running the abbey, as well as my partner in life."

The carriage swung around a corner and threw them together. She felt the warmth of his body through her gown. Laura lost the thread of her argument as a surprising sense of yearning filled her. "I don't dislike the idea of children," she said, tentatively.

His smile stretched into a grin, his teeth white against his olive skin. "I'm pleased to hear it."

The carriage deposited them outside the Opera House in Covent Garden where they joined the milling crowd dressed in their opera cloaks and finery. As they moved through the entrance hall, Laura caught snatches of conversation. Men were discussing the Boer War. She had questioned her father about it. Although he was reluctant to tell her much of the unpleasant details, the broadsheets had filled in the gaps.

She'd read John Stuart Mill who said that although war was an ugly thing, moralists and patriots who think that nothing is worth a war are much worse. She would like to have Lord Lanyon's opinion.

He tucked her hand into the crook of his arm, and they climbed the red-carpeted staircase together. She glanced up at him, curious to discover more about him. "If women were in charge of the country, there would be no wars," she said, becoming purposefully provocative to draw his response.

A dark eyebrow raised a fraction. "You may be right."

"If our country was in danger, would you fight?"

"Every able-bodied man would." His fingers tightened around her arm. "What a solemn discussion. Let's enjoy the evening, shall we?"

Chastened, Laura wondered if she'd shocked him. Or worse, had he found her immature?

From the lavish opera box, she gazed down on the stage, soaking up every nuance of the music as the pianist created magic. She turned once to glance at Lord Lanyon and found him watching her, a soft smile on his lips.

Later, as they stood awaiting the carriage, she remained deeply affected by the superb virtuoso. "I enjoyed tonight very much. Thank you for inviting me."

"I enjoyed watching you." The look in his gray eyes sent her pulse racing.

"You didn't lose yourself in the music?"

"Music and art are agreeable, Laura. But true passion comes from living."

"Life would be dry as dust without them."

The beginning of a smile lifted the corners of his mouth. "But we don't have to live without them, do we?" He assisted her into the carriage and sat beside her, taking her gloved hand in his.

She should protest at the familiarity of his gesture, but she liked the firm decisiveness of his hand clasping hers. The carriage rolled away, the horses trotting down Bow Street.

"I suspect you wish for a spirited conversation," he said. "And I promise we will talk of these things at another time. I have something more important to discuss."

Laura drew in a deep breath. That meant he wanted to see her again. She had been afraid he might not.

"My estate in Cornwall demands much of my time, as do my parliamentary duties." His gaze settled on her mouth, causing her pulse to flutter madly. "I don't have time to court you, Laura. I must return to Cornwall in a week. And it will be some weeks before I can return to London. I'd like this settled between us one way or the other before I leave."

She blinked. "Settled?"

"I require a wife, someone who can take on a good deal. I've come to believe you would perform many of those tasks with grace and competence. I like to think you would enjoy it."

With a soft gasp, she dropped her gaze to her lap. How could he have made such a swift assessment of her abilities? She couldn't help being flattered. "My plans don't include marriage."

"You've made that plain, but I hope to change your mind. Are you sure you want those things above all else? What a terrible waste that would be, and what a half-life you would resign yourself to. You are made for more than becoming a fighter for women's rights, Laura. You have a great passion for life. Are you going to deny that part of you?"

He undid the pearl button on her glove and peeled it back, exposing the skin on the underside of her wrist. The warm touch of his lips made her tremble.

She eased her hand away. He was so sure of himself, and of her, apparently. She swallowed her annoyance at how much he unsettled her, wishing he wasn't quite so intriguing. "You feel you know me on such a short acquaintance?"

"I know enough. And the rest, I look forward to discovering." There was a wealth of experience in the depths of his eyes. Sadness too, which was not surprising.

If she did contemplate marriage, she doubted he'd have the qualities she sought in a husband. He was rather enigmatic. Would they share true intimacy, love?

"Will you marry me, Laura?"

She stared at him tongue-tied, her thoughts scattering. She'd always felt in control with the men she met, but Lord Lanyon was a very different proposition. He made her question her plans for her future. She'd been drawn to him at their first meeting, but he would not be an easy man to know.

"I shan't marry for years, if at all," she said stiffly, dismayed by her response to his charm. "I don't believe in the institution. Marriage stunts a woman's growth. It's the legal subordination of a woman to a man."

His lips twitched. Was he laughing at her? "That would depend on the husband. And the marriage."

She bridled. "Then it's rather a gamble, isn't it? How would one know for certain until they lived with someone?"

"I agree that one must trust the person they pledge their life to. But there are many delights in marriage you are discounting."

"I believe most can be obtained outside of marriage." She felt bold expressing such a view, but if she hoped to shock him, he merely shook his head.

"Not children."

Heat flooded her cheeks. "Perhaps not. But I also have other pursuits in mind."

"What are they?"

"I don't wish to bore you."

He seemed to enjoy her struggle for composure. "Nonsense. Everything about you interests me."

Laura wished he wouldn't look at her like that. As if he found her endlessly fascinating. She was quite sure she wasn't. If it was feigned, it was a clever ploy, for what woman wouldn't enjoy it? "I want to continue to work for women's independence. And I'd like to travel. See the wonderful art and sculptures I've only viewed in books."

"I applaud your desire to fight for women's rights, but the movement is in its infancy, Laura. These things will come, but it will take years. Join the fight when you really can make a difference. As my wife, I would be proud to assist you with that sometime in the future. In the meantime, we can travel, visit the art treasures of the world. The Louvre in Paris, all the splendor Rome has to offer, the Parthenon in Greece."

She breathed in deeply, as visions of those wonderful places filled her head. "You have been there?"

"I have visited them all, and more."

"Then you may not wish to view them again."

He smiled. "But I would. I'd love to show them all to you."

She gasped when his hand squeezed her waist, which seemed like an act of possession. Leaning forward, he took her chin in his big hand and gazed into her eyes, his warm and imploring. "Will you think about it, at least?"

His deep voice beguiled her, and she was dismayed at the magnitude of her own desire, even as a warning voice in her head urged her to delay. "I would not want to raise your hopes."

He lowered his head to hers. "You already have."

He meant to kiss her. She closed her eyes, inviting his touch. His mouth grazed her earlobe and feathered soft kisses across her cheek, then firm lips claimed hers. He inhaled sharply. His strong arms encircled her, his kiss masterful, practiced. But there was raw hunger in his kiss too, along with intent. She was shocked by the awakening response he stirred within her.

He ended the kiss, his mouth hovering close to hers, his breath warming her lips where the imprint of his remained. "Say yes, Laura. We'll have a wonderful life together."

She was annoyed to find herself trembling. She must not forget what such a life could mean. Village life would never equal the excitement of London. She would be isolated from like-minded people. She might feel more trapped than she did now.

Laura pushed him gently away, for when he was close, he consumed her thoughts. "I need time. It's too soon."

"Do you believe in destiny?"

"I suppose I do."

"I believe we were destined to be together."

She couldn't discount it entirely, the way she'd been drawn to him from the moment they met. She'd never felt that for any man. She wanted very much to be with him. But she didn't fool herself why that was. They shared a strong physical attraction. Still, what he offered *was* exciting. To become his baroness and live in an ancient home. The cost was her liberty. Might she have the romance without marriage?

Laura sank against him, wanting him to kiss her again, her deep breaths failing to calm her. She sought to offer some form of argument, to slow things down, but her mind, usually so clear, became befogged at what she saw as his assault. He rushed her, overwhelmed her, and she suspected he meant to. And he would continue until he got what he wanted. She already knew that about him. Men born into privilege never expected anything less.

He cradled her face in his hands and plundered her mouth again more urgently, his breath deepening. The carriage rocked as it negotiated a corner. Laura had no idea where they were, or who might see them behaving so scandalously. Neither did she care. She slid her fingers through the silky hair at his nape and returned his kiss, desire unfurling, warming her body.

It was he who drew away. "I think it best we stop." He reclaimed her hand and knitted his long fingers with hers.

Regaining her breath and what was left of her composure, Laura sank back into a corner of the carriage, a heartbeat away from his disturbing presence.

"There's an exhibition of Art Nouveau style at the Grafton Gallery in Mayfair tomorrow. Is it of interest to you?"

He knew just how to entice her. "Yes. I saw it advertised."

"Then see it with me. Tomorrow afternoon at two. Your mother might like to accompany us."

"Perhaps she would. Thank you."

Her mother would be overjoyed. If Laura sent him back to Cornwall without seeing him again, her life at home would become unbearable. And even though she couldn't marry him, she did want to spend more time in his company.

"I've sent Mary to bed." Mother had waited up for her, and as Laura undressed, she told her about his invitation, but not his proposal. "Lord Lanyon has invited you too, Mother."

"I'm to arrange the flowers in the church tomorrow. He was the perfect gentleman? He didn't behave inappropriately?"

"Of course not." Trying to settle her own rampaging emotions was enough. She could not deal with her mother's.

"Lord Lanyon's intentions would be entirely honorable. You have no need of a chaperone." She hung up Laura's dress. "Do you like him, Laura?"

"He's interesting."

"Find out more about Wolfram. Get to know him."

"I'm not considering marriage, Mother."

"It's what he obviously expects. He's a busy man. You should not give him a false impression."

Was she? Laura suffered a wave of guilt. She only knew that she would be deeply disappointed not to see him again.

CHAPTER THREE

The next afternoon, Lord Lanyon accompanied Laura around the gallery. She had a refusal prepared should he press his suit again, but he did not mention it. She felt oddly piqued. Had he given up on her so easily?

The exhibition proved fascinating. The William Morris collection absorbed her, and when they left, she bubbled over with enthusiasm. He agreed with most of her comments while revealing a good eye for color and design.

As the carriage approached her home, she found it extremely difficult to end their association.

"I have the day free tomorrow," he said. "I fancy a picnic if it remains fine. Might I entice you to accompany me to Richmond Park?"

She should refuse him. Cut it off cleanly now. And with words to that effect forming in her mind, she met his sensual gaze. "That sounds perfectly lovely," she found herself saying. "I'm not sure it will be permitted, however." Laura hoped her mother would agree. It appeared that she wasn't ready to see him walk out of her life. Quite yet.

"I shall reassure your parents that I will take good care of you," he said with his usual confidence.

And of course, his confidence was well placed. Her mother

beamed when Laura asked her. "Yes, you may go. Your virtue shall be perfectly safe in a carriage. Richmond Park will be filled with visitors during this dry spell."

Mother immediately turned her attention to Laura's clothing. "The bronze straw trimmed with feathers and flowers, I think." She tapped her chin with a finger. "Teamed with the flannel Eton jacket and skirt in Dresden blue over a lawn shirt-waist. Dressy, yet suitable for an informal outing."

After telephoning the next morning to confirm, Nathaniel arrived, dashing in cream wool trousers, a striped gray and white coat with silver buttons, and a straw boater on his dark hair. They traveled in a brougham, a carriage following behind. It was perfect weather for a picnic, the sky a deep Wedgewood blue and barely a cloud in sight.

Her white parasol shielded her face from the sun, as Laura strolled with him along a meandering path through a meadow of wild grasses, thick with bluebells and harebells. Behind them, two servants carried a wicker basket into a grove of oak trees where King Henry VIII hunted deer centuries ago. A herd still grazed over a rise, a huge stag keeping guard. It occurred to Laura that Lanyon might have brought someone here before. He seemed sure of his destination. They passed a family party gathered beside the pond, the air filled with the children's sweet voices as they tossed bread to the ducks.

A servant spread out the rug in a sheltered spot, while shooing away a gray partridge intent on building a nest. The hamper was unpacked, and the champagne cork popped. Then they were alone.

"I trust this will be sufficient. My hotel prepared it." A feast of ham, roast fowl, lobster, bread rolls, salad, and strawberries and cream for dessert.

She laughed. "My goodness. We could feed an army."

Laura sipped chilled champagne from a crystal flute, while very aware of the big man beside her.

Despite her need for independence, the significance of her carefully laid out plans seemed to diminish when she was with him, her gaze constantly drawn to him. Was she foolish to consider that married life might offer her more freedom than that of a spinster? Her parents' marriage hardly inspired confidence. Her mother seemed content to assist her father socially in his career. If she ever had dreams of her own, she'd never spoken of them.

Laura was caught by his male strength and grace as he spread his long legs over the rug, a respectful distance from her. She took a bite of lobster, which was fresh and cold and smelled of the sea. She'd never been to Cornwall.

"Your mother told me that you lost your sister to illness," he said, his eyes filled with sympathy. "I wanted to say how sorry I am."

"Almost three years ago, now."

It seemed less, for Liza had been taken from them so quickly. She and her sister hadn't shared the same interests. While Laura's time was spent reading books, studying art and playing tennis, Eliza and Mother enjoyed decorating the new house and spent hours discussing clothes while studying the fashion magazines. But she and Eliza had still been extremely close. When Laura was in low spirits, Eliza buoyed her up and vice versa. Laura swallowed. Death was so final; it made a mockery of planning the future.

She pushed her plate away. "Did your wife die from an illness?"

"No. A fall."

By his tone, she gathered it wasn't something he wished to discuss. He wiped his hands on the linen napkin and propped himself on his elbows. "We might help each other to put the sad past behind us."

Laura sucked in a breath. He made it sound very appealing. Despite his relaxed pose, Laura sensed the restless energy in him, as if he could spring into action at any moment.

"I have yet to have your answer to my proposal," he said. "But first, is there something that concerns you? Anything you'd like to ask me?"

She'd lain awake the night before, trying to understand her own mind. She needed to know more about his life, what his marriage had been like. Had he recovered from her death? It would be inappropriate for her to ask. Now was not the time to speak of the departed. Laura felt alive and sensed he felt the same. "Tell me more about Wolfram," she asked instead.

"It was once an abbey. Wolfram was built in the most glorious place on God's earth." His voice held a rasp of pride. "I can't put its appeal into mere words. You must see it." His gaze caught hers. "Do you want to see it, Laura?"

"I've never seen the sea."

Her attraction to him had been powerful and immediate, and not merely physical. There was so much more that drew her to him. Laura had forced herself to contemplate how she'd feel if she sent him away then read about his marriage in the social pages of *The Times*. Her chest tightened at the surprising sense of loss.

"I promise to worship you, body and soul, Laura Parr." His heavy-lidded gray eyes held an invitation to more earthly pleasures than spiritual.

She touched her bottom lip with her tongue. An ache had been sparked by that first indelible kiss in the carriage. A searing need which was new to her. "Do we have to marry? I rather thought we might become lovers."

Raising his gaze from her mouth, his eyes widened and he chuckled. "Lovers?"

Embarrassed, Laura toyed with her hat. "I don't find it amusing."

"A gently reared young woman like you, my mistress?"

"I fail to see how the way I was raised has anything to do with it."

His eyes darkened, grew serious. "You were meant to be a wife, not a mistress. Revered by her husband, not treated like a whore."

He expressed it so brutally. He meant to, she was sure. Under Laura's numb fingers, a daisy fell off her hat. She flicked it away; she'd never liked the shape of the straw anyway. "I've never wanted to be tied to anyone."

Nathaniel pushed himself into a sitting position as if he was ready to leave. Was he irritated? "My dear Laura, you are innocent in the ways of the world. If I wanted a mistress, I would look for someone very different from you."

She flushed. "Because of my inexperience?"

He nodded. "That, and other...considerations."

"Am I not desirable enough for a mistress?"

"You are most desirable. If we were not in plain sight, I could show you how much. I might still..." He leaned forward and kissed her. The noise of people enjoying the sunny day beyond the shrubbery receded as her pulse pounded in her ears. She breathed him in, the smell of clean male overlaid by his fresh cologne. How quickly he'd become familiar to her. It was a restrained kiss, but her blood still sang through her veins.

He edged a respectable distance away. "Say yes. Or I'll kiss you again, and this time, your reputation may well suffer."

Laura almost shivered at his threat. It was vexing how unsophisticated he made her feel. She could throw caution to the wind here on this blanket in broad daylight, but he was quite controlled. She admitted to being hopelessly beguiled. It appeared that marriage would be her only choice if she wanted him in her life. And she did. "I'll marry you, Nathaniel."

His gray eyes sparkled, and he raised her hand to his lips. "Darling, I promise you will never come to regret it."

She realized in that moment that he'd been confident of her answer. Was she so easy to read?

He sat back, and a corner of his mouth twitched. "I have to ask. You're not marrying me just to escape your mother, are you?"

Laura gave a gurgle of laughter. "A little perhaps." She studied his face, the strong chin, his sensual mouth and lustrous black hair. She wanted to ask him if he believed in love at first sight, but she feared he would accuse her of youthful romanticism. "I like the idea of standing by your side, aiding you in your endeavors."

He raised his eyebrows, a grin tugging at his lips. "I like that too."

"And should I wish to do more," she continued, testing the waters. "You would permit it?"

He leaned forward and kissed her nose. "Providing you don't go off on your own to study art in some foreign city, or take a lover."

There was a steely note beneath his words. Laura felt confident she would never wish for another lover; the man before her would fulfil all her dreams of love. But she had inherited her determination from her father. And one day she would take up the suffrage cause again, when the time was right.

Nathaniel jumped to his feet. He leaned down to take her hands and drew her to her feet. "Now I must do the proper thing and ask your father for your hand."

His servants appeared and began to pack things away. There was so much food uneaten. "Could the food be given to the poor?" she asked. "Or a children's orphanage?"

He smiled. "It will be done."

They walked back to the carriage hand in hand. Her parents would be pleased. Her mother especially. While she could never take the place of Eliza, perhaps distance would improve their uneasy relationship. Her pulse thudded as life blossomed like a rose opening to the sun. Admittedly, Nathaniel had wooed and enticed her to accept him. But she no longer feared landing herself in a dreary marriage in a remote part of England. No place where Nathaniel was could ever be dreary. And she looked forward to a chance to become fully herself; to immerse herself in a new world where her energy and need to be useful could make a difference, and with a husband she was already half in love with.

After departing from his newly betrothed's residence with Lord and Lady Parr's best wishes for his marriage to their daughter, Nathaniel leaned against the leather squab and crossed his arms, his doubts reappearing to plague him. He had not been entirely honest with Laura. He had little faith in a happy marriage. Was it wrong to hope he could offer her a good life, while not giving too much of himself? His parent's marriage ended in scandal and disaster. He could still taste the sour horror of betrayal and refused to be hurt deeply again. For all her bravado, spirit and intelligence, Laura was an innocent. She must be protected while Wolfram remained a cauldron of unrest.

He placed his booted foot over his knee and sighed. It was done. There was no going back, and he didn't wish to. Laura's effect on him was like water to a man dying of thirst. She lifted his spirits and imbued him with an emotion that had been absent for a long time: hope. But try as he might, he still couldn't shrug off the fear of what he might have unleashed into her life.

CHAPTER FOUR

Laura sat across the table from her aunt in her Camden townhouse. The room was a riot of flowers, birds and peacock feathers on curtains, sofa cushions, rugs and the wallpaper. The furniture, carved with flowers and feathers, was stained to a black ebony finish and gilded, and the blue and white porcelain stacked on the shelves displayed a similar theme. Vases of lilies perfumed the air, and pots of orchids lined the windowsill.

In the midst of this exotic splendor, Laura's sweet-faced Aunt Dora appeared like a plain brown bird in her shapeless linen dress.

Laura swiveled the large solitaire diamond ring on her finger, causing a brilliant flash of color. "Mother doesn't want me to contribute anything to this wedding. I had to fight her tooth and nail to wear a tailor-made suit to Cornwall. Perfectly suitable for train travel, but she is firmly of the belief that men hate to see women in suits. She finally agreed when I chose pink brocade from the House of Redfern."

"Catherine is in her element. You can't deny her this moment, Laura." Although Aunt Dora refrained from mentioning that there would be no more weddings after Laura's, it hovered in the air.

Laura took a bite of crumpet while her aunt poured her another cup of tea. She loved to come to this cluttered little house. Her visits to her aunt, a well-respected poet, often proved to be a delightful surprise, especially when her rooms were crammed with artists and writers. Oscar Wilde had once attended one of Aunt Dora's soirées.

Her aunt's sleek black cat leapt onto her lap and stared unblinking at Laura with marble-like green eyes. "Not now, Satan." Dora lowered the cat to the floor. The animal stalked away with a malevolent glance in Laura's direction.

"He is a widower, you say. What was his wife like? Does he speak of her?"

"No, just that she died in a fall. I got the impression that he didn't wish to talk about it, and so I didn't pry."

"Well, you have a right to know what you're getting yourself into. It would be nice to learn if he had a happy marriage, don't you think? I believe if a man is a good husband for one woman, he will be again for another."

Laura bit her lip. "Yes, I suppose so." She'd been uneasy about asking him. Did Dora sense something? "I have no doubt that Nathaniel will make an excellent husband," she said in a firm tone.

Dora cleared a space on the table and tucked back the sleeves of her gown. She bowed her gray-streaked, brown head over the well-worn pack of Tarot cards and removed the significator, the Page of Wands. This card always represented Laura. Cutting the deck, Dora divided it into three, then into one again. She pushed the cards across to Laura. "Shuffle and cut three times."

She loved her aunt especially for her strong, unshakeable convictions. Aunt Dora was her mother's unmarried stepsister and considered the disreputable member of the family, although there were male ancestors who would surely be more worthy of the title. Adding to her sins, Dora dressed in a fashion Laura's mother disparagingly called bohemian. Aunt Dora remained unruffled by criticism, saying merely that she would rather be known as bohemian than bourgeois. An arrow, which found its mark and enraged her mother, as Laura's maternal grandfather had also made his money in trade.

Determined not to allow her mother's influence to extend as far as Cornwall, Laura looked for a good outcome from the reading as she shuffled the cards and handed them back. Dora then laid out ten cards in their familiar, cross-like pattern.

"My goodness," Laura exclaimed, as The Tower and the Death cards emerged. Although she didn't understand much about Tarot, she knew they were not the cards one wished for.

"Change," Dora muttered, groping for her spectacles. "It's everywhere. Understandable."

"Good change?"

"Good and bad."

Laura shivered. She pointed to another card. "The Lovers. That's a good sign, surely?"

"Reversed." Dora tapped it. "Placed as it is, it reads as a happy ending to a period of difficulty. And it crosses the King of Pentacles, a dark-haired man of means, which could mean that only through you can this man complete himself."

"Oh!" Laura didn't know what to make of it. She focused on the happy ending bit.

Dora reached for the deck. "That will do."

"Wait!" Laura pointed at another. "What about the King of Cups?"

"A fair-haired man, one you must watch out for."

"Why?"

Her aunt frowned. "I don't know, but in an unexpected way he will bring an end to a difficult time."

"I don't like the sound of that. What about the Knight of Cups, here?"

"The emotional seeker. He represents your quest—your search for something that's difficult to obtain."

Aunt Dora began gathering up the cards.

"That wasn't much of a reading," Laura protested, faintly alarmed. "You usually say so much more. I suspect there's a lot you aren't telling me."

Dora looked her most mysterious, destroying the arrangement of cards. "Some things are better not to know."

"You are naughty, Aunt Dora. Can't you tell me more?"

Her aunt shook her head. "What month was Lanyon born?"

"November."

"Scorpio. The most murdered sign of the zodiac. And the most likely to commit murder."

Laura laughed. "He has managed to survive until thirty-two without being murdered or thrown in prison."

"You can laugh, Laura. But you're Cancer. You'll have trouble understanding a Scorpio man. They can be remote. It will be difficult for you to ever know him completely, even though you will fight hard to understand him."

"I like a challenge."

Nathaniel hadn't kissed her again, although to be fair, the opportunity hadn't presented itself. Since the engagement appeared in the newspaper, and Nathaniel's return from Cornwall, they'd been caught up in a whirlwind of parties and dinners with her parents. It had become impossible to talk privately. She would be treading on eggshells until she learned more about his life and understood how the past might affect their future.

"I haven't been alone with him since we became engaged. We've been so busy with social occasions. Not to mention fittings for the gown and the trousseau." Laura knew her aunt would have no interest whatsoever in learning her Mother had engaged Worth for the wedding gown and Lucile for lingerie and tea gowns. She rose from the table to give her aunt a fond hug. "I'm so glad you're coming to the wedding. Heaven knows when I'll see you again. We are traveling down to Wolfram Abbey the day after the ceremony."

"Do you know the abbey's history?"

"The prior was John of Wolfram during the 12th century, Nathaniel tells me. Of the Cistercian Order. The abbey was dissolved in the 16th century after the prior was executed on a charge of treason."

Her aunt's gaze settled on her, her brown eyes just as shrewd as her mother's. "No honeymoon?"

"Nathaniel can't spare the time. We plan to have our honeymoon later."

Aunt Dora replaced the Tarot on the shelf. "If you ever need me, you know where to find me, dear."

Laura stood as the dressmaker pinned the hem of a new ensemble. Made for her trousseau, the promenade costume was of flowered silk and lace appliqué. After it fit to her mother's satisfaction, they drove home in the carriage.

Lady Parr turned to Laura as the carriage left the crowded London streets. "I haven't explained what you might expect from the marriage bed."

Laura grimaced. "Oh, Mother, you needn't."

Her mother's glance was sharp. "You and Lanyon haven't…"

Laura didn't know when they might have found the opportunity. She turned her ring on her finger. "He's been most respectful."

Her mother nodded. "I was sure a man of Lanyon's ilk would never overstep the line. But if he'd gone back to Cornwall without a commitment we might have lost him."

Laura flushed. Did her mother see her like a business arrangement, as her marriage to Father appeared to be? Did she feel any real affection for her remaining daughter?

"Men expect their wives to be accommodating in the bedroom," Mother continued. "You must endure, Laura, no matter how little you wish it. It is Lanyon's right as your husband. It would be most unwise to refuse him."

Refuse him? Laura had no intention of it. "Didn't you ever enjoy that with Father?"

Lady Parr cleared her throat. "In the first few years, it wasn't entirely disagreeable. I hope you will find it pleasurable. It is an act for the procreation of children. Once that is done…" She glanced away. "I have a booklet you might like to read."

"It's really not necessary, Mother. You don't need to prepare me. Lovemaking was often spoken of in some detail at Cambridge."

"Of that I have no doubt," Lady Parr said dryly. "I'm surprised you came home untouched."

"Your maid was with me, Mother. No doubt Agnes gave you a

running commentary on everything I did while I was there."

"She said you spent a good deal of time with a lecturer, a Mr. Farmer."

"He is a friend. A group of us gathered together over luncheon to discuss the lectures." Laura had written to her university friends and advised them of her marriage. They had all sent her their best wishes. She had not heard from Howard Farmer, however, and wondered why. She'd been aware that he found her attractive and felt rather awkward about it.

Her mother snorted. "A poor professor who would always work in some university town would not have suited you, Laura. You would have become bored very quickly."

Laura was relieved when the carriage turned into their street and the conversation ended. To distract her mother, she talked about the flowers chosen for the church. She wanted to retire to her room and think about Nathaniel.

CHAPTER FIVE

Rain clouds threatened on the day of the wedding, held at St Margaret's in Westminster. Laura's mother expressed her displeasure, but even Mother had no control over the weather.

Laura was thrilled with her gown. It was not what her mother wanted, but her parent was in a conciliatory mood and agreed to the style Worth proposed. The gown of ivory champagne satin damask had a floral pattern in satin on the boned bodice, with short sleeves of Micheline lace. Laura's hair had been drawn back into an elegant chignon and cream rosebuds adorned her veil. Her bouquet was of cream roses and pale pink peonies. Cousin Georgina, Laura's matron of honor, and Phoebe, another cousin, held up her long train. Both women wore deep rose pink, their wide-brimmed hats laden with pink roses.

Three hundred guests including the prime minister and other notables attended. Laura walked down the crimson-carpeted aisle on her father's arm to the strains of the "Bridal Chorus" from Wagner's *Lohengrin.*

Handsome in his gray morning suit and top hat which matched his eyes, a boutonniere in his lapel, Nathaniel stood at the altar with his best man, Horace Tothill, an old friend from university, and his two groomsmen, Ambrose Chesterfield and Phillip Dunn. Nathaniel's side of the church was filled with friends and associates, as he had no relations; he was an only child and his parents were both gone.

"You are breathtaking." Nathaniel's silver-gray eyes and dazzling smile banished her nervousness.

Laura handed her bouquet to Georgina and took her place beside him. With a squeeze of her hand and an encouraging murmur, her father stepped away. In a sonorous voice, the minister began.

When the ring slid on her finger and they were pronounced man and wife, she smiled into Nathaniel's beautiful eyes with a bubble of joy.

Laura clung to her new husband's arm and laughed up at him as she and Nathaniel emerged from the vestry.

The rain, which had been threatening, arrived as they attempted to leave the church. Everyone scattered as the downpour filled the gutters. Filthy brown water overflowed and spread across the pavement. Laura hesitated on the step, holding up her train.

Nathaniel scooped her into his arms. He ran across the wet pavement and deposited her in the carriage, then followed her inside.

Smoothing her skirts, which had suffered only a little water damage, Laura smiled at him. "You are my gallant hero."

The laughter faded from his eyes. "I hope to be."

The reception was held at the Savoy Hotel in the Strand where they were to spend the night. In the columned, gilt-mirrored ballroom, Laura danced the wedding waltz with Nathaniel, the train of her gown over her arm, his gaze bathing her in admiration. Having made up her mind to marry him, she had not questioned her decision again. On the previous night, she had slept soundly and had woken filled with joy and a sense of purpose.

How strange. Although she hardly knew Nathaniel, she felt, as she believed he did, that they were destined for each other. She had not banished all her plans and resolutions, however. She knew herself too well. Her studies might lie in the past, but university had given her a thirst to continue broadening her knowledge and to be tested in other ways. Nathaniel had said his wife would have many duties. She was keen to embrace them, but women were forging careers in England, and she wanted to be a part of it. She would tell him when the time was right.

The best man, Horace Tothill, claimed a dance. "You have married a good man, Lady Lanyon."

"I know it, Mr. Tothill." She had judged Nathaniel entirely by instinct, dismissing rational thought, and didn't doubt that she was right.

"Once in Wolfram, you may hear something to the contrary. If you do, I hope you will continue to believe in him."

Surprised, she stared at the attractive, fair-haired man. "I would like to ask what you mean by that, Mr. Tothill, but I suspect you won't tell me."

He smiled. "It must come from Nathaniel. He has chosen well. You seem a calm, patient woman."

Laura nodded. She was not by nature the soul of patience. With so much lying ahead of her, she shelved his advice away for when it might be useful. But it left a whisper of unease behind.

The wedding breakfast over, Laura stood on the bottom step of the hotel staircase and threw her bouquet. She was glad when her favorite cousin, Phoebe, caught the posy. When the last of the guests departed, Laura slipped upstairs to their suite to change. She sent Mary back to Wimbledon with her wedding clothes, then came down to join her parents for a farewell drink in the hotel dining room.

Her father drew Nathaniel aside for a brief conversation. Laura tried to hear what they discussed, but they kept their voices low. She kissed her mother, who held her against her soft bosom. "You've done very well, Laura, and made us proud."

At last, I've done something right. She hugged her father and kissed his bristly cheek.

He winked at her. "Have a grand life, Lady Lanyon."

Lady Lanyon. Laura drew in a breath. She was a baroness and had left her father's protection forever. Upstairs in their suite of rooms, her handsome husband would make love to her. She welcomed it but shivered with anticipation.

"You're not cold, my love?" Nathaniel asked.

"No." She searched his eyes for a sign that she was his love. That it was not merely the overused endearment she feared. After a whirlwind courtship, they hardly knew each other. But she was determined to make him love her as dearly as she knew she would love him.

Tomorrow they departed for Cornwall, and heaven only knew when she would see her family again. It was with a mixture of excitement and trepidation that Laura took Nathaniel's hand, and they mounted the stairs.

Entering their hotel suite, Laura crossed the green and gold Savonnerie rug. The room's elegance had pleased her when she'd come upstairs earlier with Mary to change. The pastel floral drapes at the windows matched the wallpaper, the furniture of rosewood. The half tester bed had made her quiver with nerves.

Her nightgown, frilled and tucked with lavish ribbons, lay on the green satin bedcover. Laura spun away as her heart beat madly. "We have our own bathroom."

Nathaniel tipped the hotel page. He removed his gray tailcoat before opening the bottle of champagne just delivered, pulling the cork from the bottle with a pop.

Laura removed her hat before the mirror. Her trunk had been sent on to the railway station. Tomorrow's ensemble hung in the closet with a change of underwear, her toiletries on the dresser.

Nathaniel handed her a glass of champagne and clinked his against it. "To my beautiful wife."

Laura was glad of the champagne. She toasted him in return. "To my gallant husband."

She hadn't dared drink wine at the reception, not under her mother's gaze. Laura had been afraid it might go to her head. The champagne was delicious, dry and fizzy. She drank deeply, hoping it would settle her nerves.

"Your maid will help you undress. It's been a long day. You must be tired."

"I've sent Mary home. She prefers to remain here close to her family. I shall have to find another lady's maid."

"Dorcus is a good maid," Nathaniel said. "But perhaps not quite to the standard you're used to. She will do until you can find another."

Laura longed for him to kiss her. What had happened to the man who had pursued her with such passionate intent? He seemed restrained. Was this how husbands behaved?

He flicked open the buttons on his gray satin waistcoat with his long fingers. His broad chest strained against his shirt as he undid the top button and pulled off his cravat. His movements were unhurried, while his gaze remained on her, making her tremble. She wanted him to sweep her up, carry her to the bed and ravish her before the fear set in that she would disappointment him. She wished she'd questioned her friends at university more closely.

She put down the glass and went to the window. "Oh look! The Thames. How magnificent it looks from here."

"I have seen the river. I want to see you. Come here, sweetheart," Nathaniel said from behind her, his hands on her shoulders.

He sat on the upholstered chair and drew her down onto his lap. As she leaned against him she could feel the rapid beat of his heart. Was it a sign that he was as moved as her, that he desired her?

"I hope I can make you happy."

"You do make me happy," she said, surprised. She'd been so concerned about pleasing him; she hadn't thought he might have similar concerns.

"Cornwall will be different to anything you've known."

She smiled. "I certainly hope so. Mother can no longer order me about. It's a heady thought."

His laugh rumbled in his chest. Looking up, she saw that his eyes had cleared of some indefinable worry.

She stroked his chin, feeling the beginnings of stubble. "Soft," she said, "and prickly at the same time."

"I am cursed with a heavy beard."

He smiled and his arms tightened around her as he began to talk of his home, Wolfram, the ancient abbey and the tiny fishing village that bore its name, the deer-filled woods and sea, the soul and the heart of the Cornish coast. It touched her deeply when his voice grew gruff with emotion.

Laura waited for him to mention Amanda. She was filled with curiosity about his first wife. Did her loss still hurt him deeply? But of course, he did not. She would have to be patient. With that thought, she vowed to banish his sadness with the force of her love.

"It's growing late, and we have an early start in the morning." He rose with her in his arms and set her on her feet.

His touch upset her balance, and she placed her hand against his chest as he began to remove the pins from her hair, gathering them up in his big hands. He placed them neatly on the bureau. He was an orderly man, she realized as her fiery tresses swung heavily to her waist.

He gathered the locks in his hands. "Beautiful. Streaks of gold amid burnished copper."

"Mother complains I go out in the garden too often without a hat." Laura held her breath when he turned his attention to her clothes.

Nathaniel's quiet intensity made her terribly unsure. He helped her out of her jacket, and then unbuttoned the pearl buttons on her blouse. Stripping the exquisite pin-tucked, lace-trimmed garment from her, he laid it over the back of the chair. Her skirt and petticoat pooled at her feet, and she stepped out of them.

He seemed very much at home with women's clothes. But as a married man of course he would be. Her mind reeled. Had he sought feminine company since…? She knew of the high-class brothels in London where men of his ilk visited beautiful women practiced in the art of lovemaking. Eavesdropping on her father's conversations had proved fruitful, but now she wished she hadn't. Would Nathaniel like her body?

"Turn around, sweetheart." His fingers burned their way down her back as he unlaced her corset. The new pink lace affair fell away, and she pulled her camisole over her head. Shy about her naked breasts, she bent to untie her satin garters, then sat hunched over to remove her stockings. In her haste, she snagged the silk as she rolled a stocking down her leg.

"Bother," she muttered.

"Allow me."

She leaned a hand on his shoulder as he knelt, his fingers warm against her thigh. She couldn't resist threading her fingers through his dark hair, shot through with amber lights. It was silky to the touch. With a smile, he handed her the other stocking, then went to the bureau to remove his cufflinks.

Intent on climbing under the covers as quickly as possible, Laura pulled off her lace-trimmed bloomers and scampered into bed.

Nathaniel turned as he slipped his braces off his shoulders. A smile warmed his eyes. "In bed already? Don't you wish to use the bathroom?"

"I'm all right for the moment," she said in a tight voice.

He sat on the bed, as if to reassure her. "You're a lovely woman, Laura. Really quite beautiful." He dropped a quick kiss on her lips, his rough chin rasping against her cheek. Then he drew away, running his hand over his jaw. "I need to shave." He disappeared into the bathroom.

Every nerve in her body alert, Laura lay back on the pillows. She would not sleep a wink tonight.

When he returned some minutes later smelling of soap, she smiled at him, having settled with the covers drawn up to her neck.

"Don't hide yourself from me," he said. "I enjoy looking at you."

She liked looking at him. He had a broad chest with a mat of dark hair tapering to his waist. He was beautifully proportioned and had obviously lived an active life. Well-defined muscles rippled with each movement beneath smooth olive skin. New brides might swoon at moments like this and reach for their smelling salts. Laura had no such intention. She had never seen a man without his clothes.

After Nathaniel's trousers joined the rest of his clothes, she tucked her hands between her legs, discovering the heat and need there. He walked over to the bed completely unaffected by his nakedness. Were men always thus?

She'd grown rather hot and swallowed. "I might have a bath."

His eyebrows rose, and a wry smile lifted his lips. "Very well."

She grasped her nightgown to fling it over her head. "I,

um…won't be long."

He tugged the garment out of her hands as the blankets fell away. Laura lay exposed to his gaze, fighting the urge to cover herself. "What a lucky fellow I am to have such a beautiful wife."

"I'm a lucky woman."

"Ah, Laura," he murmured. "Go. Have your bath. Put on your nightgown if you must." He stretched out on the bed, as she hastily threw her nightdress over her head and ran across the carpet.

"Are you all right in there?"

Laura had brushed her teeth, bathed and dried herself, adding a dab of perfume. Wearing her nightgown, she hovered before the mirror, splashing cold water on her cheeks that embarrassment had made rosy. "I'm coming," she called. He must be completely out of patience with her.

She returned to the room to find he'd turned off all the lights except one lamp. She warmed with a rush of gratitude. He lifted the covers for her, and she slipped into the bed. "I'm sorry I was…"

She gasped against his lips as he brought his mouth down on hers. When he drew away, she thought he was smiling but wasn't sure in the dim room.

"This is pretty," he said, fingering the lace of her nightgown. "Shall we remove it?"

Nathaniel pulled it over her head and gathered her close, running his hands over her back and hip. At his touch, a pulse throbbed deep inside, and her breathing quickened. She loved his warm skin against hers when he took her mouth again in a long, passionate kiss, their breaths mingling, his invasion of her mouth incredibly intimate. He tasted of sweet wine. His gentle hands on her body left a trail of sensation. She gasped as he softly stroked her most intimate place. The rush of pleasure his skillful fingers produced brought a moan to her lips.

He took a nipple in his mouth. She couldn't help a mew of pleasure. Warmth pooled at the base of her stomach. Nathaniel turned his attention to her other breast with an appreciative moan. Laura's body throbbed and she was having trouble gaining her breath.

The room filled with the sound of their raspy breathing. She traced her fingers from the soft, dark hair on his chest, down over his flat, hard stomach, but faltered somewhere near his bellybutton. Nathaniel held her hand and guided it onto himself. His skin was hot and silky and so hard it made her quiver. A flood of moisture gathered at her core.

"I'll be gentle." He kissed the hollow at the base of her throat. "Your first time might be painful."

She tensed, but she wanted him so much, she closed her eyes to hide her nervous excitement from him.

"Look at me, sweetheart. I want to see your beautiful eyes when I make love to you." He spread her thighs and settled between them. Trying not to stiffen, Laura clutched his shoulders as he nudged her entrance. She whimpered at the burst of pain as he pushed inside. He paused. "All right?"

"Yes," she whispered, rather unsure, but determined not to fail him.

The pain eased as he began to move within her, stirring up emotions she could not have imagined and could barely comprehend. If only she could relax, she was sure she would enjoy it more. She loved the smell of him, the weight of him, his smooth skin and soft hair beneath her hands and the profound closeness she felt when joined with him in this intimate act of love.

Love? She pushed the thought away.

Nathaniel kept up a steady rhythm, stirring up a needy, demanding sensation in her stomach. He groaned and withdrew, leaving her unfulfilled and on the verge of tears.

He kissed her then stroked gently down her body to the sensitive, hard nub throbbing at her core and circled it with a finger. When she cried out at her release, Nathaniel kissed her. He put his arm around her and settled them back on the pillows. She laid her head on his shoulder.

"Not too uncomfortable?"

"No," she whispered. She wished she could tell him it had been wonderful. But the experience had not been as fabulous as the women at university had led her to believe. Her limbs seemed leaden, her eyes difficult to keep open.

He stroked a long finger down her cheek. "You will come to enjoy it more, I promise."

Nathaniel had been considerate of her needs, an attentive lover. To be joined in that intimate way with him, to belong to him was extraordinary. She was quickly falling in love with him. If only he had communicated his love for her. She supposed she had hardly inspired it. When she'd thought of their lovemaking, she'd never envisaged lying like a lump while he did all the work. She would learn to be a good lover, she thought with a resurgence of determination. Lying here against him she felt deliciously warm and safe. She pushed her concerns away as sleep claimed her.

Laura opened her eyes to daylight. Nathaniel was already awake watching her. He pressed a light kiss to her mouth. "Good morning."

"Good morning."

He propped his head in his hand. "How are you, sweetheart?"

She smiled. "Hungry."

"Then let's have breakfast. We have a train to catch."

"I can't wait to show you Wolfram." He kissed her briefly again and leapt out of bed, leaving her oddly lonely. "Care to use the bathroom first?"

She still felt shy. "No, you go first."

He'd said their lovemaking would be better the second time. Her tiredness had vanished, and she was keen to try, but admitted she was sore and needed a bath. She admired his naked body as he crossed the bedroom toward the bathroom.

"That's where our life together will really begin," he said as he closed the door.

Nathaniel stood in the hotel's ornate bathroom lathering soap over his chin. Poor girl, what kind of a future had he given her in a moment of weakness? He would never be able to give fully of himself or to give her what she needed. His lips firmed, and he finished shaving, bent to splash cold water onto his face then gazed at his reflection. His eyes darkened with regret. What had he done to her?

When he emerged from the bathroom, Laura had slipped on a negligee, a modest thing with dainty embroidery. She perched on the edge of the bed, a brave smile on her lips, all coltish bare legs as she put on her slippers, her red hair tumbling forward around her shoulders. She had given up so much for him. Compassion gripped him. He would do everything in his power to protect her.

CHAPTER SIX

"This is your first time traveling by train?" Nathaniel asked, his gray eyes full of amusement.

Laura nodded, embarrassed by the sheltered life she'd led. Her parents had insisted she travel in the family carriage with her maid wherever she went.

"The journey to Penzance takes nine hours," he said. "We'll have to change at Plymouth."

The train rumbled beneath her, the wheels click-clacking on the tracks. It seemed as if they'd already been traveling for days, having risen so early to go by carriage to Paddington Station. It would be close to five o'clock when they reached Penzance. Nathaniel's carriage would then take them on to Wolfram.

"I prefer train travel whenever I go to London for Parliament," Nathaniel said. "There will be short periods when you will be alone at the abbey. I hope you won't be lonely."

"Of course not, I'll be too busy," Laura said in a firm tone, her ribcage tightening with unease.

She tugged at her collar. The train carriage was humid with the windows shut against the smoke. Every seat filled, even in the first-class compartment. It was difficult to talk to him with a crying baby and a demanding young child sitting opposite, so she couldn't broach any private concerns.

"Rest your head against my shoulder," Nathaniel said, taking her hand.

Laura settled closer. She watched the green fields, woodland and quaint market towns rush past the window. The speed was remarkable, and the noise! Horses danced away to the far corner of their paddock as the train roared past. The carriage rocked on the track, but at least it didn't bump one about like a horse-drawn vehicle.

The novelty of traveling in a train had worn off by the time they reached Plymouth and changed trains. Finding the movement hypnotic, Laura closed her eyes.

"Wake up, Laura. We've arrived."

Laura sat up so quickly her head spun. She rubbed her eyes. The train had pulled into the station. Nathaniel stood and began to pull down their bags from the shelf overhead.

After he helped her down onto the platform, she turned to survey her new home, but a mist hung over Penzance. Laura could see little beyond the end of the street.

"There's Ben Teg." Nathaniel strode toward the road where a fair-haired young man jumped from a smart brougham and hurried to meet them.

"Teg, this is your new mistress, Lady Lanyon."

Teg touched his cap. "*Dynnargh dhis*, my lady."

"Good afternoon, Teg," Laura said, thinking she must learn some Cornish words. "Will this mist make it difficult for us to travel?"

"Not for a Cornish lad, Your Ladyship. I'll get you safe and sound to the *porth*."

Although she found Teg hard to understand, Laura liked his friendly, open face. "I imagine the *porth* means a harbor?" she asked Nathaniel in an undertone.

"It does. You'll become familiar with the language in time." Nathaniel placed his portmanteau and Laura's carpetbag in the brougham and assisted her up the step. "Teg has been with the family all his life, and his father before him."

When the sun broke through the bank of clouds, the temperature seemed to rise several degrees. It was warmer here than in London, and she sweltered in her brocade suit. She would change as soon as she reached home. *Home.* The word sent a shiver of excitement through her. She was impatient to see Wolfram.

Laura opened her parasol, as Teg, along with another servant, stacked the trunk and bandboxes into the trap.

Teg jumped up onto the seat of the brougham and took up the reins. "Walk on." He cracked his whip, and they set off along a lane bordered by paddocks and high hedge rows.

They had only been traveling a matter of minutes when an obstacle struck the carriage door on Nathaniel's side with a bang. Whatever the projectile was bounced away into the ragged gorse bushes before Laura could catch sight of it.

"What was that?" she asked, as Nathaniel stood up to stare back along the road. Unaware, or seemingly unaffected, Teg slapped the reins, and they turned a corner where shrubs and trees blocked the road behind them.

Nathaniel took his seat. "Someone might wish to voice an opinion," he said in a humorless tone.

"Opinion? Of what?"

Nathaniel placed his arm along the back of the seat as if to protect her. "I was jesting. It was more likely to be a stone on the road, thrown up by the wheel. Forget it, please. I want you to enjoy your first day here, instead of worrying over little things of no importance."

She shivered. He had not been joking. Nathaniel's words were clipped; he was angry, although not with her.

The beauty of the place made her push the incident away. They followed the river through a green valley ringed by forest. A flock of birds disappeared into the misty distance as if by magic, their calls muted. Dry stone walls crisscrossed the countryside. Black-faced sheep paused to watch the carriage pass by.

When they topped a rise, the clouds shifted. Laura caught her first sight of the sea, like golden gauze under a westerly sun.

She craned her neck. "I can see the water!"

"A pity we have fog today. But you will come to love the mists here at Wolfram as I do."

She wasn't entirely sure she would ever relish the suffocating fog, not if it was anything like London, but she patted his hand, which rested on hers. "I know I shall."

Small cottages crammed into a warren of narrow cobbled lanes as they traversed the road leading down to the bay. The seaside embraced them, warm, salty and unfamiliar. Foreign smells washed over Laura. Gulls cawed overhead in the misty sky, the view over the water vanishing into thick fog.

They arrived at the water's edge where a row of narrow-fronted houses, a shop and an ancient Tudor inn faced the harbor foreshore. Fishing boats bobbed along the seawall where a wash of surging waves sent a curtain of spray over the paved quayside.

Nathaniel motioned to the inn called The Sail and Anchor. "We'll take some refreshment." He jumped down and turned to assist her.

Laura suffered a wrench of disappointment. She was eager to reach the abbey. "Can't we go home?"

"The causeway's underwater, Your Ladyship," Teg explained, standing at the horses' heads. "We must wait for the tide to turn before we can take the carriage across."

Laura raised her eyebrows and stared at Nathaniel. "There's a causeway?"

"It's high tide. Shouldn't be more than an hour before we can proceed."

Laura was silenced, incredulous that he had not seen fit to explain this to her before. The prospect of being cut off from the mainland unnerved her as she stared out over the misty stretch of water. Beyond a glowing description of the abbey's history, Nathaniel had told her little that really mattered. Not that they were to live on an island. And nothing of his first marriage. She bit her lip, needing to be reassured.

He took her arm in a purposeful grip. "We'll take the boat, Teg. I'll leave you to bring the luggage. Lady Lanyon is impatient to see her new home."

Teg touched his cap "Right you are, Your Lordship."

Laura walked with Nathaniel along the harbor foreshore to where a fishing boat unloaded its catch onto the wharf, and squabbling gulls dived in a hungry frenzy. The men nodded as she and Nathaniel approached, studying her with ill-concealed curiosity. She'd never smelled anything like the overpowering stench of fish, but she managed not to take out her handkerchief. Instead, she smiled at the men. "It seems you've had a splendid catch today."

"Better than most, madam," one craggy-faced man replied, tossing his knife into a bucket.

Nathaniel paused. "My wife, men, Baroness, Lady Lanyon."

The fishermen removed their hats and murmured a welcome. She found their manner guarded. Nathaniel was too formal. Perhaps he didn't associate much with the village folk. She most certainly would.

"Here we are. The steps are slippery. I'll carry you down," Nathaniel said.

A rowing boat tied up at the wharf bobbed about in the water. Nathaniel hefted her into his arms and descended, then set her on her feet on a step beside the boat. Laura eyed it with alarm.

Nathaniel held her arm and assisted her as the craft rocked alarmingly under her feet. "Sit there in the middle."

Uneasy, Laura obeyed. Her woolen suit was completely unsuitable for scrambling about in boats. Unstable in her high-heeled boots, she clung to the hard, wooden seat as the boat danced on the waves. The ocean swirled beneath them, deep and forbidding. What had she gotten herself into?

CHAPTER SEVEN

When Nathaniel sat opposite Laura and picked up the oars, Teg untied the mooring rope and pushed them away from the dock. Nathaniel began to row, steering the boat out into the bay. Within minutes, they had left Teg and the wharf behind.

The ocean churned in a wash around them. Laura glanced in dismay at her best boots as the boat dipped, and spray splashed over the sides to pool in the bottom. What if they were swamped? She couldn't swim. The prospect of her heavy suit and footwear dragging her down made her suck in deep breaths of briny air.

She refused to express her concerns and watched her new husband with reluctant admiration, both annoyed and impressed with how calm and capable he was. It was impossible to imagine anything untoward happening with him in control. He grew up here and was at home on the sea. There would be no nasty surprises, she repeated silently like a mantra. The wind picked up. She clung to her hat that must now resemble a limp, old cabbage leaf, grateful that it shielded her eyes from the surprisingly sharp glare off the water.

Nathaniel pulled hard on the oars. "Not far now."

"The abbey is on an island?" she managed to say, dreading his reply.

"No, Wolfram joins the coast farther on, but the causeway is the quickest way to the village. If you'd agreed to wait for the tide to turn, your journey would have ended in a more comfortable fashion."

"This is not unpleasant." Laura chewed her lip on the lie. "I wouldn't have asked you to row in your good clothes if you'd explained."

"What do clothes matter? Isn't this invigorating? We'll be there soon."

His voice held a rasp of excitement, like a boy on Christmas morning, she thought with a reluctant smile. The mist cleared and a narrow jetty appeared, where a small sloop rocked on the waves.

"Welcome to Wolfram," Nathaniel said.

While he secured the boat to the jetty, Laura gazed up at the abbey. Its tower, as unyielding as a mountain peak, emerged from the fog as the sky began to clear. Nathaniel lifted her onto the wharf. There was a rambling garden filled with flowering trees and shrubs spilling over a stone wall. Laura's heart leapt at the sight of something so ordinary and familiar as she followed him along the path.

Nathaniel whistled. A moment later, exuberant barking rent the air, and a pair of red setters raced down the hill. Glossy ears bounced and tongues lolled as they pounced on their master in delight. "Meet Orsino and Sebastian."

Laura laughed. "From Shakespeare's *Twelfth Night*?" Her husband constantly surprised her.

He grinned. "A favorite play."

The dogs barely acknowledged Laura; their love for their master took all their attention. After he rubbed their ears and gave them a pat, she walked with him up the path, the dogs rushing ahead.

They entered through a wooden gate in the stone wall.

The garden of purple magnolia and white azaleas that had caught her eye grew among ancient gravestones, the scent of jasmine cloying. Laura was taken aback. It looked so... forbidding. "Your ancestors?"

Nathaniel turned away. "Yes."

She silently cursed herself for her insensitivity. Of course, his late wife, Amanda, would be buried here.

He smiled and held out his hand to her. She clasped it, and they continued up the hill. Laura's breath shortened as emotion and exhaustion took their toll on her depleted energy reserves. She chided herself for her weakness, but she was tired; so much had happened, and it had been a long trip.

Nathaniel pushed open an iron gate which led into a cobblestoned courtyard. The abbey appeared, sheer walls of granite darkened to black by the fog, the long, mullioned windows reflecting a leaden sky. Above a set of wide steps, the solid pair of arched oak doors were set within a square frame of ornamental stone molding, with a solid brass knocker in the shape of a lion's head.

"Orsino, Sebastian, to the stables!" Nathaniel commanded. The two dogs whined in protest, but turned and loped off around the corner.

The door opened. A dark-haired young maid in a black dress, white apron and mobcap bobbed. "My lord."

Nathaniel frowned. "Where is Rudge?"

"Gone into the village, Your Lordship."

"This is Lady Lanyon, Dorcas."

"Milady." Dorcas dipped again.

Wondering why his butler's absence annoyed him, Laura smiled at the maid. "Hello, Dorcas. What is the housekeeper's name? I should like to meet her."

"We have no housekeeper at present, milady," Dorcas said.

"Have tea brought to the library," Nathaniel ordered.

He ushered Laura into a grand hall that reminded her of a cold, fossilized forest. Solid columns of stone like the trunks of giant oaks formed graceful arches rising to a giddy height above. The carved wooden staircase decorated with branches, leaves and fruit led up into the shadowy floor overhead. A chill radiated up from the stone flags.

Their footsteps echoing, Laura followed Nathaniel along a passageway where massive tapestries decorated the walls. He opened a door and stood aside for her to enter beneath an ornamental arch into a magnificent room, its high, vaulted ceiling a series of decorative ribs. A splendid stained glass window dominated the far wall, which was set on fire by the lowering sun. The fog had drifted away.

"We have a smaller salon, which is cozier in the winter. But I prefer this room."

"It's breathtaking." Laura was unable to suppress the relief in her voice at finding both beauty and comfort in the elegant room. Bookshelves filled with gilt and leather-bound books covered two of the oak-paneled walls. Glass cabinets held displays of delicate Chinese porcelain. The furniture was mostly antiques of a very fine quality, most particularly the round rosewood library table and the carved oak desk. A large globe rested on a stand nearby. The pair of brown leather chesterfields faced a baronial fireplace, a Canaletto landscape of the Thames hanging above. It was all undeniably tasteful, well suited to a man like Nathaniel, she thought, eyeing the leopard skin rug stretched out before the fire.

"Did you shoot that?" she asked with a smile.

He grinned. "I believe a great uncle did. I don't care for safaris."

Relieved, she made a note to have it stored in the attic. "You have an extensive collection of Chinese porcelain."

"My mother was a collector. Sit down, sweetheart. I'll have a drink with you, and then I must consult my overseer Hugh Pitney. I'll introduce you to him tomorrow."

Apart from the beautiful porcelain, Laura couldn't see a sign of a woman's influence anywhere. No likenesses in silver frames, no china ornaments, shawls or crocheted antimacassars. She sat on the chesterfield and swallowed her disappointment at him leaving her so soon. Although eager to see more of the house, she would have liked him to show it to her. But she knew he must supervise the running of his estate, especially after an absence.

Nathaniel seemed preoccupied since they arrived. As if Wolfram owned a large part of him. She shrugged at such a fanciful thought but couldn't help another creeping in to replace it. Would Wolfram ever become home to her? She sat back and smoothed her heavy skirt that she couldn't wait to change out of. While she wanted to learn more about Nathaniel's life here, now was not the time to ask. "Tell me more about the history of the abbey."

He poured himself a whiskey from a crystal decanter on the sideboard. "It was a monastery before it became an abbey. The estate has been in my family since the 16th century." He stretched his long legs out and leaned back against the leather squab. "The Jacobites hid here in 1714. Their plan was to seize Exeter, Bristol and Plymouth in the hope that the other smaller towns would join the Stuart cause. But the militia quelled the uprising."

"Your ancestors supported the Jacobites?"

"King James II was a Catholic, and King Charles II's illegitimate son, the Duke of Monmouth, was popular in the Southwest. The first Baron Lanyon supported his claim to the throne. Not wisely as it turned out."

Dorcas carried a tray with a solid silver tea service into the room, followed by another maid with golden-colored fruitcake, flat scones, thick cream and jam.

Laura had rejected any food on the train, and now her stomach rumbled. She took a bite of the fruitcake, finding it tasty. "What makes the cake this wonderful color?"

"Saffron. Traditional fare in these parts."

Nathaniel put down his glass. He stood and bent to brush a kiss on her lips. "Dorcas will take care of your needs."

Why no housekeeper? She had many questions, but he was gone before she could ask them. Laura poured another cup of tea, a smoky brew she didn't recognize. The dainty teacup was Spode china with the family crest emblazoned on it in gold.

She'd finished her tea and was eating the last crumbs of the delicious fruit cake when Dorcas returned. "I'll take you to your chamber, should you be ready, milady."

Eager to see more of the abbey, Laura rose and followed her. They mounted the wide staircase and on the next floor walked along a corridor. A chambermaid waited with linen over her arm, her eyes downcast.

"How many on the staff, Dorcas?"

"A dozen servants in the house. There be many workers on the estate though. I have no idea of the number. You be in the Daffodil chamber, milady."

"That sounds inviting," Laura said, as Dorcas opened one of the thick, arched wooden doors.

Laura almost gasped out loud. Wolfram's rooms were lofty and large, and this room was no exception. She gazed from the painted plaster ceiling a good twenty feet above, to the floor covered in a thick Oriental carpet. An entire family could sleep in comfort in the carved oak four-poster bed with gold brocade bed hangings. A massive armoire occupied a corner, with a washstand and basin, a vanity table and brocade stool against the other wall. A painting of a lady in green velvet from another age hung above the stone fireplace. Laura wondered who it was. At least it wasn't Amanda, she thought, stifling a nervous giggle. Stepping into another woman's shoes was rather daunting.

Laura crossed to the tall, narrow casement windows, catching sight of her pale face in a gilt mirror as she passed. She prodded her hair. Heavens, she looked like a scarecrow. Pulling aside the heavy brocade curtains woven in gold thread, she gazed at the view below.

A stiff breeze dispersed the last tendrils of fog and bared the causeway, a built-up carriageway, the receding tide lapping at its rocky foundations. There were the steps she and Nathaniel had climbed earlier, which led through terraced gardens down to the restless expanse of slate-colored sea. Craning her neck, Laura could just see the stable block next to a more modern building that would be the overseer's office. The trap had arrived, and two men unloaded the luggage. Nathaniel wandered into view, imposing in his riding clothes, his crop resting on his shoulder, his dogs romping at his heels.

Aware that Dorcas waited behind her, Laura turned. "I shall be most comfortable here."

Dorcas jerked her head. "His lordship be in the Fern chamber, milady."

"I beg your pardon?"

"It's the chamber next door, milady."

"Oh. Of course, thank you."

Laura pressed her lips, as a cold dismay gripped her. Was she being foolish? Her parents had separate bedrooms. But she had expected to share a bed with Nathaniel, as they had on their wedding night. Intimacy would come with time, and she supposed she must be patient, although she had expected Nathaniel to want to be with her.

"Agnes will attend to you. I'll send her to you when your trunks are brought up."

Only a few hours of daylight remained of a very long day, and Laura did not look forward to dinner when tiredness ruined her appetite. "I'll rest a while, thank you, Dorcas."

"As you wish, my lady."

When the door closed, Laura removed her boots and sank onto the bed, listening to the mournful sound of gulls through the open window. Certain her adventurous spirit would reassert itself tomorrow, she closed her eyes.

She ran blindly down one corridor after another, but the wisp of white still followed. It seemed such a fragile thing, like smoke, and yet it filled her with a terrible fear. She could not escape it. She called out.

"Laura?"

She sat up quickly, her head spinning. "I must have fallen asleep."

"I heard you call out." Nathaniel sat on the bed beside her. "Were you dreaming?"

She pushed her hair back off her forehead. "A nightmare, or should it be a daymare?" The dream was so vivid it made her tremble. She wished he would hold her, but gazing at his concerned face, she forced a smile. "How foolish. I'm all right now."

"You must have been exhausted after the journey. Do you feel rested?"

Laura slipped her hand into his, wanting to pull him down to her, but lacking the courage. "Yes. Much."

"Care for a walk before it gets dark?"

"Oh yes." She reached for her boots.

"Have you a cloak? It's growing cool."

She smoothed her rumpled suit. She had intended to change. No matter, she would later for dinner. Picking up her cloak, she handed it to him. Nathaniel draped it over her shoulders.

She put on her hat before the mirror. "Your bedroom is next to mine?"

"Yes, the adjoining chamber."

Walking toward the stairs, Laura took his arm, determined to shake off the lingering effects of the dream. "Where are we going?"

"Up to the tower, first, for a bird's eye view of Wolfram. Then we'll walk toward the park."

On the ground floor at the end of the passage, Nathaniel opened a low, arched wooden door. He stood aside for her to enter. They climbed a winding staircase and passed through a doorway at the top, emerging onto a narrow parapet encased with a stone balustrade.

"Are you afraid of heights? Shall I hang onto you?" Nathaniel asked with a grin.

"No. I'm fine."

Laura clutched the cold stone, determined not to show what an awful coward she was. She'd barely recovered from the boat trip. But the extraordinary view soon removed any sense of fear. The village spread out to the north, linked to the abbey by the thread of carriageway. She picked out the church spire among the trees and the schoolhouse tower with its bell.

"You can't see it from here, but our home farm supplies most of the food for Wolfram." Nathaniel pointed out a narrow lane bordered by ancient oaks that led away from the stables. The road branched into two forks. One led to a row of stone cottages on the ocean side. The other ambled through horse paddocks and rose to disappear into woodland.

"It's breathtaking. I can't take it all in," Laura said, overwhelmed by the size and magnificence of her new home.

He smiled. "Let's take that walk. It will be dark soon."

They left the abbey by another door, emerging into a small walled rose garden, where fragrant scents sweetened the air. Not a gravestone in sight, just a stone statue of a lady in a wide-brimmed hat.

The statue was Victorian in style. Laura wondered if Amanda had brought it here. A stone bench sat beneath a tree. "This is charming."

"I can see you sitting there," Nathaniel said.

"It will become my special place."

"There's so much of Wolfram you have yet to see. You might find another you prefer."

She intertwined her fingers with his. "I doubt it. But I'm eager to see everything."

He squeezed her hand. "And I can't wait to show you."

They walked past small stone cottages. "Who lives here?"

"Gardeners, outdoor staff and some of the stable workers lived here at one time. Most of the cottages are now used for storage; some in need of repair remain empty. I had intended to refurbish them."

Nathaniel whistled. The dogs appeared from the direction of the stables, tails wagging, and joined them on their walk.

Laura glanced at Nathaniel. Had his plans come to a halt after Amanda died?

"How big is the estate?"

"Two thousand acres if you include tenant farms and the village." He sighed. "Every century that passes, the sea erodes a little more of the land. Who knows, it may be gone one day." Nathaniel pointed to an area of trees and shrubs. "My grandfather was interested in botany. He planted what we now call the arboretum."

They strolled past the exotic species and onto the gently sloping hills of the parkland, the dogs bounding ahead. To the west, the sunset cast a pink-tinged, golden glow over the water.

"Oh, it's just lovely here," Laura said.

Nathaniel gazed down at her with a smile. "We should go back. Dinner and early to bed might be a good idea for my tired wife." The unspoken suggestion of intimacy hung in the air, enticing her. He put his hands on her shoulders and gazed into her eyes. "You believe you'll be happy here?"

She reached up to touch his cheek. "I'd be happy anywhere you are."

He took her hand and turned back toward the abbey. "You're a sophisticated young woman. You'll find few people who fit that description in these parts."

"You were educated at Oxford, were you not?"

"Feminine company, I mean."

She disliked finding doubt in his voice, which must have been reflected in her face, for he pulled her to him for a hug. Bending to kiss the top of her head, he murmured, "I have one person in mind who could."

"Oh, and who might that be?

"We'll discuss her later. I want you to myself for a while."

Arm in arm, they ambled down the lane. They halted at the cry of a small gray-brown bird. It swooped down over their heads and sat on the lowest bough of a tall ash. The dogs barked.

"Sit!"

With a thump of their tails, both dogs obeyed.

A faint chirping came from the ground at the base of the tree. Nathaniel crouched and parted the grass. "The fledgling must have fallen from its nest."

Laura squatted beside him, one hand on his shoulder. "What species is it?"

He glanced at the branches overhead. "A greenfinch. That's the mother up there."

Laura eyed the tiny bird. "The poor thing."

The bundle of feathers opened its beak with a feeble chirp, while its anxious parent called from the tree.

Nathaniel straightened and peered up. "I can see the nest. If I can get the fledgling back up there, the mother will take over."

Laura shielded her eyes with her hand. She could make out a small nest. "It's almost near the top."

Nathaniel grinned boyishly. "I've had plenty of practice climbing trees. Although not for some years." He bent and scooped the fledgling up, cradling it in his palm. "Still has plenty of life in it." He undid a button on his shirt and placed the little bird carefully inside.

He swung onto the lowest branch and began to climb. His strong legs carried him swiftly upward.

"Nathaniel, do be careful." Laura watched him disappear into the thicker foliage near the top. She stepped back and craned her neck. Holding on to a branch with one hand, he reached into his shirt, removed the bird and placed it in the nest while the parent bird flew around him.

"Well done." Laura applauded as he started down.

The olive-green and yellow male arrived to join the female, both fluttering near Nathaniel's face.

"That's not very grateful," she heard him say as a bird flew at his head.

When he lifted his hand to shield his eyes, his foot slipped off the branch. Laura put her hand to her mouth, horror-struck. He swung by his hands high above her. She swallowed a cry, afraid she would distract him, while the dogs whined and scratched at the tree trunk. Nathaniel regained his footing and moments later jumped to the ground.

Once he'd found his feet, Laura launched herself at his chest, throwing her arms around him.

"What's this?" he asked with a reserved smile.

"You frightened me. I thought you'd fall."

"Goose." He smiled and took her hand. "Don't fuss, sweetheart. I was never in danger."

As they continued down the lane, she sensed the easy warmth they'd shared earlier had waned slightly, and she wondered why her display of emotion had disturbed him.

Nathaniel watched Laura's green eyes deepen with apprehension. She looked so young in her tan cape and hat with its absurd curling feather. As he had feared, she sought a close, intimate relationship. Although he could not give her what she wanted, he cautiously considered the possibility that despite the differences in their natures, they might still be happy. When they'd reached the house, Laura's buoyant nature reasserted itself, and she giggled at something she had seen from the train. He couldn't help grinning at her silly, nonsensical recollection, which served to banish the dark mood he fought his way out of. He breathed more easily.

CHAPTER EIGHT

The banquet-sized dining room featured an oak table long enough to seat King Henry VIII and all his courtiers. Laura dined with Nathaniel at one end, silver candelabra casting a soft glow over the polished table. The butler, Rudge, had returned from the village. A dark-haired gentleman of mid-years, he appeared to be of a reserved nature. He stood in attendance pouring the wine with a sharp eye on the staff as they brought in the courses. Delicate, flavorsome aromas filled the room. Fish was the main staple, roast bream, lobster in a cream sauce, limpets, oysters, vegetables and fresh salads from the castle gardens. Dessert was *tesen aval*, a deliciously light Cornish apple cake served with thick clotted cream.

Laura's corset held her in a vice-like grip. After a few spoonfuls, she pushed away her dessert plate. "My figure will suffer, if I continue to eat like this." She smiled at the butler. "Please compliment Mrs. Madge, Rudge. She has prepared a feast!"

Nathaniel chuckled and threw down his napkin to rise from the table. "We'll work off some energy riding tomorrow." He clasped her arm. "We'll have port and coffee in the library, thank you, Rudge."

Laura sank onto the comfortable leather sofa. She rested her cheek against her hand and stared into the fire while Rudge silently served their port wine and brandy. Her wine was velvety smooth and sweet. If only her mother could see her now. The thought brought an unexpected bout of homesickness that passed when she gazed into her husband's smiling gray eyes as he sat beside her.

"You approve of the port?"

She licked her lips. "Delicious. Do we make port in England?"

"England doesn't have a suitable climate for growing grapes. This comes from Portugal." When his eyes rested on her mouth, warm desire and a thrill of expectation threaded through her.

Surely Nathaniel wouldn't accept contraband goods? She'd heard smugglers still operated along this coast. Too relaxed to give the matter any thought, she took another deep sip, then slipped off her shoes and tucked her feet beneath her skirts. Outside, the wind from the sea moaned around the house. The fire crackled in the hearth, and the strong drink made her sink back against the squab.

Laura asked Nathaniel about village residents, those who might be in their social circle who could come to dinner. "Plenty of time for that, Laura. We'll discuss it later." He rested his head back against the leather and closed his eyes.

An hour passed in companionable silence. He was tired and so was she. It had been a long, exhausting day filled with discoveries. The port made her sleepy, and she yawned behind a hand.

"I believe we'll retire." Nathaniel put down his glass.

The pit of her stomach tingled. Somehow, in his mellow voice, the innocuous statement took on a more sensual meaning. Or was it just her? She slipped on her shoes.

Rudge waited at the foot of the stairs with a paraffin lamp and lit their candles. The shock of discovering the absence of electricity and running water returned with a spark of alarm. Not even a water closet. Could she bear to live without them?

Nathaniel paused at her bedroom door. "Your maid will be waiting to assist you."

With a glance at his retreating back, she entered her room where a fire burned in the grate. Fireplaces were in constant use here. The old abbey would be chilly without them.

Agnes folded back the bedcover. "I've laid out your nightgown, milady. Do you require assistance to undress?"

"Just undo the buttons down the back. I'll do the rest, thank you."

"Yes, milady." Agnes was a typical country girl with a friendly, open face and curly fair hair. She had efficiently organized Laura's bath before dinner and proved herself an excellent lady's maid.

After the maid left the room, Laura sat at her dressing table in her nightgown, plaiting her hair. A grating noise forced her to her feet, her heart leaping as a part of the timber paneling on one wall slid open. A dark head appeared.

"I've frightened you. I am sorry," Nathaniel said with a rueful smile. "I hadn't planned to enter this way, but as you can see my hands are occupied." Dressed in a midnight blue silk dressing gown piped with gold, he carried a bottle of champagne in one hand and two flutes by their slender stems in the other.

Laura swallowed on a gasp of relief. "A secret panel! How fascinating!"

"The abbey is riddled with passages. I spent my childhood discovering them."

"You must show them to me. I love such things."

He poured her a glass of champagne and sat beside her on the bed to clink his glass against hers.

After the wine at dinner and the port, Laura feared the champagne would lull her to sleep. She laughed and shook her head.

He smiled. "Care to share the joke?"

"You, appearing like a ghost through the wall."

His smile widened. "A welcome ghost?" He removed the glass from her hand, placing it on the table alongside him.

"Most welcome," she whispered as he drew her to her feet.

He gathered her close against the hard length of his body, cradled her head in his hands and kissed her deeply. "Must you braid your hair?" he asked when he drew away.

She did but felt unable to argue with him when he turned her shoulders, and his long fingers unraveled her hair. He gathered up her tresses and held them to his face. "Silky and sweetly scented. Glorious."

"I might wear a cap," she teased.

"Don't you dare," he said huskily. "Your hair glows like fire in this light."

He slipped the dressing gown from her shoulders to slide into a pool of silk at her feet. "You're so beautiful, Laura."

Baring her shoulder, he kissed his way to the sensitive skin at the base of her throat. He eased her back onto the bed and slid his hand over her thigh, pushing her nightgown higher, slowly, as her naked body was revealed to him. Drawing the lacy garment over her head, he tossed it to the floor. So much for the care she'd taken choosing it, Laura thought, before his deft touch sent her thoughts whirling away.

"I've been thinking of this all day." His low voice was muffled against her breast.

Tonight would bring them closer. She would make it so. When his hands strayed, finding her most sensitive spots, her body clamored for him, and she threw back her head with a moan.

After Nathaniel's masterful lovemaking, Laura stretched like a cat. She lay tangled in the crisp linen sheets, her head resting against Nathaniel's chest. Endeavoring to please him, she'd become bolder, pleased when she saw how she'd moved him. Her body was sated, but her heart and soul still yearned for something more. Confused, she pushed the thoughts away. He had been a consummate lover. No woman would complain. She was too impatient.

Nathaniel rolled away from her to sit up. He reached for the champagne bottle and topped up their glasses. She plumped up the pillows and sat, feasting her eyes on the gorgeous man in her bed. It was so gloriously decadent sipping champagne beneath a festoon of gold cloth, the bed curtains caught up with golden tassels.

"We'll ride after breakfast," Nathaniel said. "In the afternoon, I'll take you to meet Miss Cilla Gain. I believe she will be good company for you."

"Does she live in the village?"

"No, in a cottage out on the point. She is an artist."

"An artist! How wonderful."

"With your interest in art you may find common ground."

"How does Miss Gain come to live at Wolfram?"

"We knew each other years ago. She arrived one day and asked me if she could turn one of the empty cottages into a studio. She isn't well off, so I allow her to live there."

"How generous, Nathaniel," Laura said with a warm rush of feeling. "Is she from these parts?"

He patted her cheek. "All these questions. I'll allow her to tell you her story herself."

"I can't wait to meet her."

Laura gazed at her husband. She was getting to know this man slowly, which didn't suit her impatient nature, but she loved all that she'd learned about him.

Some hours later, Laura woke to find Nathaniel's side of the bed empty. Her head swam a little when she raised it from the pillow. He'd refilled her glass more than once before she'd fallen asleep. Brilliant moonlight shone through a gap in the curtains. Laura donned her nightgown. She had no need for a candle when she rose to use the chamber pot. A privy was one convenience she sorely missed and was determined to rectify. Pouring water from the jug, she washed in the basin. As she dried her hands, she thought she heard a soft footfall in the corridor outside. She paused, hoping Nathaniel would return. When he didn't, she went to open her door. The corridor was dark where the moonlight couldn't reach and chilly.

She cleared her throat. "Is someone there?"

No answer. Her skin prickled as she searched the shadows. When her eyes adjusted to the darkness, she found it empty, the only movement a huge tapestry on the wall stirring in the draft.

With a shiver, Laura returned to her room. She ran her fingers along the panels in the wall hoping to open the secret door. Failing to find the catch, she grabbed a shawl and slipped into the corridor again. She hesitated outside Nathaniel's room wondering whether to knock. How ridiculous. She was his wife! She needed warmth and reassurance. Surely that wasn't unreasonable. Opening the door, she found the room in darkness, the curtains closed.

Laura paused, not wishing to wake him, but there was no soft snore, no sign of movement. She groped her way over to the bed and reached down to touch his pillow. The sheets were cold, the bed empty.

"Nathaniel?" Even as she said it, she knew Nathaniel wasn't there. He must have gone downstairs.

Stumbling to the window, she scraped her knee painfully against what must have been the corner of the bureau. She pulled back the curtains. Moonlight swept into the room, confirming that the bed was indeed empty. The pillow was smooth, the bedclothes unrumpled. It had never been slept in. Where was he then?

She paused to catch her breath, and then hurried from the room. Farther down the corridor, candlelight flowed from beneath a door. Laura crept toward it.

Hadn't Nathaniel told her that the staff was on the floor above? As she reached for the doorknob, a shadow crossed the light. Laura hesitated. She could hardly enter someone's bedroom in the middle of the night. Knocking would be embarrassing to say the least. Have you seen my lost husband? She grinned despite her discomfort. It would be such a bad beginning. But why hadn't he mentioned someone was just down the corridor? Had she mistaken him when he'd said only guest chambers were in this wing?

She trailed her hand along the wall to hasten her walk back to her room. Odd to feel a trespasser in her own home. Her bedroom seemed a haven of warmth as she hurried inside.

Shivering, more from unease than cold, Laura climbed back into bed and pulled the coverlet up to her chin. She sank down and closed her eyes, with the hope that sleep would ease her concerns, at least until daylight. An hour passed. She thrashed about unable to quiet her mind, alert for any sound. Could it have been Nathaniel in that room? If not, then who was it? And if not Nathaniel, where had he gone?

There was nothing to make Nathaniel suspect danger still lurked at Wolfram. Yet he could not discount it. Surefooted, he ran over the grounds. If he had to, he could negotiate the land blindfolded, but tonight a moonlit sky made his way easier. Not just him, perhaps, for it was on a night like that that... He shook the dispiriting thoughts from his head and glanced up at Laura's window. It remained in darkness, making him confident she still slept safely in her bed. He had stayed longer than he intended, watching her sleep. Such an innocent with her thick golden lashes resting on her creamy cheek. She had spirit though. Those remarkable green eyes of hers could flash, and she was a passionate, generous lover. He admired her intelligence and her curiosity, while at the same time, felt discomfited by them.

Cilla's friendship might prevent Laura from becoming too lonely here. But he had no idea what she would make of the artist. Cilla was, well, Cilla.

An owl hooted. The shrubbery along the wall shook, probably a badger or a fox. A brisk, salt-laden breeze blew into his face, helping to clear his fatigue. Moving slowly, ever on the alert, Nathaniel reached the water.

Nothing but the slap of waves against the seawall.

CHAPTER NINE

The following morning, the weather changed dramatically. Gazing from her window, Laura saw a clear azure blue sky and sunlight sparkling on an indigo sea. She was happy and eager to see more of her new home despite her restless night. On the way to the staircase, even the stone corridors appeared more welcoming than on the previous day.

Nathaniel had returned at daylight and told her he'd gone to check on something in his study and had fallen asleep. He was often restless at night. It seemed so plausible she was ashamed of herself and decided to delay questioning him about the candlelight in the room down from hers.

At the breakfast table, the warmth of his smile echoed in his voice as he suggested they ride over the estate. Laura returned his smile and agreed, while being a little uneasy about her riding skills. She was good at sport, but her riding had been restricted to a pony when she was a child. She was determined to master it. In her bedroom, she adjusted her riding hat before the mirror. It was a handsome green-gold felt adorned with net and a graceful feather. Her mother had chosen it for Laura's trousseau to match her new riding habit. Laura smiled to herself. They might not always agree, but in matters of fashion, her mother's taste was unerring.

Laura raised the watch that hung on a slender gold chain at her breast. Half past ten. Nathaniel had left the house after breakfast to attend to business. He promised to return at eleven o'clock for their ride. With half an hour to spare, she wandered about restlessly. Should she go downstairs and seek out Rudge? There was still so much of the house to view. She wanted to learn her duties and begin as soon as possible.

Leaving her chamber, with barely a thought, Laura turned right instead of left and found herself standing before the door which had been occupied the night before. With a steadying breath, she knocked. When no sound came from within, she tried the handle. The door opened.

She leaned back against the open door and blinked. The walls of the luxurious bedroom were of deep magenta overlaid in gold. The bed had ruby satin bed hangings and a matching silk coverlet. A rose-pink velvet armchair perched by the window. Laura shivered and rubbed her arms. The chilly room smelled musty, as though shut up for a long time. But overlaid was a scent she failed to identify. The candle in a glass candlestick on the dresser had burned down to a stub. It was tallow. Odd when she'd been told that only beeswax candles were used in the house. Laura crossed the crimson rug to open the two matching mahogany armoires.

"Good heavens!" Her voice sounded loud in the still room. Both cupboards were crammed with dresses of every hue. Taffeta silk, appliquéd velvets, organdie and India muslin, capes trimmed with ostrich or fur, and silk tea gowns of the finest quality. Silk underthings and nightgowns were folded neatly in the drawers. Laura picked up a dainty, soft gray chemise trimmed with Valenciennes lace. A delicate perfume wafted into the air.

The realization almost buckled her knees. This could only be Amanda's bedchamber. Laura quickly folded the chemise and returned it to the drawer, as if she had no right to be there. She couldn't rush away though. She was held captive by a need to understand more about the woman who had been Nathaniel's wife.

Laura turned her attention to the dresser. A row of sterling silver and cut glass perfume bottles were scattered over the top as if they had been disturbed. She picked up a lantern-shaped bottle and removed the diamond-cut glass stopper, recognizing the scent: a hint of ylang-ylang and exotic vanilla. Clive Christian Number One, Queen Victoria's favorite perfume, and Laura's mother's. Laura shoved in the stopper with trembling fingers.

A silver-plated comb and mirror set, inlaid with amethysts and crystals, lay on the muslin-covered table amid other treasures: a rope of creamy pearls flung carelessly down, a pair of golden candles in crystal holders, pink artificial roses in a crystal vase. She opened a jewel box to a Chopin *Nocturne*. Necklaces, earrings and trinkets almost spilled from it. Her fingers hovered over a coral necklace in an exotic gold setting. Her breath came faster, and her nape prickled as if someone looked over her shoulder. Laura replaced the lid and hurried to the door. Had it been Nathaniel here last night after he left her bed? The possibility struck Laura like a blow to her stomach. She didn't want to believe it. But who else could it have been? Was he still in love with his dead wife? They must talk about this. She *would* ask him.

Soon.

She feared his answer, or worse, his lies, as she exited the room. Closing the door behind her, she turned and saw him.

He stood outside her bedroom door. Frowning, he tucked his riding crop under his arm and drew on leather gloves. "That was Amanda's bedroom. Are you exploring?"

Laura flushed. "I wasn't aware it was hers." She straightened her shoulders.

"We'd best take that ride. It looks like it might rain."

"Does it?" She hurried after him, smoothing her silk cravat with nervous fingers. "The sky had scarcely a cloud when last I looked."

"The weather can change in a moment here."

He turned his broad back and started for the stairs. He invited no questions. Did he assume she didn't wish to ask any? Of course she did. Curiosity ate at her, churning her stomach. She chewed her lip and followed him. Should they have it out now? After their ride, perhaps.

What a coward she was.

With the dogs panting at the horses' heels, she and Nathaniel rode up the lane into the wood, pungent with rotting leaf mounds. They followed a bridle path, the earthy smells mingling with the tang of pine. The dogs disturbed a flock of wood pigeons, and they exploded into the air as if at the sound of a gun.

She followed Nathaniel out from the trees, emerging onto a strip of land above the bluff covered in wild grasses. "Careful here," Nathaniel called, reining in his horse.

The sea wind threatened to rip Laura's hat from her head. A hand on the crown, she attempted to steady her horse. Above them, clouds scudded across the sky and seabirds swooped. Her gaze followed a bird's dizzying path as it dived into the white-tipped waves to rise again with a wriggling fish in its beak. The cliff curved away; at the foot, the surging sea dashed against rocks in a thunderous roar. Laura licked her lips, tasting salty brine on her tongue. Out at sea, a three-masted ship disappeared into the haze. It seemed to capture Nathaniel's interest. She noted the rigid set of his shoulders.

She wanted to speak to him but held back, lacking the confidence to draw her horse close to his. The neat roan was an obliging animal, but Laura didn't trust her riding skills yet.

After Wimbledon, Wolfram seemed timeless. It had stood unchanged for centuries. So many lives played out, day by day, year by year, and generation by generation. She was suddenly aware of her own mortality. She almost laughed at her gravity as she watched her handsome husband, in command of his huge stallion. She had everything to live for. Was it Amanda's room, so carefully preserved, as if she'd just walked out the door, that brought this morbid turn of mind? Or the shifting horse beneath her and the nearness of the cliff? Her horse sidled, and that frightening drop suddenly became too close for comfort.

Nathaniel's mount stamped and snorted. He appeared deep in thought, turned away from her, gazing out to sea. The wind plucked at her hat again, and the veil of net tightened, claustrophobic against her face. Laura panicked. She pulled on the reins and turned her horse back onto the bridle path.

"Laura!" Nathaniel rode after her. He headed her off on the narrow path, pushing his horse in front of hers. "Did she bolt?"

She swallowed. "No."

"Then why did you take off like that?"

She couldn't explain. She looked into Nathaniel's face, finding concern. "The cliff…"

He backed his horse away, his face relaxing. "Goose. Come on. Let's ride to the village. You'll feel better when you meet some of the people here, and I'll introduce you to the parishioners in church on Sunday."

After he ordered the dogs home, they rode across the causeway. The whitewashed cottages in the village stood out against the landscape, their slate roofs the color of the sea. A few people came out to pay their respects as she and Nathaniel trotted down the street, but others hung back, talking among themselves. Nathaniel appeared not to notice as he helped her dismount. He had done so much for these people, so why did they dislike him? For dislike it surely was. She thought of the rock which had hit their carriage on the way from Penzance and wanted to question him, but sensed by his set expression that he wouldn't welcome it now.

"Let's take some refreshment."

He took her arm, and they entered the old Tudor inn, The Sail and Anchor on the quayside. Inside was dim with a low, heavy-beamed ceiling and flagstone floor. The air was stale and smelled heavily of hops from the locally brewed ale and cider. It was not an establishment she would choose to frequent.

Nathaniel nodded at the two people behind the bar. "Roe, a glass of port for Lady Lanyon."

The barmaid, a blue-eyed blonde with a low-cut blouse, curtseyed and gave Nathaniel a sly glance from beneath her lashes.

It was lost on him, Laura was glad to see.

The innkeeper, Roe, bowed his head. "Milady." He scrubbed at the bar with a cloth. "Excuse me, Y' Lordship, while I wipe up the tears of the tankard. Can't have you wetting the sleeve of your good coat."

Nathaniel ordered a pint of ale for himself, then led Laura through a door into a smoky parlor with small windows looking out onto the street.

Roe brought their drinks. "It's a pleasure to have you in my humble establishment." His grin exposed a missing front tooth. "Not like the rascals and sharps that usually frequent the place."

"What does he mean by referring to the drinkers here as sharps?" Laura asked after he'd left the room.

"Nothing complimentary, that's certain." Nathaniel drained his tankard. "Stay here, Laura. I won't be a moment." He returned to the bar.

Laura heard him say, "I need to have a quiet word with you, Roe."

"If you'll step into the back room, Y' Lordship?" Roe replied.

A good twenty minutes later, Laura, having finished her drink, walked to the parlor door wondering where Nathaniel had gotten to. A soldier stood at the bar talking to the barmaid. His pipe smoke seeped into the stuffy parlor. The pair glanced at her. The soldier said something Laura couldn't catch, and the woman, her breasts rising like two half-moons from her white blouse, threw back her head and laughed.

Laura's discomfort grew. Why had Nathaniel brought her here then left her to drink alone? As her frustration mounted, he reappeared.

Roe returned to his place behind the bar. "No fear, Y' Lordship. That business shall be dealt with."

Frowning, Nathaniel murmured something indecipherable and threw some coins onto the bar.

"Right you are." Roe weighed the coins in his hand. "Thanks for the strike, Y' Lordship."

Nathaniel escorted Laura into the street. He tossed another coin to a young lad minding their horses, then threw her up into the saddle.

He treated her in such a cavalier fashion. As soon as they were out of earshot of the curious villagers, Laura edged her mount closer, disappointment causing her voice to shake. "Why did you take me there?"

"Why? It's the local inn." His eyebrows met in a puzzled frown. "I've been going there since I was old enough to drink."

"I don't think it's a suitable place…" she began, then realized it sounded snobbish and unreasonable. "It's just that I didn't enjoy drinking alone."

"Yes, I'm sorry. I didn't expect my business to take so long."

An unwelcome thought had crept into her brain, and she desperately wanted to dismiss it. Nathaniel had told her the port they drank at home had come from Portugal. Did smuggling still go on in these parts? "What business would you have with that man?"

"Sweetheart, please, it's nothing of import. Don't concern yourself."

He shut her out and showed no interest in her opinion. Tense and wary, Laura gripped the reins. Had she left her mother only to replace her with a male version of the same? Her horse sensed her mood and broke into a gallop across the rocky ground of the causeway.

"Laura!"

When they reached solid ground, she was still fighting to slow the animal. Nathaniel grabbed her reins, pulling their horses close. His expression was one of pained tolerance. Laura quaked.

"Are you going to take off every time something happens that doesn't suit you? This is Cornwall, Laura. It's dangerous to let your mount have her head. This isn't Hyde Park. Things are done differently here."

Laura remembered her aunt's words. Would she ever really know him? She tried to pull her horse's reins from his grasp. "Let go, Nathaniel."

"When you have regained your good humor."

She didn't want to admit she'd lost control of the horse. His disappointment in her would be too hard to bear. "I'm not used to being treated in this fashion," she said instead. It sounded weak and wasn't what she really wanted to say; her frustration was about something else entirely. She clamped her lips together.

"Of that I am patently aware." He studied her for a moment with a perplexed expression, and then released her reins. He nudged his horse into a canter. "If you've forgiven me, we shall call on Cilla. That's if you still care to?"

"I do."

He appeared to be on friendly first-name terms with this woman. Laura was in no mood to meet her. They rode on in strained silence. The chance to question him about Amanda's bedchamber receded even further.

When they approached the narrow track along the bluff, Laura was already regretting her quick temper. Her husband's business affairs were not her concern, although he might have humored her. She faced the fear that although he clearly desired her, he wasn't in love with her. It was foolish to expect so much so soon. She grew angry with herself for being vulnerable to every perceived slight.

Roe's news had rocked him, and Nathaniel struggled to push it from his mind. Having secured the horses to the rail beside the water trough, he held out his hand to Laura, hoping she'd recovered her good nature. He could tell by the lift of her chin that Laura hadn't completely forgiven him. She was young and expected a great deal from life. He'd been aware of this when he'd married her. In the future, he would conduct his business alone. He'd wanted her company and to have her under his eye. But he refused to burden her with his problems. There were things of which he couldn't speak, wounds so deep that he would be afraid to voice them. They needed time. Unfortunately, they didn't have it. A trip to London could not be avoided. Legislation was to be introduced into parliament which would affect Wolfram.

Laura needed a friend, but there were good reasons why she and Cilla might not get on. Once again, the fear that he'd made a serious mistake bringing her here caused his shoulder muscles to knot. He shrugged, trying to ease them, and took her arm.

A muscle ticked beside Nathaniel's jaw. Laura would attempt to clear the air between them once they were alone. A garden path led to the small stone cottage. Red geranium spilled from window boxes, the front door painted a bright yellow. She took a deep breath and plastered on a smile as he knocked on the door. There was no sound from within.

"It appears Cilla is not at home," he said after a moment.

As they retraced their steps to the gate, a woman appeared in the lane riding a bicycle.

"Nathaniel! How nice." Miss Gain jumped down from her bike. "I went to buy sugar from the village shop." She grimaced. "I expected to be back in a trice, but I ran into Mrs. Hartwell and she does talk so."

Nathaniel took the bike from her. "Cilla, I've brought my bride to meet you. This is Laura."

Laura studied the woman as she came through the gate. Cilla was attractive. A tall brunette close to Nathaniel's age. Laura noted her very modern divided navy skirt which ended at calf level with a twinge of envy.

"How lovely to meet you at last, Laura."

"I've been keen to meet you, Cilla, ever since Nathaniel told me you were an artist." Laura shook her hand, her gaze falling on the man's tie Cilla wore around her neck. She brightened. Might this woman be interested in women's suffrage?

Cilla's amused hazel eyes met hers. "Please do come inside."

They entered the tiny front hall. "Come through to the back garden. I find it the best place for tea. One cannot be indoors on such a day."

The cottage was filled with light and bursting with odd things. Sculpted pieces, some finished and some not, sat amongst rocks, feathers, driftwood, books and dried flowers. Bunches of fresh flowers were shoved into vases without a care to their arrangement and placed wherever a spare space offered itself. Hook rugs covered the bare boards. An embroidered, fringed shawl hung over the back of the crimson sofa with cushions of all shapes and sizes thrown on it willy-nilly. Bright, thickly painted canvases in the loose and bold style of the French Impressionists covered the walls. Sheer white curtains stirred in the sea breeze at the open windows.

The acrid smells of oil paint and varnish fought with the floral scents. A canvas hidden beneath a cloth perched on an easel in a small dining room off the parlor. She'd made this her studio, where all the paraphernalia of the artist—a palette, half-squeezed tubes of paint and jars filled with brushes—were piled onto a table.

Nathaniel led Laura outside to a leafy, vine-covered loggia, where they sat in wicker chairs. Here they could look directly out to sea, the cliff only yards away. The sea breeze toyed with Laura's hat again, and she eased the net away from her face.

Nathaniel placed a hand on her arm and leaned toward her. "Laura…"

Cilla bustled out of the doorway carrying a tray. She unloaded tea things onto the wicker table and disappeared again.

"Yes, Nathaniel?" Laura searched his face.

He frowned and shook his head. "I can see you're not happy. But now is not the time to talk."

Laura forgot her plan to appease him. "I'm glad you acknowledge that we do need to talk."

Cilla reappeared with a cake plate, which Laura now recognized to be Cornish heavy cake.

"I didn't make the cake," Cilla said. "Mrs. Hartwell did, and she's a splendid cook. Eat up." She pulled off her shabby straw bonnet and threw it on the ground, placing her chair leg on the brim to stop it blowing away. "I'll be mother, shall I?" Cilla picked up the brown teapot and proceeded to pour the tea. "You look very well, Nathaniel." She glanced at Laura with a smile. "It's been an age since I've enjoyed decent company. And Nathaniel told me you attended university." Her eyes widened. "I've never met a woman who has done such a thing."

"I was fortunate to be able to sit in on lectures," Laura said. "I didn't write papers or take exams."

"Still…" Cilla shrugged. "I would love to hear more about it."

Nathaniel winked at Laura and nodded, as if to say this was what he hoped would happen. They'd been discussing her, apparently. "And I look forward to learning more about art."

Cilla appeared to be a fish out of water here. She was obviously very talented, but who else would share Cilla's interests? At least Aunt Dora, who devoted her time to writing poetry, mixed with other writers in London.

Nathaniel looked very much at home here, leaning back in his chair, sipping his tea. How often did he visit? A shaft of jealousy coiled inside her. Had he confessed the secrets he held so tightly in his heart to Cilla? An even more unattractive situation occurred to Laura. Had they once been lovers? Such a thought was unworthy of her. What was the matter with her?

Laura took a gulp of tea. It burned her throat. "Oh!" she said, choking. She reached for a napkin.

Nathaniel straightened, with a concerned expression. "Are you all right, my dear?"

She would hate for Cilla to suspect that they'd quarreled earlier. She smiled. "It was a little hot."

"How do you find Wolfram, Laura?" Cilla asked.

"I've yet to see much of it," Laura said. "It's so big. When Nathaniel told me about his home, I never envisaged anything quite like this."

Nathaniel frowned. "That doesn't sound like a ringing approval."

"I certainly meant it to be."

Cilla refilled her cup. "I imagine one accustomed to living in a city would take time to get used to the... differences."

Laura flushed, feeling besieged and strangely inadequate. An outsider. "I already feel very much at home."

Nathaniel's somber gray eyes searched hers. "I hope so."

She had been uncertain about so much since she'd arrived and felt unequal to the task of refuting it.

"In time," Cilla said with an encouraging smile, "you will come to love it, the lack of modern comforts and all."

Laura gave Nathaniel a small smile. "I have to admit there are a few things I do miss."

She felt grateful to Cilla for tactfully changing the subject. Now was not the time to suggest new plumbing. They discussed village affairs, and even though their conversation mostly excluded her, Laura listened with interest.

"Where did you study art, Cilla? At the hand of a master, I suspect," Laura asked when there was a pause.

Cilla's eyes warmed. "I was lucky to have a very good teacher in Paris."

"Paris! But you aren't French?"

"Mother. She was a distant cousin of Berthe Morisot's. Perhaps you've heard of her?"

"I love her work; I was sorry to hear that she died. Did you live in Paris for a long time?"

"While my parents pursued their painting careers. I came back after they both died from influenza."

Laura reached across and touched the other woman's arm. "How difficult that must have been."

Cilla nodded. "It was, for they left me very little money. But I've been content here. I can paint. I can't paint everywhere, you understand."

"It's the same for writers, I imagine," Laura said sympathetically.

Nathaniel offered little to the conversation. He was allowing them to get to know each other. But even though Cilla's former life was fascinating, Laura's thoughts constantly strayed to him. There was a reserve, a gulf between them today, that she hadn't felt before. Their cross words should not have affected them so much. Perhaps, unlike Wolfram, built to last on a foundation of rock, they'd built their relationship on the shifting sand of attraction, and the slightest disagreement caused a rift. Trouble was, she didn't really know him. He didn't allow her to. Even their lovemaking, as wonderful as it was, didn't make her feel any closer to him. She wanted so much; she couldn't bear things the way they were.

Across the sea, roiling purple clouds rolled over the horizon toward them. Nathaniel stood. "We'd best get the horses back to the stables."

They walked through Cilla's chaotic little house. A painting Laura had been too distracted to notice earlier hung near the front door. A moonlit landscape where candlelight shone out from the windows of a cottage, the woods in the distance. The painting was eerily beautiful. She stopped to examine it more closely. A woman in a red dress stood at the doorway rimmed by candlelight.

"We'd best go, Laura. That storm will be upon us before we know it." Nathaniel took her arm and hurried her out to the waiting horses.

As Nathaniel predicted, the sky darkened overhead and the wind picked up, tossing the tree branches around. As they reached the stables, rain sleeted down. They made a mad dash for the house.

"I must change," Laura said, climbing the stairs.

"I'll come up with you."

This pleased her. They would be more relaxed and open with each other within the confines of her bedroom, and they could heal the earlier quarrel.

"Your Lordship?" Rudge appeared at the foot of the stairs. Nathaniel turned and ran back down. The butler spoke too quietly for Laura to hear.

Nathaniel glanced up to where she stood waiting, his eyes strained. "I'll see you at dinner, Laura."

"What is it?"

"A small problem. Nothing to worry about."

He grabbed his oil slicker and disappeared out the front door. Yet again, no explanation offered. Feeling excluded, Laura stood there for a moment, holding the banister. The wood felt cold under her hand as she continued her climb.

CHAPTER TEN

Nathaniel leaned into the rain-laden wind. His overseer, Hugh Pitney, was close in height and matched his stride as they continued in grim silence. They took the left fork heading down to the shore. Pitney was one of a few men Nathaniel could rely on. He'd proven he could carry the weight of responsibility on his broad shoulders while Nathaniel was in London.

Nathaniel's thoughts returned to the painful past, when a dangerous man had brought chaos to Wolfram. He'd slipped through the net and disappeared, denying Nathaniel the chance to bring him to justice and see him hang. But in his gut Nathaniel was sure he'd turn up again. The man was arrogant and confident no one could land a blow on him. He'd spread vicious gossip before he left, and the villagers remained in ignorance of what had happened here two years ago.

They'd reached the stone cottage, isolated from the rest, which perched on a rise above the sandy shore below which a funnel of rock, like a pointing finger, reached out into a dark gray sea, stirred up by the force of the wind. The gale howled around them, the sand-laden wind blowing in Nathaniel's eyes. Exasperated, he swept a hand over them and blinked away the grit.

"I've expected this ever since that three-masted ship turned up," he yelled above the wind. "How did you discover this hoard?"

Hugh's brown eyes were troubled. "I stumbled upon it, milord, when part of the roof caved in and I went to inspect it."

"Good thing you did." Nathaniel gestured toward the beach. "Have you checked the caves?"

Hugh nodded. "Empty. No sign of recent activity. Crazy to store anything there in this weather, and you'd think they'd know better than to try this again after the last time."

He forced the door open as the rain became a deluge, flowing from the broken gutters. Ducking their heads, they entered the low doorway. Rain splattered down from the ceiling of the tiny entry, but the main room remained dry. Boxes were stacked over the floor.

"How did they get this lot past the coastguard?" Removing a pocketknife from his coat, Nathaniel squatted down and levered a box open. "Tobacco." He sat back on his heels with a shake of his head. "Not been here long. They probably meant to move it by boat before we discovered it." He straightened. "The storm has held them up. Any thoughts as to who is behind it?"

"It's hard to say, milord. The catch has been poor of late. Some are finding it tough."

"Get the constable over here." Nathaniel rested his boot on a box. "I'll wait here for him."

Hugh drew the collar of his coat around his ears and shouldered his way out into the rain.

Left alone, Nathaniel wandered around the musty room, opening random boxes. The same smuggling ring. With a different man at the top. They'd have to round them up quickly this time, before more damage was done. Mud stuck to a man, he already had evidence of that. Disgusted and disillusioned, Nathaniel put a hand to his hair and swore. Could things get any worse? He'd lose any support he had in the Lords if word of this reached London.

He groaned. Laura! After Amanda's death, he'd been determined never to bring another wife to Wolfram. This would frighten her. Hell, she'd only just arrived, and everything was so new to her! He didn't want her to think life would always be this grim. It wasn't going to be, not if he had to personally round up everyone involved. Anger and despair seeped into his bones like poison.

"Wine, my lady?" The butler stood hawkeyed as the servants brought in the first course.

"Thank you, Rudge."

Nathaniel had not yet returned.

She'd been determined not to ask Rudge where Nathaniel went, but she couldn't swallow a mouthful of food until she did. "Where did his lordship go, Rudge?"

Rudge lifted the decanter. "I beg pardon, my lady. Lord Lanyon didn't see fit to inform me."

Laura wondered if he just refused to tell her. Whatever message he'd relayed to Nathaniel had sent him rushing away. She glanced away from the butler's unfathomable, black eyes. He didn't like her. It perplexed her, for she believed she'd done nothing to warrant it. "What message did you give his lordship?"

Rudge blinked. Laura realized with satisfaction that she'd surprised him. Was the butler not used to his mistress taking an interest in the running of the estate?

"His lordship's overseer, Mr. Pitney, sent word, my lady. A problem had arisen which required his lordship's attention."

Laura sprinkled salt onto the soup, although she didn't wish to eat it. "What sort of problem is it that cannot wait until morning?"

"I'm afraid I couldn't say, my lady. Would you care for more wine?"

Laura nodded, realizing she'd drunk a full glass. As the ruby liquid swirled into her wineglass, she discreetly studied him. Rudge was younger than she first thought. The shady side of forty, the gray at his temples and his manner lent him a gravitas one associated with age. "Have you been with Lord Lanyon long, Rudge?"

"Four and a half years, my lady."

"Then you served the first Lady Lanyon."

"Yes, my lady."

"She was a good mistress?"

Rudge put down the wine carafe and stepped back into his position. "Yes, my lady."

"I believe she was quite lovely."

"Yes. A very fine lady." He clasped and unclasped his gloved hands. "Do you not care for the soup? Shall I serve the next course?"

"The soup is delicious, but I'm not very hungry tonight." She pushed her plate away, wondering if she made him uncomfortable. Her curiosity and perhaps the wine had made her speak out of turn. Somehow, she didn't much care. She took another sip of the fine claret. "Is there a likeness of her here? I haven't seen one."

"His lordship had the portrait removed."

Laura sat stunned. Amanda's room was kept as she left it, yet any picture of her had been removed. It made no sense. She rubbed her brow. Unless Nathaniel could not bear to look at one.

"There's a portrait stored in the library," Rudge said. "I could show it to you after dinner should you wish it, my lady."

Laura toyed with her wineglass. Candlelight flashed rainbow colors across the cut glass. "Perhaps I'll wait for Lord Lanyon to do so. Serve the next course, if you please."

After dinner, Laura asked for coffee to be served in the library.

Rudge stood beside her as she sat by the fire. "Do you require anything more, my lady?"

"No, that will be all."

"I could show you the portrait now, if you wish?"

Rudge seemed very eager for her to see it. Should she refuse? Or would she know better what she was dealing with if she viewed it? She finished her coffee and put down the cup. "Very well."

"If you'll come this way, my lady."

Laura rose, wondering if she'd been rash, and followed Rudge to the far end of the room. Opening a cupboard, Rudge carefully removed a large painting wrapped in a cloth cover. His mouth twisted into an odd smile. "This used to hang above the fireplace in this room." After he pulled away the fabric, his thick fingers caressed the gilt frame. Then he turned the painting toward her.

Had Rudge been obsessed with Amanda? The suspicion sent a shaft of unease down her spine. Not about to give him satisfaction, she studied the painting without comment. The composition was an unusual one. The artist had placed his subject in this room, with the magnificent stained glass window, the baronial fireplace, even the leopard skin rug just as it was now. Again, the feeling that it happened just a moment ago made Laura drag in a sharp breath.

Amanda stood in the center of the stone-flagged floor with a flowery hat in one gloved hand, as if she was about to go out or had just returned. She looked directly at the painter; a smile curved her lips and her blue eyes held laughter, her blonde hair drawn back from a pale brow into a smooth knot. Her gown was of a blue stuff that matched her eyes, and she held a dainty blue parasol at her side.

"She was lovely." Laura wished Amanda hadn't been quite so beautiful.

"Yes, she was." The crisp reply came from behind her. "Put the painting away, Rudge."

Laura whirled around. Nathaniel stood at the door.

"That will be all, Rudge," Laura said, not taking her eyes from her husband.

Nathaniel threw himself down into a chair by the fireplace. He'd changed his clothes. "Bring me a brandy before you go, Rudge."

Her throat tight, Laura remained silent until the door closed behind the butler. "I'm sorry, should I not have seen it?"

"You are interested in my first wife." Nathaniel sounded exhausted. "I should tell you more." He passed his hand over his eyes. "I will tell you more, Laura. Just not now."

Guilt heated her cheeks. She should have waited for Nathaniel to show it to her. His hair was wet, and she longed to move closer, to lean her head against his shoulder and learn what troubled him, but she seemed frozen on the sofa. "What called you out in this dreadful weather?"

"An estate matter. I'm sorry I was not able to dine with you."

"I can't imagine what would require your attention so late."

"Any number of things." His dark eyebrows snapped together.

"Running an estate this size doesn't fit neatly into normal business hours."

Noting the edge to his voice, Laura gave up. She rose. "You should eat, Nathaniel. Would you like me to arrange for a tray to be brought?"

"Thank you, but I'm not hungry."

It seemed they both had lost their appetites. "I believe I shall retire."

He raised his head to look at her. "You're tired?"

"Yes, a little."

In truth, she quivered with nervous exhaustion. Suddenly, the long day without a shred of affection from Nathaniel overwhelmed her. How could she compete with Nathaniel's memories of a beloved wife, who would stay forever young and lovely? Life here proved so confusing, so hard to grasp hold of, with a secretive, distracted, uncommunicative husband and a butler who measured her poorly against his previous mistress. Was it an impossible task to make Wolfram her home? But what choice did she have?

Nathaniel stared at the half-glass of amber liquid. "I'll follow you up in a little while."

Upstairs, Laura donned a modest nightgown buttoned up to a high collar and dismissed Agnes. She tried to still her anxious thoughts. Hating that she was so unsure of herself and her position here, tears flooded her eyes. Where was her eager lover now? She climbed into bed. Had she failed so miserably? Did he no longer desire her?

The clock on the mantelpiece ticked away the hour.

Nathaniel stared into the fire, which crumbled into orange sparks as it died. Laura's curiosity concerning Amanda was understandable. Yet, how could he explain, put into words what had taken place here and not have her doubt him, as so many others had done?

His tired mind tried to come to grips with what he'd discovered and who might be behind it. When smugglers targeted Wolfram two years ago, Ben Jerkins, who worked at the home farm, had been arrested and hung along with four other men from the village. Although Nathaniel was sure Mallory was behind it, there was no proof, and his head gardener had disappeared soon after Amanda died.

At the time, Nathaniel had been glad to see the back of him. In a murderous mood, he was sorely tempted to deal with the man personally. As the villagers turned their backs on Nathaniel, he discovered that Mallory's parting gift was to spread hateful lies accusing Nathaniel of murdering Amanda.

Nathaniel had hired an investigator to keep tabs on him, and to make sure that if Mallory ever set foot again in Wolfram, he'd be ready for him.

Mallory's villainy still affected him and would continue to do so while some believed Nathaniel to be a murderer. There wasn't a damn thing he could do about it. The familiar horror rolled over him, and he took a long swallow of brandy. He felt incapable of dealing with it. The very thought of his wife with a man such as Mallory made him ill. Had Mallory used Amanda? And after she made demands of him, had he killed her, fearing she might give him up to the police? Nathaniel wished he could find out the truth.

He would have to inform the Customs and excise investigators in London about this new outrage. He found very few he could trust. There was no saying who might be involved. Upstairs Laura waited for him, and he tried to banish his concerns from his mind before he went to her.

Until these people were behind bars Laura would need to be protected. He would not sleep until all this was at an end, and the lack of it was taking a toll on his temper. But tired as he was, his need for her drew him to his feet. Her lovely face, her warm voice and lush curves, her silky skin beneath his hands, her hands on him. Laura's innocence and honesty made him crave to be the man she thought she married. He couldn't bear the thought of living without her, yet would she want to remain here? Or would she begin to gaze at him with suspicion? He didn't think he could bear it if she did.

Reaching the upper corridor, he slowed his steps toward her door. Every night he urged himself to take a chance. To respond to her obvious need to understand him. And each night he pushed it away. He knew he would fail again tonight.

CHAPTER ELEVEN

The panel slid back. Laura's heart leapt at the sight of him, as it always did. He threw off his robe, and the candlelight played lovingly over his strong, naked body, muscles rippling beneath olive skin. Pulling back the covers, he climbed in beside her. His skin was cool against hers as he gathered her up in his arms and pressed a kiss against her neck.

"You're so warm, and you smell wonderful, sweetheart."

Laura slid helplessly toward desire. Her body had come to expect it and now demanded the sensations only his lips, hands and body could produce. No matter how desperate she was to confront him, the touch of his mouth on hers, probing and insistent, sent every thought skittering away. Only one sure thought remained. When he entered her she cried out in joy, relishing the opportunity to be affectionate and give him all her love, even though he might not return it.

Nathaniel lay beside her, and she heard him sigh. She raised her head on an elbow. "Darling, what is it? What worries you so?"

"Estate matters. And I have to travel up to London this Friday; I'll be there for a week."

Her heart sank. "I thought the next trip was some weeks away."

"I can't always know when my presence will be required in parliament. I did explain that to you Laura when we first met. This is the way my life must be."

She tried to banish the disappointment from her voice. "I do understand. It's just that I expected us to have more time together. We have delayed our honeymoon."

"I am sorry. But you shall come with me. Stay at Wimbledon, visit your parents. I'll put up at a London hotel, but I will hardly be there. I'm busy during the day and must attend dinners that you would find dreadfully dull."

She pulled the sheet over her breasts. "You wouldn't want me to stay with you?"

"Not want you?" Nathaniel laughed and shook his head. He reached out and traced a line down her throat. "I've wanted you in my life since I first set eyes on you. So much so, I assured myself you would be happy here."

He sounded doubtful. Did he regret marrying her? Laura moved away, not wanting his touch to distract her, as her eyes filled with tears. She left the bed lest he should notice and pulled on her nightgown. "I wish I understood you, Nathaniel. Sometimes I fear you don't want me near you."

"That's nonsense!" Shrugging into his dressing gown, he followed her across the room. "Sweetheart, I'll be busy, tired and I fear short-tempered. You wouldn't be comfortable in a hotel suite. You can see your friends, go shopping with your mother."

At her vanity table, Laura picked up her pearl-handled hairbrush, its familiar smoothness reassuring beneath her fingers. She began to brush, but her movements were jerky and she snagged a curl.

Nathaniel removed the brush from her hand. His firm strokes felt wonderful. "I need to gather support for an important bill. The people here rely on me."

"But I've been asked to open the church fête on Saturday. I did tell you. It's my first official act as your wife." She'd expected him to be there.

He met her gaze in the mirror. "There'll be other fêtes. Make your excuses; they will understand that you must accompany me to London."

"I don't like to, Nathaniel. They'll think I don't care, and I want them to like me." And she was in no mood to come under her mother's measuring gaze. Certainly not now when she felt so unsure. "And I wish to address the servants, familiarize myself with the running of the household. We have no housekeeper. That cannot go on. You must employ one."

"Yes, quite so." Nathaniel put down the brush, swept aside her hair and touched his lips to her nape. "Perhaps you're right. It's an opportunity for the villagers to get to know the new baroness, who's a charming, lovely lady." He smiled. "I know they will warm to you. While I'm gone, you must take any concerns to my overseer, Hugh Pitney. He's a good man and will assist you."

She turned on the stool. "I will miss you terribly." She placed her hand at his nape and drew his head down for a kiss while she prayed that he would miss her as much.

"And I you, sweetheart." He swept her up in his arms and returned to the bed.

Nathaniel leaned back against the leather seat as the steam train chugged northward. The journey provided him with time for contemplation without distraction. He had instructed Hugh to keep a sharp eye on Laura during the daylight hours. The wheels were set in motion for an investigation into the smuggling, which the harbormaster and the revenue agents would orchestrate. He prayed something would come of their inquiries soon. The smugglers had been put on notice. They would be scattering to avoid the revenue men, and there was little reason for them to return now that their spoils were gone.

Could he and Laura ever settle into a peaceful life together? Nathaniel wasn't sure he believed it, but he clung to the possibility like a drowning man. He stared sightlessly out of the window. Would she continue to gaze at him with such warmth and affection? Having her love and her trust, when so many doubted him, was important. Whether he deserved it or not, it had become everything.

CHAPTER TWELVE

After seeing Nathaniel off on his way to the station in Penzance for the London train, Laura walked back to the house. Would he miss her as much as she would miss him? There was still a wall between them she seemed unable to breach. Was it because she'd failed to measure up to Amanda? She couldn't bear to think he might regret marrying her. One thing she was confident of, however: she did not disappoint him in the bedroom, for his hunger for her had not abated. But she'd begun to suspect that his confidence of her passion and his prowess to satisfy her smoothed over any disagreements between them. Nothing would change unless she demanded more openness from him. She was bewildered by how meek she'd become. She didn't know herself anymore. She'd always been spirited, a fighter, but fear of discovering Nathaniel's affections remained with his first wife had silenced her. If it were true, it was something she couldn't fight.

A stroll before lunch would have the dual purpose of ordering her thoughts, while discovering more of her new home. There was still so much she had yet to see.

Donning her hat, Laura strolled along the tree-lined lane past the row of stone cottages. One house looked very much like the one in Cilla's painting. Yes, there was the band of tall firs isolating it from the rest. She hesitated, then opened the creaky, rusted gate and entered the weedy front garden that had been a riot of color in Cilla's painting. Shading her vision from the sun's reflection, Laura peered through the dirty window into an empty room. Nathaniel had said they were unoccupied, but when she opened the front door and walked into the tiny parlor, she found the room partially furnished. A sofa flanked the fireplace, a table beside it. A fire had been laid in the grate as if someone was soon to arrive to light it. A branch of candles and a box of matches sat on the mantel. Feeling she had made a mistake and wandered into someone's home, Laura hurried out the door.

As she walked to the gate, a man on a chestnut horse appeared in the lane. The overseer, Hugh Pitney, pulled up his mount and raised his hat to greet her before riding on. She recalled having seen him earlier that day. Was Mr. Pitney following her? Laura bit her lip. Nathaniel must have instructed him to keep an eye on her. It was nonsensical. Was she not safe here? Nathaniel was as bad as her mother.

Laura continued her walk, glad that Mr. Pitney had made himself scarce. In among the trees of the park, she breathed in the pungent aroma of damp leaves, warm bark and fungi. Dappled patches of sunlight broke through the canopy overhead, brightening the shrubs and trees bordering the well-trodden path.

A squirrel scampered over a fallen log. Rustling in the bushes made her turn, her heart thumping, until her common sense took hold. It would be a deer or some other small animal. Not given to flights of fancy, she considered it foolish to find the silence, broken only by bird calls, ominous. Nevertheless, she picked up her skirts, increased her pace and hurried toward the patch of sunlight ahead.

She hadn't considered her direction and was a little shocked to find herself at the top of the cliff. She was about to go back the way she'd come, but stared instead at the awe-inspiring view. It was undoubtedly beautiful. There was a rim of dark gray on the horizon above a churning silver sea.

When Laura looked down at the crashing waves below, she grew dizzy. She hadn't been aware that heights affected her in this manner. Caught by a gust of wind, her skirts flapped, and when she smoothed them down, the wind ripped her shawl from her shoulders. She grabbed at it, but found herself only a few yards from the edge. Her throat tightened, and she stepped back on shaky legs. The fringed Cashmere shawl floated well beyond her reach. Like a sail in the wind, it soared out over the cliff and disappeared beneath the swell of white-capped waves below.

Laura held on to her hat, which threatened to join the shawl. She turned and marched along the narrow track through the trees. Instead of continuing in the direction of the village, she walked along a lane bordered by a high hedge.

"Damn it!" she muttered, remembering the pretty shawl had been a present from Aunt Dora.

"My goodness. Is that you, Laura?" Cilla rose from the garden with a trowel in her hand, a straw hat in a sad state of disrepair on her head. An apron covered a pair of what appeared to be men's trousers rolled up at the ankle. "This is a nice surprise."

Laura smiled. "I've been exploring." She wasn't sure she was up to facing the artist when she felt so low. But perhaps she'd unconsciously brought herself here, for Cilla might supply the answers to her questions.

Cilla grinned. "Please excuse my gardening attire. These were my French lover's and are so much more useful than a dress. You're just in time for lunch."

Laura hesitated. "Thank you, but I should return to the house. They'll be expecting me."

"Nonsense." Cilla opened the gate and stood aside. "My maid is here today. I'll send her over to tell them you won't be in for lunch."

"Well, if you're sure."

"I'd love the company."

Wondering if Cilla was ever lonely, Laura followed her along the path. "In London, some suffragettes prefer men's clothes, to make a statement I suppose. But I doubt the villagers would approve if I did it here."

Cilla chuckled. "They consider me to be a batty artist, so they tolerate me. But barely. You would cause a frightful scandal, however. Are you interested in women's suffrage?" She looked surprised. "I wouldn't expect a baroness to bother with such things."

"I wasn't always a baroness." Laura bit her lip at the fractious tone of her voice. It wasn't Cilla's fault that she now struggled to understand who she was and what she wanted. "I was very much involved when I lived in Wimbledon."

Cilla's hazel eyes brightened. "I hope you intend to continue to support this excellent cause."

"Yes, I do."

"And Nathaniel approves?" Cilla's tone was mild, but her sidelong glance alerted Laura that she doubted he would.

"Of course," Laura said airily. She needed a distraction and paused to look at the painting of the cottage garden in the moonlight. An impressive, moody work. "I walked past this cottage earlier."

Cilla folded her arms and leaned against the wall. "That place is empty now."

"Who used to live there?"

"Theo Mallory. Head gardener at Wolfram." Cilla dropped her arms. She turned and walked through the sitting room.

"I've met the head gardener, and his name isn't Theo. Does he still work here?"

"Not anymore."

Although she sensed Cilla's reluctance to discuss it, Laura persisted. "Who is the lady in the red dress at the door of the cottage? Real or imagined?"

Cilla swiveled, eyebrows raised. "She was real. Tell me, what has Nathaniel told you about his wife's death?"

Embarrassed, Laura shrugged. "Just that she died from a fall."

"Then perhaps I shouldn't talk of it. Come and keep me company while I prepare us a simple lunch. I have cauliflower soup and herby pie. If that appeals?"

"Sounds delicious. As you're now without your maid, please allow me to help."

Cilla smiled as she removed her hat. The green and brown scarf tying back her hair brought out warm lights in her eyes. "You may set the table. Such pleasant weather, we'll eat outside."

Laura discovered she was hungry. As she ate the delicious pie, she and Cilla chatted about the William Morris collection she and Nathaniel had seen. It was a pleasure to talk to someone who shared her interest. But when they'd exhausted that subject, the question that burned in Laura's brain begged to be answered.

"Can you at least tell me how Amanda died?" She reddened as the words popped out without prior thought. "I assumed a fall down the stairs."

"You haven't asked him?"

"I was gearing myself up to do so."

Cilla frowned. "There's no reason why Nathaniel won't tell you."

Laura dropped her gaze and flushed. "I think he still mourns her."

Cilla pushed away her plate. She rested her elbows on the table. "Well, you're going to find out eventually, and you've a right to know. I'm not surprised he hasn't brought the subject up though. You're right. I believe he remains very troubled."

Laura took a sip of water, her mouth suddenly dry.

"When Amanda failed to return to the house at dusk, Nathaniel gathered together an army from the estate and the village to search for her. The next day they found her body washed up on the rocks. She'd fallen from the cliffs. The weather was fine, so that wasn't a factor. We get dreadful storms here sometimes." Cilla dropped her gaze to the table and drew a pattern on the tablecloth. "We were very good friends. I miss her dreadfully."

"A horrible accident," Laura said.

"That was the coroner's finding when an inquest was held."

"Why would Amanda wander about alone heavily pregnant?"

"She liked to walk. Exercise made her feel better." Cilla gazed out to the horizon and frowned. "There were rumors. Don't ask me to repeat them, Laura. It would be merely unsubstantiated gossip, and I like to think I'm above that. I feel a sense of loyalty to Nathaniel. He has been kind to me."

Laura swallowed at the horror of such a useless death. She fell silent, recalling her fright when her shawl blew over the cliff.

"The servants and villagers have little better to do than gossip," Cilla said. "Such a tragedy. I imagine it will pass into the annals of history, as mysteries do. Try not to believe anything you might hear about Nathaniel though."

Laura stared at her. "Nathaniel?"

"I'm sorry I mentioned it. Let it go, Laura. You have your own life to live. Amanda's death will never be solved."

For Nathaniel's sake, Laura could not dismiss so sad a loss that easily. "But her unborn baby. Nathaniel's baby."

"I've no doubt he'll relegate it to the past where it belongs when you give him an heir."

Laura almost gasped. It seemed so coldblooded.

Cilla pushed away from the table. "Let's have tea inside, shall we?"

They stacked plates and cutlery onto a tray and sat in the sitting room.

The friendly atmosphere had waned slightly. "I'm sorry, I'm sure you don't want to talk about it either, Cilla. It's just that I need to know."

"Then talk to him."

Frustration filled Laura's eyes with tears. "I know, it's just..." She put down her cup, spilling tea in the saucer. She couldn't explain that she was afraid she could never fill Amanda's place in Nathaniel's heart.

Cilla rose and placed her arm around Laura's shaking shoulders. "You are troubled, aren't you? I think you should give it time. Be patient, Laura."

Laura sagged back in the chair. "Do you believe love to be a necessary ingredient to a successful marriage?"

What she didn't understand weighed her down. Why Nathaniel left her bed after they made love, and why he pushed her away when she tried to express tender feelings. Where he went every night. And she knew he did because she'd figured out how to open the panel. He had said once they were destined to be together. Had he meant it? Did he still believe it?

Cilla's eyebrows rose. "Surely you aren't referring to yours and Nathaniel's? Why, he's besotted with you. I didn't expect him to ever marry again. I am sure he'd decided not to. Yet here you are."

Laura picked up her cup with shaky fingers and took a gulp. The strong, hot tea warmed her and helped her regain her composure. "I must beg your pardon, Cilla. Burdening you with my troubles is unforgiveable. It's because I've no one to confide in. Nathaniel has been distracted since we came here. He's been caught up with estate problems." She brushed away the annoying tears on her cheek. "I've felt so isolated."

Cilla smiled. "You have nothing to apologize for. You are welcome to talk to me at any time."

"No. I've become a bore. Please tell me more about yourself. What brought you to Wolfram?"

"My father was born here in the village. He and my mother returned after they married, and I spent my childhood here. Until Nathaniel went away to school, he was part of a group of children who roamed the land together. My family was not of his class, of course, but children care nothing for that, and no one seemed to object at the time."

She leaned back in her chair. "My parents returned to France when I was a young woman. It was wonderful at first." She looked down at her hands. "Then they died of influenza within a week of each other, leaving me destitute. I had to sell my paintings cheap on the left bank of the Seine to eke out a living. And after my lover died, I couldn't bear to remain."

"How dreadful," Laura said. "Were you about to marry?"

"Marriage isn't for me, Laura. I prefer a bohemian life. It's impossible to live as I wish in a small village like Wolfram. I ran back here in distress, but I shall return to Paris once I have sold enough paintings."

Laura realized what a sheltered life she'd led, never having to worry about where her next meal came from or the roof over her head. Poor Cilla. To think she'd been jealous of her, fearing she and Nathaniel might have had a relationship. Would she never have any sense where he was concerned? Jealousy was such a humiliating emotion, but born out of insecurity, and that was as much his fault as hers.

"A contact in London is arranging for an exhibition of my work," Cilla said, breaking into Laura's thoughts.

"How wonderful. You are very talented, Cilla. I know you'll become very successful." Cilla would feel more at home in a big city. She would be among like-minded people. Laura understood that. She still felt like an outsider here herself.

"You're kind, Laura. I should like to paint you. Perhaps when you feel more settled, you'll consider it."

"I should like that. I considered you to be more of a landscape artist, but I see you are adept at portraits too."

Cilla tilted her head as if already considering the possible composition for Laura's painting. "I've painted a few portraits."

"The lady in the blue dress at the abbey?"

"That's mine."

"I thought so. It encapsulates a brief moment and says so much about Amanda. She looks happy."

Cilla's smile widened. "I think I captured Amanda's essence. She had that wonderful ability to grasp life with both hands. Not let anything stand in the way of what she wanted. How did you come to see the painting? I heard it was taken down."

"Rudge. He almost insisted I see it."

Cilla raised an eyebrow. "Did he? Awful man."

"And your painting of the cottage? Was Mallory living there then?"

"Yes."

"Where is he now?"

"He went away after Amanda died. I haven't seen him since."

Curiosity sent prickles over Laura's neck. Was there something more that Cilla did not want to tell her?

Cilla glanced at her easel.

Laura rose. "I must go."

Following Cilla into the tiny front hall, Laura paused in front of the painting again having found Cilla evasive. "Why choose to paint Amanda at the door of that cottage? It seems a humble setting for her."

Cilla stared at her hands. They were capable hands, the fingers long and pointed. Artist's hands. "Mallory and Amanda were in discussion about the planting of the rose arbor. In her crimson gown, she looked striking against the rustic backdrop, like a rose among weeds. I rushed away, determined to capture it. And the very next day I did from memory."

"It seems odd that Mallory left so soon after her death."

"He was in love with Amanda. We used to laugh about it."

"Did she and Nathaniel have a good marriage?" Laura rushed on as Cilla shook her head. "I'm sorry. I don't know why this is important to me."

"Hard to know what happens behind closed doors." There was sympathy in Cilla's eyes. "Would my opinion mean much to you?"

"I don't know what's gotten into me." Laura swallowed the lump blocking the back of her throat. "I'll leave you in peace."

"Love can be a curse for those who love too much." Cilla opened the door. "You didn't make me feel uncomfortable. Please come again soon."

Laura returned the way she'd come and steeled herself to walk beside the cliff. Perhaps it was here that Amanda had plunged to her death. The idea made the place even more forbidding. Why would a young woman in the eighth month of her confinement come this way? Had the stunning view fascinated her? Once safely past, Laura stopped to glance back. It certainly could not have been here, for no one would go close to the edge, unless they planned to jump. And surely no woman carrying a baby would do such a thing.

CHAPTER THIRTEEN

Sitting alone at the long table in the dining room, Laura toyed with the roast mutton stuffed with oysters. Rudge stood by the door, his gloved hands clasped together. In the silence, the gilt clock on the mantel and the patter of the rain against the window sounded abnormally loud.

Laura pushed the food around her plate as she took in the details of the room, noting what pleased her and what didn't. The well-proportioned room was decorated in gold and soft olive and was a little too dreary for her taste. A buffet displayed an impressive array of decorated china and ceramics. Above it, shelves of glassware sparkled. An antique, embroidered screen dressed a corner. She dismissed the stuffed birds in a cage but liked the gold wallpaper above the oak wainscoting. The faded green velvet covering the row of arched windows needed to be replaced. She had a strong desire to make this house hers, and this room was the perfect place to begin. The Victorian style was far too heavy. It was time for something lighter and more cheerful.

"I believe new curtains are needed for this room," Laura said, as much to herself as to Rudge. "These are a cold green." It would be a start, before she redid the whole room in floral pastels, primrose yellow, leaf green, or the lilac of wisteria with gray.

"Lady Lanyon…" Rudge cleared his throat. "The first Lady Lanyon, that is, planned to change them."

Laura welcomed anything she might learn about Amanda. "Did she have something in mind?"

A smug expression stole into his eyes. "Pompeian red velvet, I believe, my lady. Lady… the first Lady Lanyon had excellent taste."

But it was not Laura's. "I can see we would have agreed on the need for warmth."

Rudge's eyes brightened. "There were samples, I believe, which would still be here. I could find them, my lady. Should you wish?"

"Please don't bother. I prefer the charming chintzes in fashion, something floral which will pick up the colors in the carpet and tone well with the oak. I'll have the dining chairs recovered to suit."

Rudge's mouth firmed and his gaze dropped to his highly polished shoes. "As you wish, my lady."

"I'll write to a decorator. I agree that a touch of Pompeian red velvet works well in this room. It will be perfect to cover the dining chairs."

Laura felt Rudge's gaze on her back as she left the table and wandered the room. He never stepped beyond the bounds of propriety or raised himself above his station, and yet his hard eyes always looked upon her with cool dislike. It made her want to assert her authority. If Rudge didn't warm to her, at least he would respect her.

"That leather corner chair shouldn't be in here. Please have it moved into the library. It will be more comfortable for Lord Lanyon than the chesterfields." She faced him, finding little had changed in his expression. "Why did the housekeeper leave?"

"Mrs. Bright succumbed to an illness, my lady. About a year ago, it was. Lord Lanyon has yet to replace her."

"I can't imagine how the house has continued to run without one. I shall begin to interview possible replacements immediately." Laura paused at the door. "Oh, and have the cage of stuffed birds removed. Potted plants can fill the space. Orchids and ferns are a good choice." She walked out the door. "I believe I'll retire, Rudge."

In the great hall, as he always did, Rudge lit a candle for her. Laura said goodnight and gathered her skirts in her hand to mount the stairs. The nights were long and lonely without Nathaniel. But next time, she would go with him.

It was still early when she blew out her candle. Although her mind seemed determined to sort through all she'd gleaned from Cilla, more questions arose than answers, and she soon fell into an uneasy sleep.

Laura struggled to adjust her sight to the dark room. She leaned on her elbows, listening to the noise that awakened her: scraping and a soft shuffle. She threw back the bedclothes and fumbled for the matches, which eluded her panicky fingers. After several deep breaths to steady her hand, she gripped them. Striking a match, she lit a candle and sighed, relieved to find the room empty. The noise had ceased, but what had caused it? It sounded close by.

Once she'd donned her dressing gown, she opened the door and tiptoed out into the corridor. At the far end, she glimpsed movement. The flash of white vanished so quickly she began to doubt she'd seen anything beyond a shaft of moonlight. The candle raised high, her shaky hand threw a pale, trembling light over the wide corridor.

Convinced the glow had come from near Amanda's bedroom, Laura took two steps toward it. Her legs felt oddly heavy, and she was short of breath. Without Nathaniel's protection, she was vulnerable. She turned and ran back to her room, shutting her door and locking it. In bed, she hugged her knees, her ears straining for the smallest sound.

Gradually accepting that the noise must have been the wind which had picked up during the night, Laura lay down. She faced facts. She'd been overconfident in believing that Nathaniel would fall quickly and deeply in love with her, and that their love would blot out his still raw past. It seemed both unreasonable and childish to expect it. He had never attempted to open himself to her and explain his true feelings. Might he feel disloyal to Amanda if he did? Overwhelmed, Laura closed her eyes.

The dream she'd had on her first day here returned. A lady, light as a cobweb, hovered above her. Her face in shadow, her hair pale as morning sunlight. Fighting her way out of sleep, Laura opened her eyes. She was too hot. She threw off the cover and pounded her pillows. Grayish-lavender shadows hugged the corners of the room as the dawn broke. Laura lay with an arm above her head, gazing at the golden canopy above, sternly assuring herself it had only been a dream. It didn't work. She remained convinced that what she'd sensed close by was either a ghostly presence, or more disturbingly, an earthly one. She wasn't sure which terrified her the most.

Teg carried wicker baskets from the house, full of Mrs. Madge's fine pasties and her famous Cornish heavy cake, plus jars of rhubarb, apple and blackcurrant preserves. He packed them in the brougham before driving Laura to the vicarage.

She had dressed carefully in an outfit of dove-gray crepon featuring a short bolero jacket over a lace vest, the high crown of her yellow straw hat adorned with feathers and ribbons.

When they drove up, the fête was already underway. A group of inquisitive villagers gathered as Laura alighted from the carriage. A small welcoming party came forward to greet her as she and Teg made their way to the tables and handed over their baskets from which delicious, warm-baked smells wafted. Mrs. Madge's offerings were eagerly accepted. Before Laura had moved on to inspect some of the other stalls, all had been sold. Mrs. Madge would be gratified to hear it.

Couples performed a round dance on a stage set up for music and dancing. A male tenor followed with a rendition of "Sweet Nightingale," his fine voice carrying across the air:

> *Don't you hear the fond tale*
> *Of the sweet nightingale,*
> *As she sings in those valleys below?*

Once the song had ended and the clapping died away, the vicar assisted Laura onto the platform. A circle of faces ten-deep was raised to watch her, some smiling, some curious. Still unsure of the Cornish ways and language, Laura swallowed to banish her nerves. If her dreams were to be realized, speaking in public would be a skill she must acquire.

"*Dydh da!*" She greeted them first in Cornish that she'd learned from Teg. She had prepared a speech, but discarded her notes, talking freely about her love of her new home. Gazing down at the smiling faces, she added an amusing anecdote about a northerner who couldn't swim, and her shock when her husband rowed her to her new home on that first day. She finished with praise for the committee ladies' hard work and how splendid a fête it was.

Relieved that it went well, she was helped down to enthusiastic applause. In the church hall, she took tea with the committee ladies; a plate of cake balanced on her lap as she listened to a discussion of village life. It warmed her to be part of it, and she yearned to do more.

"It is so very nice to have a baroness at Wolfram again," said a woman in purple, her hat laden with artificial fruit. "Especially one as elegant as yourself, my lady." "Why, thank you, Mrs. Matcham." Laura smiled at the woman, whose cheeks were flushed pink. "I have been admiring your hat; it's such a summery affair."

"Oh. Thank you, my lady." Ms. Matcham turned a deeper pink and patted her hat. "So sad, what happened." She leaned forward. "Don't you let those gossips distress you. Lord Lanyon is a fine man. We don't believe a word of it."

Before Laura could think of a tactful reply, Mrs. Brown, one of the committee ladies, cleared her throat. "Mrs. Matcham, I wonder if you'll arrange for some more hot water. I believe we're running out of tea."

When Mrs. Matcham moved out of earshot, Mrs. Brown said, "I do apologize, my lady. There's some here far too free with their opinions."

Laura quickly masked her shocked surprise. "That's perfectly all right. I'm sure Mrs. Matcham meant well, Mrs. Brown. I am not at all thin-skinned, and I treat gossip with the contempt it deserves."

After tea, Laura crossed through the throng toward Teg and the waiting carriage. A female voice came from the crowd behind her. "Such a nice lady to have married a murderer."

Shocked, Laura stopped and, shaking with distress, forced herself not to spin around and face them. She allowed Teg to assist her into the brougham. How could anyone suspect Nathaniel of such a crime?

"Such cruel nonsense," she muttered, as she settled herself on the seat.

"There are some here who like to stir up trouble where none is warranted. Pay no attention, my lady," Teg said over his shoulder, as he urged the horses to walk on.

"I don't understand such spite."

"A few here don't believe the inquest went far enough into the first Lady Lanyon's death. Some relish a mystery, my lady; they worry away at it like a cancer. But Lord Lanyon is well liked by most."

That wasn't enough for Laura. She firmed her lips at the unfairness as a surge of anger and dismay gripped her. What lay behind this view? Was Nathaniel and Amanda's marriage an explosive one? Were they known to argue? A passionate relationship was often a combustible one. But she had never found a shred of violence in Nathaniel. He was gentle with her and his animals. His staff was loyal and obviously respected him.

Laura felt like weeping and began to understand the problems he wrestled with. She wished there was something she could do. But perhaps there was. She would involve herself more in village affairs. It was easier for her to mingle with the people than it was for Nathaniel, who, although he worked hard to improve their lives, must always seem a little too far above them. And it would give her a chance to mention those things he did for them, like this bill which was about to be passed in parliament, something many may not be aware of.

"Teg, Mrs. Moffat mentioned her mother was sickly. I plan to call on her. Do you know where she lives?"

"I do, milady."

Laura would take her some baked treats to brighten her day, and perhaps she might be able to offer some help. She would visit the village school. Her university education could be put to good use to spot where improvements might be made. Discreetly, of course.

Once she'd begun, Laura's ideas gathered force. As mistress of Wolfram it would be expected of her to visit the poor. She would meet with the clergyman to learn of their needs. She could form a charity; many of the women there today would like to join it, she was sure. And she would defend Nathaniel to her last breath.

Laura was glad of the breeze to cool her heightened color as the carriage gathered speed. Suddenly, the village appeared to be held back by the past. The end of this year would be the start of a new century, and the village would move forward with it, if she had anything to do with it.

CHAPTER FOURTEEN

The days without Nathaniel dragged by slowly. Laura kept busy taking on new tasks. She inspected the linens, the china, the glassware and silverware, and familiarized herself with the household accounts. She organized the flowers for the library, even though there was no one there to enjoy them but her.

She roamed as far as she could from the abbey, returning only when her feet grew sore or it began to rain. She spent evenings in the library reading about Wolfram's fascinating and exciting past.

A local woman came to inquire about the role of housekeeper but proved unsuitable. Laura could not employ anyone without Nathaniel's agreement. She decided to cast her net further afield. In the meantime, she mentally rolled up her sleeves and went about with Dorcas making notes, keeping her mother's instructions in mind. Nathaniel, like most men, didn't understand the importance of a well-run house. Laura laughed to herself. How like her mother she sounded!

When she discussed menus and preserves with Mrs. Madge, the cook mentioned they were shorthanded in the kitchen. Laura took note of it as she went to examine the kitchen gardens. She discussed the plantings with the gardener to ensure the right produce and herbs were grown to supply the table. While it was the man of the house who usually hired staff, she must convince Nathaniel to permit her to take on some of the responsibility. She smiled. She believed women to be more practical and to have a better understanding of human nature, although she would not tell him so. There was also the need to have more uniforms made for the staff; poor Dorcas' and the other maids' dresses were quite shabby. Laura's activities helped to keep her from worrying about the disturbing gossip.

Days before Nathaniel was due to return, Laura sat in the rose garden with the brassbound rosewood writing slope she'd discovered, which might have been Amanda's, attending to her correspondence. It had rained earlier, and the air was moist and heavy. A faint breeze sluggishly stirred the leaves of the chestnut tree above her and lifted the corner of her letter. Eloise Travers, a friend from Cambridge, had filled several pages with news of her latest literary conquest. She was employed to review for *The Bookman*, a monthly magazine. Laura paused from adding her heartfelt congratulations, tinged with a little envy, to admire the arbor of pink and white roses intertwined into a fragrant arch. Amanda and Mallory had exhibited some skill in creating it. Had there been more to their relationship? Hadn't Cilla said Amanda found the gardener's infatuation amusing?

Dismissing such unpleasant thoughts, Laura penned a dutiful letter to her mother, fearful that her parent would fill in the gaps and guess things weren't as good as they might be. Laura chewed the end of her pen. She had no heart to embellish her words. Instead, she attempted to distract her mother with a request. Might she or her acquaintances know of a housekeeper with good references prepared to come to Cornwall? Laura elaborated on her refurbishment of some of the rooms. Running a house had proved to be more challenging than she imagined, and she'd developed a grudging respect for her mother's ability to manage Grisewood Hall. Laura added a footnote of love and encouragement for her beloved father, who she knew was overworked and apprehensive as the Boer War raged on in Africa.

Her last note was to Aunt Dora begging her to come and visit them soon.

The butler brought several letters on a silver salver. "These have just been delivered, my lady."

Laura gazed up at the man's stern face from beneath her wide-brimmed hat as she took them. "Thank you, Rudge."

"Shall you take tea in the library, my lady?"

"I believe I shall have it here. It's nicer outdoors."

"Very well."

As he returned inside, Laura eyed his stiff back, then dropped her gaze to the letters. There was an invitation from the vicar and his wife to dine at the vicarage. She would reply today. It would give her an opportunity to ask him how she might assist the poor and set up her charity. Another invitation to tea had come from two aged spinsters, daughters of a viscount, who lived at Thrompton, a small manor house a few miles outside of Wolfram. Nathaniel had mentioned them to her.

She opened a letter of thanks from the women's committee; everyone enjoyed her speech, and they asked if she would open the annual flower show this spring. She set about replying. Laura murmured her surprise at the next. Her old university chum, Howard Farmer, had sent his belated best wishes for her marriage. They had often debated together, and he'd once come to play tennis with her at Wimbledon. He now taught classics at the University of London. If she ever wished to see him, she was not to hesitate to contact him there. She smiled, glad for him.

The last was addressed to Nathaniel. Why had Rudge brought this to her? The envelope bore one line, a hasty scrawl: *His Lordship, the Baron Lanyon.* One word in the corner caught her attention: *Urgent!* Laura hesitated for a few seconds, then seized her pearl-handled opener and sliced through the envelope, removed the letter and smoothed it out. It was exactly like the envelope. A scrawled, brief message, not dated, nor signed.

Baron, the man you sought has been seen in St Ives. He may plan to return to Wolfram. I pray the Lord protects you and yours.

The signature was impossible to decipher.

Her stomach tightening, she read it again. Protect them from what? Her hand shook as she tried to think what she should do. Should she contact Nathaniel? Would he disapprove of her opening his mail? It appeared too urgent to ignore, even if the writer did enjoy a dramatic turn of phrase. There wasn't a telephone at Wolfram, but there was one at the post office in the village. Nathaniel had given her a number to call in an emergency. Would he consider this urgent? She gathered up her letters, aware that she couldn't leave it for his return.

In her bedroom, she took out her riding habit and rang for Agnes. Was it possible to install a telephone at Wolfram? She hated to be so isolated when Nathaniel was in London.

When a knock came at the door, she held her bodice together, expecting her maid. "Come in."

Rudge stood at the open door. "Your morning tea is served in the rose garden, my lady. As you instructed."

"I find I have to go out, Rudge. I need to telephone his lordship. Send Agnes to me, will you?"

"Certainly, my lady." Surprise registered on Rudge's chiseled features before he returned to his usual impassive expression. Surely he must have known the urgent letter would be dealt with? Why else add it to her correspondence?

In her green habit, Laura hurried to the stables where the groom saddled her horse. Trotting toward the causeway, she saw a man crossing from the village onto Wolfram land. She reined in her mount and waited for him to reach her. He walked with a confident swagger. Dressed in nankeen trousers, with a tan leather jerkin beneath a cloth jacket, he swept off his hat. Blond hair gleamed in the sun. He had a good-looking, rather insolent face.

His eyes swept over her approvingly. "You can only be Lady Lanyon."

Laura's horse pinned her ears, disliking the delay. "You know who I am, but I'm at a loss to know who you are, sir." Annoyed by the familiarity of his tone and the bold look in his brown eyes, Laura steadied her mount, anxious to get to the post office.

"Theo Mallory at your service, my lady."

"The head gardener at one time, Mr. Mallory, were you not?"

"The very same, my lady."

"To what do we owe this visit, Mr. Mallory?"

Mallory frowned and replaced his hat. "I have business with Lord Lanyon."

"His lordship is in London. He's not expected back until Saturday."

He walked beside her. "Then I'll see him then. I've taken a room at The Sail and Anchor."

Curious, she watched his expression. "I believe you lived in a cottage on the grounds at one time."

Theo's laugh possessed a scornful ring. "I did, my lady. Thank you for reminding me."

What was he doing back in Wolfram? Something about him made her uneasy. "I bid you good day, Mr. Mallory." She urged her horse into a trot. The tide lapped at the granite rocks just below the road. "How long before high tide?" Laura called back.

"An hour or so."

"Then I must hurry." Laura nudged her mount.

He followed behind her. Mallory's manner was too informal, disrespectful, and although she was curious, she had no time to give to him now. She rode into the village, going over the conversation she was soon to have with her husband. It would not be an easy one.

At the crank of the telephone handle, a hollow voice came over the line. Laura asked the exchange for the number Nathaniel had given her. Would he consider this to be important enough for her to call him? Shouting into the mouthpiece, she repeated her request.

Moments later, she heard Nathaniel's voice come on, sounding as if he was on the other side of the world. She had planned to be brief, but hearing his deep voice, her emotions got the better of her. She relayed the contents of the letter in a breathy voice. "The letter was marked urgent!"

There was a pause, and when he spoke it was impossible to judge his tone. "I'll be home by Saturday evening. Wait a moment." His voice grew fainter as he spoke to someone with him. "Laura? There's a vote in the House. I must go. I'm sorry. Sweetheart..." The line crackled.

"What? I can't hear you," Laura yelled.

"...miss you."

"Oh, Nathaniel, I miss you too," Laura cried. Had she heard him correctly?

The crackling on the line ended, and suddenly his voice was so clear he might have been standing there with her. "I'll attend to the matter when I return home. Goodbye, sweetheart."

She hung up the phone, relieved Nathaniel hadn't expressed anger at her opening his mail. Outside the post office, Theo Mallory leaned against a lamppost smoking a cheroot.

He threw it down and straightened. "Did you settle the matter which had you in such a hurry, my lady?"

"Please don't concern yourself with my affairs, Mr. Mallory." Her lips firmed as she beckoned the lad to bring her horse.

When she took the reins, Mallory came to her side. "Allow me to give you a leg up, Lady Lanyon."

"Thank you." It would be a direct snub to refuse him, and with a group of villagers watching she didn't like to. She placed her booted foot in his clasped hands, and he threw her up. She arranged her skirts over the sidesaddle. "Do you intend to remain in Wolfram long, Mr. Mallory?"

"That depends. I have important business here." He touched his hand to his hat in what should have been a respectful gesture, but his brown eyes held an overly familiar expression that drew her ire. "Such a picturesque place, Wolfram."

His smirk made his meaning plain. Her fingers itched to raise her crop to him. She quickly turned her horse's head and rode toward the causeway. The water was alarmingly close to overflowing onto the road. She rode back to the abbey, relieved that Nathaniel had not seemed concerned about the letter, although it was impossible to be sure. In a few days, he would be home. She tamped down her impatience to see him.

At the bright prospect, she urged her horse into a canter.

At dusk, wrapped in a warm shawl, Laura walked in the gardens before dinner. The cool evening was a favorite time when the scents of flowers and trees intensified, the birds calling as they nestled in the trees. She went down the steps, skirting around the abbey to the gate leading into the graveyard. After a pause, she entered and walked beneath the magnolia. The grass and weeds needed to be scythed. Some of the old gravestones were almost covered. Laura bent down to read the inscriptions on some of them. She located Nathaniel's father, but strangely, his mother was not there. Farther down the hill, she discovered the one she admitted to herself she'd come to see.

Amanda Elizabeth Lanyon. Born: 1868. Died: 1897.

Her soul has now taken flight
To glorious mansions above,
To mingle with angels of light
And dwell in the kingdom of love.

A posy of dead wildflowers lay beside the grave.

Could Nathaniel have put them there before he went to London? Was it he who chose the beautiful epitaph? The salt-laden breeze strengthened, stirring the branches above her. She shivered and wrapped her shawl more closely around her shoulders. Strange to feel like an intruder, but she did as she closed the gate.

The sound of voices made Laura pause at the steps. Theo Mallory stood some distance away, his foot resting on the stone seawall. His back to her, he was deep in conversation with one of the grooms. The groom raised his hands, his manner apologetic, his mutterings carried away on the wind.

Mallory straightened. "See that it's done," he ordered, his voice loud enough for her to hear.

The groom nodded.

Laura hurried through the gate before they caught sight of her. What brought Mallory here? As she climbed the steps to the front door, a thought made her gasp. Mallory had acted as if *he* was the master of Wolfram.

After dinner, Laura took her usual spot in the library, thinking about what she'd seen. Finally, she rose to search the shelves for a book to make the night seem less long. She discovered a slim volume with a red leather cover. It appeared to be written about a garden, so without opening it, she took it upstairs with her to bed.

Settling against the pillows, she opened the volume and sighed with impatience. It was an old Arabian text translated into English and not at all what she expected. Something made her persevere, and soon the sensual pleasures detailed in the prose made her breath catch in her throat and her face burn. She closed the book as if fire leapt from its pages and gazed again at the title: *The Perfumed Garden*. She had never known such a book existed; it was so blatant and undeniably arousing. A graphic and beautiful account of sexual love. Intrigued, she opened the silken pages again. She read until the candle guttered, then tossed and turned in the dark for hours as her imagination placed her and Nathaniel into the scenes in the book.

After Laura's phone call, Nathaniel's fingers remained clenched around the handset for several minutes before he hung up. He should have been there. Laura's voice had faded in and out, the line atrocious. His blood drummed in his veins while he hoped the bad line had hidden the surprise and horror in his voice. Would Mallory turn up at Wolfram? He had enough gall to do it. It was doubtful he'd arrive before Nathaniel, but if he did, Laura was unlikely to meet him. Still, he would count the hours until he could return. The only calming thought was the knowledge that Hugh would do as Nathaniel requested and keep his eye on Laura.

CHAPTER FIFTEEN

Laura still felt uneasy the next day. She stared out of her bedroom window, her restless gaze taking in little of the landscape. What had happened to her dreams of a rich, cultured life, sharing her husband's thoughts and dreams? Annoyed with herself, she stared upward, where wisps of cloud drifted across the pewter blue sky. The weather in Cornwall was so changeable: calm with blue skies one day, stormy the next. It mirrored her thoughts.

As there was no sign of storm clouds lurking out over the horizon, she decided to ride to the estuary. Nathaniel hadn't had time to show her more of the coastline said to be a beautiful part of Cornwall.

After breakfast, Laura set out alone, taking the road which led away from the village into undiscovered terrain. Now familiar and comfortable with her roan mare, Velvet, a good-natured horse, she rode past fields of cows and horses. A dray loaded with produce passed by on the way to the house. The driver smiled and touched his hat. Laura decided she must visit the home farm next.

Trotting along a road heading west, she called "good morning" to a man who straightened from his garden and removed his hat. Farther on, a woman bobbed as she walked to the market with a basket over her arm.

"It's a fine day, isn't it?" Laura called out.

"That it is, my lady."

The cottages grew sparser, and then the road followed the rivulet, which fed into a wide lake alive with bird life. Long-legged, wading birds flocked noisily over the reeds. Wild grasses covered the rounded, sandy hills dotted with wildflowers. Laura left the road and urged her horse up a trail over the hillocks. Buffeted by the wind, the ocean's roar in her ears, she peered down upon a sheltered bay, which looked like a giant had taken a bite out of the coastline. Laura dismounted and tethered her horse to a spindly tree. She walked over soft sand to the deserted shore.

At the water's edge a set of footprints crossed the damp sand. Someone had walked here not long ago, for the waves were now sweeping the sand clean.

A gust whipped off her hat. Laura grabbed it as the strong wind toyed with the bun at the nape of her neck, unraveling her hair from its pins. She gave into it, removing the remaining pins and combs while staring out to sea, her locks and her skirts billowing around her. The horizon was a hard line of dark metallic gray beyond the turbulent water. She took a deep breath and felt alive in a way she'd never experienced before. The ocean was so vast it was both humbling and awe-inspiring. With a rush, she realized that Wolfram had become home to her. Her passion for this small piece of England, and for Nathaniel, filled her heart. She hugged herself with her arms. Shelley's poem, *Mont Blanc,* rushed into her mind, and she murmured a line:

> And what were thou, and earth, and stars, and sea,
> If to the human mind's imaginings…

"My, my. We have an educated lady among us."

Furious, Laura swung around. With that insolent smile, Theo Mallory had emerged from a pile of boulders and retraced his footprints across the sand.

Laura disliked being alone with him. More annoyed than afraid, she kept her features deceptively composed as he approached, destroying her peace. His manner, coupled with what Cilla had told her about him, made her wary.

She nodded, coolly polite. "Mr. Mallory."

"Lord Lanyon does have excellent taste, I'll give him that. Your hair is like a red sail at sunset," Mallory said with a bland half-smile. He held up a hand, as if he wished to stroke her hair.

"Your opinion is not welcome, Mr. Mallory." Laura attempted to gather her hair into some semblance of order. "I came here to enjoy the beauty and solitude."

He laughed. "This is not Lanyon land, my lady, although I admit there's very little around here that isn't. I have as much right as you to enjoy the scenery." His gaze roamed over her body.

Laura resisted the urge to cover her chest with her arms. "It appears my pleasure has evaporated."

Having twisted her hair into a rough bun, she secured it with combs and turned away to walk back to her horse. On the crest of the hill, Hugh Pitney appeared on his chestnut.

"It seems you have company," Mallory said, eyeing him.

So, Nathaniel *had* asked him to keep an eye on her. Right now, Laura could only be glad. Curious, she looked back at Mallory. Praise generally worked on an arrogant man. "I believe you worked closely with the former Lady Lanyon in the design of the rose garden."

His gaze sharpened. He smoothed back his golden hair. "That's correct."

"Then I must congratulate you. The arbor is a work of art."

He shifted his feet. "We had great plans for the Wolfram gardens, Lady Lanyon and I," he said softly. "Many plans." He stared up at Pitney again, who'd made no move toward them. "They crumbled to dust when someone killed her."

Laura took a sharp breath. "What makes you think she was murdered? The coroner's finding was accidental death."

He scowled. "Am... Lady Lanyon was nervous of the cliffs. She would not have gone too close."

"You were not her ladyship's confidant, surely."

"That I was."

Why Amanda had allowed such familiarity from this man was beyond her. "I find that difficult to believe, Mr. Mallory. Why you?"

He shrugged. "Why not me? Perhaps there was no one else."

She ignored the insult aimed at Nathaniel. "Who would want her dead?"

He looked at her, his eyes distant. "Ask your ice-cold husband, my lady. He may well know the answer."

Mallory strode away before Laura could reply. Not that she could have, for words had dried up in her throat. He disappeared behind the rocks, as she stood gasping with anger. Mallory's heated response could well be an attempt to hide his own culpability. She was about to mount her horse and join Mr. Pitney when something in the water caught her eye.

"Oh!" A glossy seal's head emerged from the water, so foreign and strange that she laughed. Its sleek gray body rode the waves. Transfixed by the amazing creature, she failed to see the ship that had rounded the point until it was almost in front of her. The three-masted vessel sailed close to shore. She had seen it before, when on the cliff with Nathaniel. Laura raised a hand to shield her eyes against the glare, but she couldn't make out anyone on board. The ship sailed out of sight around the point. She'd never seen a vessel of that size moored in the harbor, only fishing boats.

She ran back and took up the reins, leading Velvet to where Mr. Pitney waited.

"That Theo Mallory is a bad man, my lady," he said, as he helped her to mount.

"In what way?"

"Not my place to say. But I'd keep him at a distance."

She drew up the reins and turned her horse toward home. "I have every intention of it."

Mallory's attack on Nathaniel must be pure spite. What did he have against him? Cilla had said he was in love with Amanda. That was certainly possible. But how did Amanda feel about him? Although Laura found him obsequious, she could see how some women might enjoy his flattery and flirtatious manner.

The painting of Cilla's with the scarlet-dressed woman sprang into Laura's mind. Laura was certain there wasn't a crimson dress in

Amanda's closet. She seemed to favor colors which suited her blonde hair and blue eyes. And she would hardly wear a dress like that during the day. Might Cilla have painted Amanda in scarlet because it added color to the painting, or could it have been a condemnation? Laura sensed a mystery and was impatient to learn more. Might it be the key to unlock Nathaniel's reserve? Or was she becoming fanciful?

On Friday, Laura accompanied Teg to Penzance. Nathaniel's train pulled into the station with a loud hiss, filling the air with sooty smoke. Laura straightened the skirts of her new outfit as she waited for him to alight. She hoped her new pink, green and white pique gown with its gilt buttons and Eton jacket, and the straw hat with the matching green silk band, would please him. When he stepped onto the platform, he looked so tired and strained that she had to hold herself back from rushing into his arms. She smiled as he kissed her cheek.

Teg drove them through the green valley toward Wolfram. "Was your trip a success?" Laura asked.

"Yes, thank you, my dear."

Their shoulders touched as the carriage swung around a corner, but it seemed as if there was a wide gulf between them. Nathaniel would make love to her tonight. The thought made her treacherous body respond. She wished she could keep a cool head around him. Nathaniel would lose himself in the lovemaking, and for a while, he would be hers. But no matter how closely he held her, she seemed unable to reach his heart. Was it unreasonable of her to want more?

Nathaniel's voice broke into her thoughts, discussing his week, pleased with the support for the changes to the Poor Law Act. He was behind a bill to set up orphanages in Southern England, the first to be for homeless girls in Bodmin. She watched him, proud of her handsome husband and she said so. She was rewarded with a warm smile. But then he passed a tired hand over his eyes.

"It was kind of you to come to meet me, but unnecessary, Laura. Please don't bother next time."

"I thought you'd be pleased." She wanted to add that she couldn't wait another minute to see him, but felt too shy to utter it.

"I'm sorry, sweetheart." He squeezed her gloved hand. "It's all in its infancy. I don't wish to bore you."

"But you weren't," she said. "It's a very good cause."

"It is good to see you." His gaze roamed from her hair down to her waist. "That is a pretty dress. You look as lovely as a flowering peach tree." He drew down her glove and kissed the inside of her wrist, "the fruit too tasty to resist."

"Hush, Nathaniel," Laura murmured, aware of Teg's sturdy back near enough to hear every word, but she was pleased, and her pulse leapt at the touch of his warm lips on her skin.

He smiled and tucked her hand through his arm. "It's wonderful to be home."

While he was in a good mood, she decided to broach the subject of the phone call. "Nathaniel, that letter…?"

The warm spark disappeared, and the gray depths of his eyes became unfathomable. "I told you I will deal with the matter, Laura."

Laura bit her lip. Her spirit, which might have deserted her in recent times, rose like a smoldering fire in her breast. She would have this out with him in the privacy of their bedroom. She accepted the irony of it, that this would be the catalyst for change.

When they settled in front of the library fire after an excellent dinner, Laura described to Nathaniel the swatches of fabric for the dining room curtains she'd ordered from London. "A bright chintz would bring this room to life," she added, noting Nathaniel's unenthusiastic response.

He frowned. "My mother chose those curtains. There's so little of her here, I suppose I've been reluctant to replace them."

Laura flushed, feeling awkward. But that must have been years ago. Odd that although there were portraits of family members stretching back through the years, she'd found none of his mother. "Is there a likeness of your mother here? I must say I'm curious to know what she was like."

Nathaniel sighed. "They are all at another one of my properties. I've been meaning to have them brought here."

How very strange. Consumed with curiosity, she longed to ask him, but he turned the page of his newspaper, apparently inviting no further questions. Had Amanda faced the same problem? "I'm sorry. I didn't know."

"How could you?" Nathaniel reached across and squeezed her hand before returning to his paper.

Was that to be the end of the matter? Nathaniel's expression gave little clue to his mood. Laura continued regardless. "I know you will wish to vet my ultimate choice, but I've interviewed a local woman for the position of housekeeper. Another in London has expressed interest. She comes with a referral from one of my mother's friends." Her mother's reply to her letter had arrived almost by the next post. To Laura's relief, she hadn't asked any awkward questions.

Nathaniel's face remained hidden by the broadsheet. "Nathaniel? Did you hear what I said?"

He lowered the paper. "I did. You have been busy."

She eyed him apprehensively. "You don't approve?"

"Of course I do, sweetheart. Wolfram needs a housekeeper. But a woman from London may not be suitable. She would be unfamiliar with our ways, and she could have difficulty with the language."

She firmed her lips. "I must tell you about the fête."

He smiled. "Ah yes, the fête. Did it go well?"

Laura failed to mention the accusation of murder she'd overheard. She suspected he'd bat it away like everything else this evening. "I visited Mrs. Moffat's mother who's been sickly. She was very glad to have company and loved the warm shawl I brought her. I have great plans to visit the school, and I've asked the vicar's help so I might visit the poor."

"I have only been gone a week, and so much has been achieved!" He raised his dark brows. "I am proud of you, sweetheart. But no wonder you look tired. You can't do it all at once, you know." He smiled. "I see I was right. I knew you would soon become a graceful asset who the people of Wolfram would come to value." He drank the last of his brandy, stubbed out his cigar and rose. "Shall we retire?"

It was a perfunctory response to say the least. Exasperated and disappointed, Laura followed him from the room. Being told she was an asset was not the reaction she wanted from him. He was pleased with her plans, but she detected a certain reserve on his part. It appeared everything was to remain forever undisturbed, like still water hiding the turbulent current beneath. She was not so easily dismissed. With each step on the staircase, Laura's frustration built. By the time she'd reached her chamber, she felt ready to explode. But with a soft caress of her cheek, Nathaniel entered his bedroom and left her to simmer.

Nathaniel entered his bedchamber to undress. He pulled off his cravat, tossed it onto the chair and began to undo his waistcoat buttons. Any mention of his mother and his life before Laura came here made his throat tighten. It had to be addressed. Keeping it from her was wrong, but he needed time to set things to rights. She had flashed those green eyes at him earlier with a challenge he'd felt unable to meet. Just now, all he wanted was to bury the past and live in the moment. To take her in his arms and feel the knots of strain unravel as her soft body and her warmth became a balm to his senses.

He should have insisted she accompany him to London. He'd lain awake every night worrying about her and missing her, and after her telephone call advising him of the letter, worry had almost crippled him. His every thought remained in Cornwall, when he needed to be clear minded and focused on garnering support for the bill. He could no longer ignore how vulnerable his need for her made him. Although he wasn't a fearful man when it came to his own hide, what he felt for Laura was something beyond his understanding. He should have known. His failure to gain control over his emotions in the past hadn't served him well.

In his dressing gown, he opened the panel, finding Laura alone. She stood with her camisole half over her head.

"May I be of help?" He stepped into the room.

"No, thank you," she murmured, her voice muffled.

She dragged the camisole off with a tearing sound and stood in her lacy bloomers, an arm placed defensively across her chest, her hair swinging and every deep breath seemingly of anger. Yes, anger, Nathaniel thought, eyeing her. He paused midway across the room, admiring his beautiful wife and knowing himself to blame.

"You are angry with me?"

She frowned. "Is there nothing I can do here that you truly approve of?"

CHAPTER SIXTEEN

In two strides, Nathaniel reached Laura, the touch of his hands on her bare shoulders reminding her of the only thing that was right between them.

"Sweetheart, what's this about? Have I ever criticized anything you've done?" Nathaniel laughed, which only made her more furious. "Why are you so angry at me?"

Laura fought for control, realizing that her anger stemmed not from their earlier conversation at all, but from the way he continued to hold her at arm's length. She had foolishly hoped for more, and it was deeply disappointing. "Don't attempt to humor me, Nathaniel."

He brushed a damp strand of her hair from her cheek. "When you're angry, your eyes flash like emeralds."

She turned her face away, searching for some way to penetrate his remoteness. "Someone said that once." Howard Farmer, after a heated debate at the university.

Nathaniel took her chin in his hand. "Who? Who was it?" His voice was mild, but his eyes narrowed.

Surprised at his reaction, she tilted her head. "You're not jealous, surely?"

"I want to strike down every man who looks twice at you." He gathered her into his arms, his voice thick and unsteady, sending a shiver through her. "You are very desirable, wife," he whispered, kissing the soft skin beneath her ear.

Was this all she meant to him? Laura pushed him away. "I'm still angry with you, Nathaniel. You shut me out. It's insulting. Don't try to sweet talk me now."

"Laura..."

"No!" She turned away from him, stalking to the other end of the chamber to put some distance between them, where she could breathe. Where she could think.

Nathaniel followed her. He slid an arm beneath her knees and picked her up. The display of manly strength robbed her of speech and fueled her frustration, bringing it to a fever pitch. "Put me down!" She struck ineffectually at his hard, muscled arm with her fist. Ignoring her protests, he walked to the bed and threw her unceremoniously onto it.

She lay there panting and stared up at him. A slight smile lifted his lips and warmed his gaze. "Does a quarrel inflame your passions, Laura? If so, I'm all for it, but for the life of me, I can't think of anything to argue about. Although I wish to investigate your concerns, right now I'd much prefer to make love to you." Placing a hand on either side of her head, he leaned down and took her mouth in a passionate kiss.

Laura pulled back. "This is the only way you know to resolve an argument." But at the determined look in his eyes, a lurch of excitement ran through her like lightning, and helplessly caught, she traced her bottom lip with her tongue where he'd kissed her.

"It takes two to argue, my sweet." He grinned, reading her like a book. His fingers circled the tips of her breasts. "My God, you have a fine body. You are made for love."

"There's more to me than this, Nathaniel."

"I agree. So much more. You are intelligent, and I love how optimistic you are, how you grasp life with such passion. I am very grateful to have you for my wife, Laura."

He was adept at pretty speeches. But did he love her? She burned to ask him. But demanding his declaration of love would render the words valueless. It must come from him willingly to be real. "You give me no chance to show those qualities when you reveal very little of your thoughts and evade my attempts to understand you."

He inclined his head in acknowledgement. "Then I'm profoundly sorry you feel that way. I thought you were happy here."

"I am happy here, Nathaniel. It's just that…" Darn it, she couldn't demand he tell her about Amanda now; it would sound like she was jealous of a dead woman.

"We shall talk, but right now, I want to hold you. May I? I have missed you."

He trailed his fingers down her cheek and paused at her throat. The smile in his eyes contained a sensuous flame, but she glimpsed something else: a softness and vulnerability, as if he understood her and felt badly about it. She'd seen little of that since they came to Wolfram.

She narrowed her eyes, fighting to resist his appeal. "I'd like to hear more about London."

"London was the same as ever, foggy and crowded. The bill failed to pass the House of Lords. Francis Bolton and I discussed our next move over too much wine. I retired early every night." He kissed her cheek. "And I saw your parents."

She hit him on the shoulder. "You saw my parents and didn't think to tell me?"

He laughed and grabbed her wrist, pressing a kiss to her palm. "You've hardly given me a chance. I ran into your father at Westminster. As your mother had come to the city for a meeting of some sort, we caught up for luncheon. I was able to tell them that you were in good health and happy." His gaze grew serious. "You are happy to be here, aren't you, Laura?"

"I never want to be anywhere else on earth. Wolfram is my home now."

"My darling." Nathaniel kissed her ear.

"Are they both well?"

"Fighting fit, I believe," he murmured, smiling down at her.

She lay back and raised her arms to draw him down with her. "Tell me more please."

He laughed ruefully. "You should not do that if you wish me to continue our conversation."

She tucked her hands under her head and grinned, enjoying her sense of power. "What are ladies wearing this season?"

A dark eyebrow rose. "Eh? You want me to speak of fashion?" He pushed back his black hair. The unconsciously graceful gesture made her want to pull him closer. She curled her fingers into her palms and resisted.

"I do."

He stroked his slightly shadowed chin. "Let me see. Your mother wore a tobacco-colored coat with a fur trim, ermine, I suspect." He smiled. "I particularly noticed the fur because I thought it impractical, and her large fur muff made me suspect at first that she'd brought along her Pekingese dog."

Laura giggled. "And her hat?"

"I'm not good with such details." He thought for a moment. "Black with gold trim, I think." He waved his hands over his head. "More ermine somewhere on it. Entirely too much fur I would say, although I don't confess to being up on the latest fashion."

"Are corseted waists still in fashion?"

"I was pleased to observe many in evidence." He lowered himself beside her, and his lips brushed below her ear. "Don't tell me waists are in danger?" he asked, his voice husky.

Desire heated her blood. She should not let her handsome husband roam free in London. What was she thinking? Thoughts fled as his gaze settled on her mouth.

"Are we done talking?"

"Yes." Her voice was barely a whisper, as she responded to his kiss.

"Have you missed me, sweetheart?"

"Yes." If only he needed her as much as she did him. "Yes, Nathaniel, very much."

She couldn't maintain her anger and moved to bring him close in the way that worked, at least for now. She pulled at the belt on his dressing gown, and after he shrugged out of it, she pushed him back onto the bed, leaning over him, seeking to take the upper hand to gain some sense of power over him. A smile tugged at the corner of his mouth. He lay acquiescent, allowing her to have her way. Even as she swept her hand over the smooth olive skin of his chest following the trail of dark hair down to boldly touch his arousal, she expected him to take control. But she had a way to surprise him with the knowledge gained from the book.

Laura kissed her way down his muscled stomach, and his soft dark hair brushed her cheek. How good it felt to kiss him there, his erection both silky and hard. Passion coiled deeply within her, her need for him tightening her stomach. Breathing hard, she gasped and rejoiced when his hands settled in her hair and he moaned. Amanda might have a claim on his heart, but in this earthly pleasure, at least, Laura sensed her power. In this bedroom, he was truly hers.

"That's so good," he murmured.

Growing in confidence and eager to learn what he liked, she ran her tongue along the hot length of him and took him in her mouth. He groaned, his arousal growing even harder beneath her fingers and lips.

Nathaniel suddenly pushed her away. He sat up, his dark eyebrows slanted in a puzzled frown. "Where did you learn to do this?"

He looked so furious and unapproachable. Did he believe she'd been unfaithful? Laura wanted to berate him, but she held her tongue, needing to understand what drove him. Was it Amanda's behavior with Mallory, innocent or not, that made him so suspicious?

"It's in a book." She gestured toward the volume on the table beside the bed.

Nathaniel snatched it up. Turning the pages, his smile widened. *The Perfumed Garden!*" He chuckled and shook his head. "My bewitching wife!" His heavy-lidded eyes gazed appreciatively over her naked body. "Shall we read it together? A different chapter every night?"

Thrilled by his response, Laura could only nod.

He seized her bloomers and pulled them down, throwing them on the floor. "We write our own chapter tonight." He gently pushed her down.

He began to explore her body as if trying to commit to memory every small part of her. Murmuring her approval, she abandoned herself to the whirlwind of sensation.

"I love the soft skin on the inside of your thigh." His fingers found the folds covering her sex. When he probed gently, he stoked the fire already alight within her until she bit her lip to keep from crying out.

"No. Please. I want to..." Averting her face to hide her blush, she eased him back and climbed astride him.

"Yes." His eyes gleamed. "That's good, sweetheart." He pushed into her.

She had dreamed of being in some way completed by a man, but she had never imagined such pleasure as this existed. Leaning back against the pillows, he cradled her buttocks and rocked her against him. On her knees, Laura let all her defenses go. She rose and fell and directed her own pleasure, watching as raw need darkened his gray eyes. Their rhythm increased as she raised her hips to meet each thrust. She was growing close to that exquisite ending she sought when he withdrew. He moved her to the edge of the bed. Her legs cradled against his hips, he drove into her. She was barely aware of her mews of pleasure as he led her to the brink and she toppled over with a cry. Soon, he followed with a groan.

Nathaniel lay close to her, breathing hard. She rested her head on his chest, her quick breaths filled with the smell of his skin, his maleness mingling with his bergamot cologne, and listened to his slowing heartbeat.

"I rather like you in a rage." He propped his head on his hand. "Now tell me what's made you so unhappy."

Her anger had fled as a deep, expansive warmth spread through her. Comfortable in his arms, she'd begun to wonder if she'd been unfair when he'd come home so exhausted. She sleepily talked of inconsequential things, leaving those more important matters for a better time. She could not destroy their closeness with intrusive questions now.

Her eyelids drooped. Fighting sleep, she tangled her fingers in the tufts of dark hair on his chest. Time might solve many of her concerns, although some did demand answers. Even though she sounded like an unreasonable, jealous woman to utter them. Did he visit Amanda's room at night? Why did he keep Amanda's bedchamber just as it had been when she was alive? Had he loved Amanda so desperately that he could never love Laura in the same way? Why did some of the villagers think him a murderer? She bit her lip and hated herself for being a coward, but she dreaded that this newly found closeness would evaporate, perhaps forever, if she learned the truth. Could he have been involved in some way with Amanda's death? For him to fob her off and attempt to hide the truth from her would be the end. He'd said that one must trust the person they married. And despite everything, she did.

"None of this would be enough to upset you," he said.

She took a deep breath and licked her tender bottom lip, swollen with his kisses. "I want to know the reason behind that urgent letter."

"The letter? Is that what this is all about?" He seemed relieved as he rolled off the bed and slipped on his gown. "I've been looking for a man who used to work here. He has questions to answer about some stolen property. That's all."

"Who is he?"

"He was once my head gardener. Theo Mallory."

Laura sat up. "But Mr. Mallory is here in Wolfram."

Nathaniel looked up from tying the belt of his gown, his eyes wide. "You've met him?"

"He came to see you on the day I telephoned. He's putting up at The Sail and Anchor."

"I could do with a drink. Like one?"

"No, thank you."

Nathaniel disappeared into his room. He came back cradling the crystal tumbler of brandy in his long fingers. "Did you speak to him?"

"Briefly. I didn't like him."

He scowled. "Was he disrespectful?"

"I thought he lacked manners."

Nathaniel nodded. "That's Mallory all right. I'll seek him out tomorrow."

"What has been stolen?"

He took a sip from his glass. "Nothing stolen from here, but goods were hidden in one of the estate cottages."

"Why hide them there?"

"They were smuggled in by sea from across the Channel. I've had trouble before." He ran his hand through his hair. "I didn't expect it to occur again."

"Mallory is behind it?"

"I suspected he was part of the earlier smuggling attempt several years ago, but the police couldn't get anything on him. And then he disappeared."

Laura's sleepiness fled. She reached for her gown. "The constabulary will deal with him, won't they?"

He threw back the last of the brandy and rose. "They will. It's late. Go to sleep, sweetheart. I must catch up on some paperwork. I'll go down to my study."

"Do you often work there during the night?"

"Sometimes. I'm a restless sleeper."

Laura wanted to ask him where he'd been on the night she discovered his bedroom empty and a light under Amanda's door. She hesitated. The evening had begun so badly, but she refused to end it that way. "I hope you sleep tonight, darling. Good night."

He feathered a kiss on her lips. "Sleep well."

The door closed. Perhaps in time, as they grew to understand each other, any differences and misunderstandings might cease to matter. *If* he loved her. It would be too painful for her to stay in a loveless marriage, even though her mother would be outraged and would never understand should Laura leave it.

Laura washed and dried herself by the fire, then donned her nightgown and climbed into bed, pulling the blankets up over her shoulders. She breathed in a blend of Nathaniel's sharp cologne, her flowery perfume and the heady odor of their lovemaking. Wrapping her arms around the pillow, she admitted she was as able as he to escape her troubled thoughts in lovemaking. Blowing out the candle, she lay in the dark recalling their conversation. Nathaniel would deal with this Mallory, of that she was sure. She yawned. She'd learned very little of what really concerned her but was now too tired to care. Tomorrow, she thought, drifting off to sleep.

After breakfast, Nathaniel left with Mr. Pitney to see to estate matters.

Laura walked with him to the stables and watched as the pair rode away to the home farm, the dogs at their heels. Was Nathaniel going to see Mallory? He hadn't mentioned the man again.

Returning to the house, she went downstairs to the kitchen to consult the cook about the weekly menu. It hadn't appeared on her writing desk in the morning room, which was a cozy chamber she'd appropriated for her correspondence since the weather had turned breezy and cool.

As she entered the kitchen, everyone came to attention. Laura was pleased to note that it looked orderly and clean. A tasty aroma rose from the oven. She was suddenly aware of the fuss she caused. The scullery maid dropped a pot she was scrubbing into the sink and wiped her face with a soapy hand, her eyes like saucers. A kitchen maid leapt up from destalking a colander full of berries and fell into a stumbling curtsey. The cook, Mrs. Madge, paused with flour up to her elbows and a rolling pin in her hand.

"Milady." Mrs. Madge grabbed a towel and hurriedly wiped her hands.

"Good morning, Mrs. Madge," Laura said. "I'd like to discuss the menus. It's his lordship's birthday in three weeks. We plan a celebration."

Having thought it through during the night, she had discussed this with Nathaniel at breakfast. She suggested inviting the vicar and his wife, the two spinster ladies from Thrompton, Misses Parthena and Orpha Fairfax, Cilla, and another couple who lived some miles from the village who were friends of Nathaniel's she had yet to meet.

"I don't know about Cilla," Nathaniel had said, after approving of her other suggestions.

"But why not Cilla?" She could not believe it was a matter of class. While Nathaniel's rank lent him a certain air and consequence, he was never arrogant or snobbish.

"She may not be comfortable in such company," he said. "But ask her if you must."

"She can always decline." Laura wanted a friend there, someone she knew.

"I'll come right up and bring my receipts," Mrs. Madge said. She put a hand to her white mobcap, her face lined with more than advancing years, perhaps some unknown sorrow. However, she was an excellent cook and confidently knew it.

"First, I'd like to inspect the wine cellars," Laura said.

Mrs. Madge's eyes widened. "Oh! As you wish, milady."

Laura resisted a smile. Rudge generally presided over the choice of wine, but this was her first dinner party. It was going to be special. Her father had taught her a good deal about wine as she was growing up.

She followed Mrs. Madge's black bombazine back along a stone passage and down a short flight of steps. The ceiling lowered and the granite walls seemed to close in. Laura held her skirts up above the damp floor, breathing in the musty air. Beyond the wine cellar, the steps continued down into a black well.

"Where do they lead to?" Laura asked.

"The cellars. There's a door at the very bottom, opens out onto the water's edge, milady, but it's a long, damp walk and is seldom used."

They entered a cobweb-strewn cavern filled with shelf upon shelf of dusty bottles of wine.

The young kitchen maid who had been preparing the berries appeared. She clutched her apron. "Mrs. Mallory, what should we do next with the pie?"

"Leave it, girl," Mrs. Madge said crossly. "I'll return in a moment."

Laura widened her eyes. "You're Mrs. Mallory?"

Mrs. Madge nodded. "I'm not called by that name here. The lass is new from the village."

"Are you a relative of Theo Mallory?"

Mrs. Madge wiped her palms on her apron. "He's my son."

"I met him recently."

The cook put her hand to her cap. "He's a man you can trust, milady. He won't cause any trouble here." Her face creased into lines of distress. "He never did."

Laura turned away to examine the bottles. "This for the meat courses, this for the fish, and this will be perfect for the dessert wine." Remembering her father's elaborate dinner parties, she chose *Chambertin Latour* champagne. She trailed along the rows and chose another, a sauterne, while dying to question the woman further about her son.

"I'll make a note of these, milady. And tell Rudge." She sounded as though it was the last thing she wanted to do.

"Thank you, Mrs. Madge."

Mrs. Madge shifted her feet and clutched her apron in her hands. "If that's it, milady, I'd best return to my pie."

Laura stood aside for the woman to pass through the doorway. "You must be pleased to see your son again."

Mrs. Madge halted, one foot on a step. "He should never have lost his position here. The gossips brought it about, of that I'm fair sure. Vicious they were, saying he was mixed up in that business."

"My husband would never act upon gossip, Mrs. Madge." What business was the cook referring to? Did it concern just the smuggling, or had Nathaniel been jealous of how closely Mallory and Amanda had worked together?

"Not normally, no. He's a good man, milady, but..."

Laura paused at the door. "What is it, Mrs. Madge?"

"I understand that his lordship was overcome by grief, milady. I fear it affected his judgment. He thought the worst of poor Theo, even though there was no evidence. And my son had to go off to find work elsewhere. A very talented gardener he is too, milady."

Mrs. Madge put a hand to her scarlet cheek, apparently realizing the inappropriateness of her comment. "If I don't get back, that green girl will do something silly, and there'll be no dessert for luncheon. If you're finished here, milady?"

"I am, thank you."

"I'll have that menu up to you in a trice, milady." Back in her kitchen, Mrs. Madge regained her confidence with a brisk shrug of her shoulders. "I'll consult Mrs. Beaton's receipts for suitable dishes for your dinner. But I have some lovely ideas of my own."

"I'm sure you do. Thank you, Mrs. Madge."

Laura returned to the ground floor thinking there were two different Theo Mallorys: the one Laura had disliked on sight and the one Mrs. Madge thought she knew. But mothers always loved their sons no matter what they did. Laura knew she would be the same. She prayed every night for a baby. Her mother had commented on the lack of news in her last letter. She'd expected a healthy girl like Laura to fall pregnant quickly. Laura sighed. A child would help banish the sadness of Nathaniel's past. It would be like a new beginning.

CHAPTER SEVENTEEN

Nathaniel rode with Hugh into the village. In The Sail and Anchor tavern, Mallory lay on his bed in his rented room, dressed in a richly patterned dressing gown decorated with yellow dragons. There was a paucity of furniture, just a wooden table and chair on bare boards. The rank smells of unwashed bodies, stale ale and smoke from the tavern below fouled the air. Mallory's coat and a spare shirt hung neatly on the chair back. A basin, clothes brush, hairbrush and razor were lined up over the table along with an empty tankard.

A red mist passed over Nathaniel's eyes at the sight of him, and his hands formed fists at his sides. He steadied himself. His aim was to get this man behind bars and see him hang.

Mallory rolled off the bed and stood. Running his hands through his hair, his bloodshot eyes flickered to Hugh's face then back to Nathaniel's. "Good of you to return my call, Lord Lanyon. I trust you've brought my money."

"For what?"

His fingers wrestled with the top button on his shirt. "I was called away before I was paid my wages."

The man had gall, he'd give him that. He also had grandiose ideas above his station. But would he have taken a chance and come back if he'd murdered Amanda? It was hard for Nathaniel to dispel his long-held belief that the man had pushed Amanda over the cliff. What else might have caused him to run? Had he been scared off by Amanda's murderer, suspecting he was next? Or was it fear that one of the gang would give him up to the police? Mallory was certainly scared now. It was in his stiff shoulders and the way he refused to meet Nathaniel's eyes. He'd gotten the gardening job because of Mrs. Madge, but Nathaniel had never liked the man. Thought the world owed him a living. And he no doubt saw Amanda as a means to better himself.

It might be two years ago, but recalling the chain of events leading up to Amanda's death brought it back fresh and stark. After Nathaniel had returned from a trip to London, he suspected Amanda's relationship with Mallory had progressed to an affair, although she'd denied it. The trauma he suffered as a child because of his parents' breakup and his mother's subsequent death, and then his taciturn father who'd ignored his existence, came rushing back. It almost brought him to his knees and left him hopelessly sad, hollow and empty.

Having wrestled his emotions into some semblance of order, he eyed Mallory coldly. Nathaniel was damned if he knew what Amanda had seen in him. Was it his blond looks? Surely not his oily charm. It surprised him that although he wished to serve bloody justice on this man, he did so without a twinge of jealousy.

Nathaniel rested his booted foot on the chair and leaned his arms on his knee to distract himself from grabbing Mallory by the scruff of the neck. "Glad to see that you had the good sense to return to Wolfram. You can clear your name of the recent spate of smuggling, if, as you say, you are innocent."

"You think that's why I'm here?" Mallory smoothed back his hair. "I've never been involved in smuggling. Not back then and not now. My nose is clean."

A man like Mallory would never pass up the opportunity to make money, through good means or bad. "Yet you ran off with your tail between your legs. The sign of a guilty man, wouldn't you say?"

Mallory attempted a leer, but it failed to match his watchful eyes. "I didn't run. I went after a lady I fancied. And now I need money to marry her. Money that you owe me, milord." He spat it out with another unpleasant smile. "I doubt you'll want me to spread it about that you don't pay your staff. Not to those who already think ill of you."

"Why you returned is of no interest to me. There are questions you must answer," Nathaniel said.

"You will tell the constable all you know or rot in jail until you do," Hugh said in a rough voice, stepping closer as if about to thump the truth out of him.

Nathaniel cast Hugh a warning glance. The villagers were ignorant of Mallory's sordid past. Any action they took against him themselves would only make matters worse. "I find it interesting that you've turned up at this particular time, however."

Mallory shrugged into his coat. "And if I choose to tell the constable to go to the devil?"

"Then he will find a reason to lock you up until you agree," Hugh interjected. "We're close to rounding up the gang. And guilty or not, you'll be tarred with the same brush. If you don't come clean with what you know, it could go very badly for you."

Mallory swallowed. "I didn't have anything to do with it, I tell you. I've been miles away! But I keep my ear to the ground. If I tell you who's behind it, will you give me my pay and let me go?"

"I can't make any promises. If you're cleared of any wrongdoing, then yes." Nathaniel jerked his head toward the door. "We'll escort you to the police station."

Several hours later, he and Hugh left Mallory with the constable. Having spilled all he said he knew, Mallory demanded to be allowed to go about his business.

"Not a bad day's work," Hugh said.

"Good that we now have the name of the scoundrel running it from London," Nathaniel said. "Let's hope next time the local lads will think twice before they get caught up in it."

"Once their mates hang." Hugh glanced at Nathaniel. "Mallory lies with ease; he's in this up to his neck."

"Then it won't go so well for him, will it?" It was good to hear Hugh thought the same. That Nathaniel's low opinion of Mallory did not color his judgement.

"He's acted to save his own skin. And it's not the first time."

It chilled Nathaniel to admit it, but if Mallory had stayed around after Amanda died, he would have taken matters into his own hands and beaten him within an inch of his life. But then Mallory was gone and it was too late. Time had the advantage of him dealing with this with a cooler head.

"Want to tell me about it, Your Lordship?" Hugh asked with a sideways glance.

"I don't think so, Hugh," Nathaniel replied, aware he'd fallen into a grim silence. "But I'll buy you an ale."

After lunch, Laura walked over to Cilla's cottage to invite her to Nathaniel's birthday dinner.

Cilla was dressed in her painter's smock. There was a smudge of red paint on her fingers, and the smell of oil paint and turpentine wafted through the rooms. In her studio nook, a painting rested on the easel, covered with a cloth.

"May I see it?" Laura asked.

"I never reveal my work until it's completed," Cilla said, her smile lacking humor.

"Very well." She smiled at the older woman, pleased to see her. Cilla was capable of extravagant and flamboyant gestures. But right now, she was the closest thing to a friend Laura had in this part of the world. "A landscape or a portrait?"

Cilla shook her head. "You *are* impatient. Care for tea?"

"No, thank you. I came with an invitation." Laura explained about the dinner as they sat together on the sofa.

"Nathaniel's birthday. He will enjoy that."

Laura grimaced. "I hope so. I don't know many people here yet, apart from you and another couple Nathaniel has invited. There's also the vicar and his wife and the Thrompton ladies. I think Nathaniel will invite Hugh Pitney as well. You will come?"

"Of course I shall. You can't have odd numbers at the table."

Laura eyed her, wondering if Cilla was being serious. "Nathaniel doesn't seem to welcome a fuss. Perhaps it's due to his childhood. His mother died while he was away at school. I don't suppose you remember her."

"Vaguely. She was a pretty woman. Seldom here—caught up in social affairs. I doubt Nathaniel saw much of her."

"Even so, a boy would be sad to lose his mother so young."

Cilla tilted her head. "I dare say."

Laura realized her motives were painfully transparent and her need to understand her husband far too obvious. "Theo Mallory has returned to Wolfram. Did you know?"

"I heard. Nothing much happens in Wolfram Village without everyone knowing."

Except for how a young mother-to-be could plunge to her death over a cliff. "Why did Mallory leave his position here, do you know?"

"Nathaniel probably fired him. If he did, he had good reason."

"He would never be unfair. He's a stickler for correctness." Except in the bedchamber, she thought with a rush of remembering. She rose and walked around the room, bending to smell lilies in a vase on the table.

Cilla examined a fingernail, picking at crimson paint. "A maid from the abbey told me she thought Amanda carried Theo's baby. Not true, of course."

Shocked, Laura stared at her. "Is she still in Nathaniel's employ?"

"Mina left Wolfram about the same time as Mallory. I thought maybe she went with him. She was jealous of Amanda. Wanted Mallory for herself."

"How can people be so vile?"

"They can and frequently are," Cilla said, her eyes bleak.

Laura's thoughts had been centered on Nathaniel and Amanda. Had venomous gossip been leveled at Cilla too? "Gossip is very often untrue. Vicious stories made up by people with too much time on their hands. Have you heard anything said about this in the village?"

"Not a word. The staff wouldn't spread that lie. They are very loyal to Nathaniel. Some in the village suspect Nathaniel killed Amanda. And if a rumor spread that she was carrying Mallory's baby, it would have given Nathaniel a good reason to have killed her, don't you think?"

Laura stared at her, horrified. "You are sure that she and Mallory weren't lovers?"

Cilla annoyed Laura by shrugging. "Who knows what people get up to? If Amanda had wanted him, she would have had him."

Laura frowned. It was a harsh thing to say about a friend who could not defend herself. "That's not very nice."

"No. But realistic." She put a hand on Laura's arm. "Come, my dear. It's all in the past. Most unfortunate to have that man back here again though, dredging up all the memories. But Nathaniel will likely banish him from Wolfram."

"I would rejoice if he did. I disliked Mallory on sight."

"Yes, I believe you would, Laura."

"Why is that?"

"You're more intelligent than Amanda."

Do men prefer less complicated women? Perhaps her mother was right. Troubled, Laura left Cilla and walked across the park. Amanda might be gone, but she left a tide of misery and pain in her wake. She found the possibility that Amanda had carried Mallory's child difficult to believe. More likely the spite of a disgruntled maid. Nathaniel must be aware of the gossip. Tears welled up, and she whisked them away. She wanted to fly to him and comfort him but feared he wouldn't welcome it. Not when he'd made Amanda's bedchamber a shrine he still visited and left flowers on her grave. For surely it must be him. Who else could it be?

The huge oaks threw deep violet shadows across the lawns. The trees were turning, and there was a new crispness to the air. Autumn was upon them. The season would be beautiful here. *"Season of mists and mellow fruitfulness,"* Laura quoted. The sickly poet, Keats, had a good reason to feel melancholic. But autumn always seemed a sad season to Laura too. She loved to be outdoors and disliked the end of bright summer days, the long, dreary nights of winter approaching.

As she walked, a worry she'd dealt with during her sleepless nights gripped her with a new sense of urgency. What if she couldn't give Nathaniel a son? They made love almost every night. Why wasn't she with child? Her mother had said that was why Nathaniel had married her, and although Laura hadn't wanted to believe it, it was true that he needed an heir. Could their marriage be happy if the years went by with no children to bring them closer?

She drew in a sharp breath. She must see Aunt Dora. She was even prepared to believe the Tarot. If a reading gave her some hope.

Reaching the lane, a sense of purpose drove her to hurry. She would write immediately and try to persuade Dora to forgo her London soirées for a visit to Cornwall. Even as Laura formed the words of her letter in her mind, she suffered another stab of guilt. She hadn't yet invited her mother.

CHAPTER EIGHTEEN

That evening, Nathaniel took his time over dinner and was rather pensive. It had grown late when they settled in the library.

"What happened today?" She'd given up waiting for him to explain.

"Hugh and I suspect Theo Mallory could be mixed up in this new smuggling ring, and we have little doubt he was involved in the last one." He took a large swallow of brandy. "But he agreed to accompany us to the police station."

Laura was surprised and pleased that he was so open with her. "Mallory is in jail?"

He scowled. "No proof. But he was eager to provide us with some names." Nathaniel rolled his shoulders. "Every man should have the opportunity to defend himself, I suppose."

Laura wondered if he was thinking he should be allowed the same.

"Pitney believes Mallory is in it up to his neck, and I agree. But Mallory did give us the ringleader in London. He plans to get his back pay and disappear from Wolfram before word gets out. It appears that this smuggling net spreads far wider than we initially thought."

"I'm surprised smuggling still goes on. I thought the government put a stop to it years ago."

He shrugged. "It will always go on where there's money to be made. It's part of Cornwall's deep-rooted history. The Cornish coast has been a favorite spot for contraband, and the locals supported the free traders. Some still do. A hundred years ago, the excise men were seen to be the villains. Contraband was blatantly moved around during daylight. Smugglers hid their French brandy in mineshafts and the caves around the coast. Their local knowledge helped to keep them one step ahead of the authorities." He paused for another swallow, then put down the empty glass. "But when times are hard, folk will try to make money wherever they can. They even hid here in the abbey at one time."

Laura thought of the noises she heard at night. She shivered. "Might they still?"

"No chance of that." He gave her a reassuring smile. "Don't be uneasy, Laura. Customs are onto them. We'll let the law deal with them."

"So, that's the end of it?" She prayed that it was. She hated to see him so tired and defeated.

"It had better be. If this isn't quickly solved, my standing in the Lords will be worth nothing. And my plans for change will lie in ashes."

Laura leaned forward, yearning to comfort him. "How did you discover the contraband?"

"Hugh found boxes containing tobacco and other items in one of the estate cottages. They'd brought them in under the cover of darkness." He rubbed the back of his head where his black hair tapered neatly to his collar. "When it happened over two years ago, I was involved with other pressing matters. I let Mallory get away without questioning him further."

"Why haven't you told me any of this?"

She caught a flash of doubt in his eyes. "I wanted to deal with it first. I didn't want you to be worried." He shrugged. "And I don't like the idea of seeing disappointment in your eyes when you look at me. I promised you a good life here, Laura. It has not been quite what you hoped for, has it?"

Did he refer to Wolfram or to their marriage? She drew in a breath, deeply moved by his need for her to respect him. "You could never disappoint me." She reached for his hand and entwined her fingers in his long, warm ones. "I shall always believe in you."

Nathaniel squeezed her hand with a grateful smile. "There may be times when you find that difficult, sweetheart."

He withdrew his hand and rose to pour himself another brandy from the decanter. He was a measured man in many ways and always stopped at two brandies after dinner. His actions showed how upset he was. Her breath caught in sympathy.

"Darling, you're a good man. I know that."

"Thank you, sweetheart. Let's not talk about it anymore tonight. I'm a little tired." He held his hands out to help her rise. "Shall we go up?"

"I've selected the menu for your birthday dinner," Laura said, attempting to lighten the atmosphere as they climbed the stairs.

"It's sweet of you to do this for me, Laura, but I don't want a lot of fuss."

"Oh," she said in a small voice. "Everyone has been invited. I asked Cilla this afternoon."

"Very well. If you must." At the top of the stairs, he pulled her against him. "I'll tell you what I'd like for my birthday," he murmured, his cheek against her hair. "To take you out in my boat. I planned to before this, but somehow I haven't gotten around to it. Winter will be closing in soon enough."

"I've only been on the water once," Laura said, her voice sounding strained. "That was in your rowboat." Her heart sank at the memory. "I can't swim."

He stroked her chin with his knuckles. "A landlubber, eh? I'll look after you, never fear. You'll grow to love it. There's nothing like the rush of waves as the sailboat speeds across the water driven by the wind." His eyes took on a faraway look as if he imagined himself there. "Sailing gives you a wonderful sense of freedom. You don't know you're alive until you're out on the ocean."

Unconvinced, she fought for a way to delay it. "But I have so much to do for your birthday dinner."

"You have a few weeks, and Rudge will take care of everything."

That was exactly what she did not intend to happen. "Despite Rudge, I will still have much to do. And these affairs require time to organize."

He arched a black brow, his eyes warm and knowing. "You don't wish old Rudge to get the upper hand, eh?" It was like the sun coming out from behind a rain cloud. Nathaniel understood her feelings. He was getting to know her, as she was him.

She grinned. "It's my first dinner party. I would like to arrange it."

"Then do so, sweetheart. We'll sail tomorrow for just a few hours. I'll take you around Wolfram and along the coast. You can't fully appreciate the beauty of Cornwall unless you see it from the water."

"I'd like that." It was a concession of sorts. He would allow her to organize her party and she would go out in the boat with him, although she dreaded it.

When Nathaniel came to her bedroom, Laura hoped to continue their conversation before they lost themselves in each other. In her dressing gown, her hair loose over her shoulders, she greeted him with a light kiss. "I can imagine you sailing around the coast as a youth. I want to hear more about your boyhood."

He settled beside her on the bed, toying with her long tresses, which always seemed to fascinate him. "My parents were busy people. I wasn't disciplined much in those days. Left to my own devices. When I wasn't with my tutor, I roamed free with the other village children. I swam, rode my pony and fished."

"Did it all end when you were sent away to school?"

"Everything changed after that." A guarded note strained his voice.

"I can see by your father's portrait that you have inherited his coloring, but you don't favor him in looks." Nathaniel's father had thin lips and a stern, rather arrogant expression. "What was your mother like?"

He dropped the lock of her hair he'd been winding around his finger. "I remember little of her. Why all these questions?" He pushed away from her and stood. "I'm sorry, Laura. That was rude of me. Must be more tired than I realized. Forgive me. I'll say good night."

The panel slid back and he was gone.

CHAPTER NINETEEN

Nathaniel had had a horrendous few days, Laura told herself. So much had happened. She tried to convince herself that she wasn't to blame for him leaving her, but she still lay in bed, tense and unsure. As sleep continued to elude her, she ran over the events of the evening. He was concerned that the rumors of smuggling would taint his reputation in Parliament. The news of smuggling was worrying, of course, but that didn't account for his behavior; his heavier than usual drinking perhaps, but not what followed. It had something to do with his mother. Dispirited, she realized it wasn't that he wanted too much from her, but too little. She could not live like this. Laura wiped her eyes, knowing she could not let it end there.

She left the bed. Having spent some time locating the spring which opened the space between their connecting rooms some days ago, she pressed it. The oak paneling slid back to reveal an empty room.

With a deep breath, Laura whirled around to snatch up her dressing gown. She left her bedchamber, her candle held high. Amanda's room lay in darkness. Laura turned and went downstairs, her footsteps echoing in the quiet house.

The great hall lay silent under a fragile silver net of moonlight. In the corridor beyond, the wall sconces sent flickering shadows over the walls. Holding her candlestick high, Laura opened the door to Nathaniel's study. It was empty, as was the library.

Puzzled, she returned to the hall, her candle fluttering. There was a draft from somewhere. Might a door be open? She retraced her steps, finding the door to the rose garden bolted shut. At the kitchen steps, the breeze strengthened, lifting her gown and swirling around her legs. She shivered with a sense of foreboding.

Below her, the cavernous kitchen lay in darkness. Laura hesitated, then her fingers gripped the banister, as a need to know propelled her forward. She stepped down into the cold room. The stoves would not be lit until daybreak. The servants' hall beyond was empty, as all the staff retired early. A current of air infused with the briny tang of the sea whipped up the stairs from the wine cellar and beyond. The door leading to the water's edge must have been left open.

Laura ventured down a few steps, as her guttering candle threatened to go out. She balked at going further. A loud scrape. The heavy clunk of a lock sliding into place. The breeze died away. The hollow sound of footsteps on the stairs followed. It must be Nathaniel, and she didn't want him to find her here.

She retraced her steps as the well of darkness below lightened. Heart racing, she hurried up the kitchen stairs. Gaining the ground floor, she began to run. She almost fell into her bedchamber and shut the door. Leaning against it, gasping for breath, she put her ear to the door and waited. Nothing, not even the reassuring sound of Nathaniel coming to bed.

Laura went to the window. Down in the garden dotted with gravestones, a shadowy figure appeared, darting over the moonlit ground before disappearing. She watched for some time, but nothing moved beyond the sway of the trees. Nathaniel had stated flatly that the smugglers had gone. Was he withholding anything that might alarm her? She shivered and sought the warmth of her bed. Huddling there, unease and frustration churned her stomach. He had pleaded exhaustion and the need for sleep. But where was he?

The next morning, Laura woke to the rasp of the sliding panel. She stretched as Nathaniel drew the bedclothes back and joined her in the bed, taking her his arms.

He nuzzled her shoulder. "Sorry, my love. I was a bear last night. Best that I left you."

His musky scent and hard body tempted her, but Laura pulled away. She propped her head on an elbow to gaze into his smoky eyes that didn't always reveal the truth. "Did you sleep well?"

"Wonderful. I feel more like a lion than a bear this morning." He untied the neck of her nightgown and kissed his way down to her breast with obvious intent.

Laura moved out of his embrace. "You weren't in your bed last night, Nathaniel." She was gratified to see surprise widen his eyes. He thought it so easy to fool her. "I doubt you were in the house."

He sat up, his dark brows meeting in a frown. "You looked for me?"

Her lips trembled. "Yes."

"Don't do it again!" Nathaniel rolled out of bed to pace the carpet.

"Why ever not?"

"Can't you do what I ask of you? It's so little, surely."

She took a deep breath. "You think it a small thing to imprison me in my room at night?"

He sat on the bed and took her hands in his strong grip. "Promise me, Laura."

She gasped. "Tell me why, Nathaniel."

"Damn it!" He flung her hands free. "You are my wife. Can you do what I ask without questioning me, just once?"

Shocked by his explosive response, Laura drew in a breath. "I will not be ordered about like a servant. And I refuse to be treated like a prisoner in my own home."

At her words, Nathaniel gave a bitter laugh. "Laura, for God's sake! You know we've had smugglers on the grounds. It's not forever, and I have my reasons. Please?"

Laura struggled into her dressing gown. "You assured me they were gone. Is it too much to ask for an explanation for your nightly sojourns?"

"You have been searching for me?" He slowly shook his head. "Have I made a mistake bringing you here?"

Laura inhaled sharply as anger and dismay coiled in her stomach. "Mother said your reason for marrying me was because you need an heir. Was that the only reason?"

His laugh was brittle. "I married you because I wanted you here with me. I wanted to spend my life with you." He raked his fingers through his hair, and a lock fell over his forehead, making him appear less self-assured. "After everything, I thought fate owed me some happiness. Perhaps I've been wrong."

She stared at him, captured by his words. He had wanted her. Now it seemed he wished he hadn't.

"Until those responsible for this are put in jail, I must ask this of you." His eyes implored her.

"What should I fear, Nathaniel? I've heard noises during the night, and there was someone in the room down the corridor."

Nathaniel's eyes widened. "Which room?"

"Amanda's bedchamber."

He shook his head. "You must be imagining it. It's an empty room."

"I tell you there was someone there. I saw their shadow move beneath the door."

He pulled her to her feet. "Come and show me."

Nathaniel opened Amanda's door as Laura's chest tightened. He stepped inside. "Damnation!"

She started at the violence of his reaction. "What is it?"

"I gave orders for all of this to be packed away before you came to Wolfram."

"But when you saw me come out of this room you said nothing."

"I believed it to be empty." His hands on her shoulders, he gazed down at her. "Honestly, sweetheart."

"It wasn't you then?" she asked, giddy with relief. All of

Amanda's possessions, her jewelry and perfume still covered the dresser. Chilled, Laura noticed that a lacy sky-blue gown had been taken from the armoire, and now lay across a chair, as if about to be worn. "And someone has been back here again. You didn't arrange this room like a shrine to her memory?"

Nathaniel stared at her as if she was mad. "Good God, no."

She swallowed. "You aren't still in love with Amanda?" Her voice dropped to a husky whisper.

"What on earth made you think I was?" With a bitter laugh, he swung away from her to sort through the jewelry on the dresser. Amanda's expensive perfume wafted into the air, and he turned with a grimace. "I must speak to Rudge." He put his arm around Laura's shoulders and ushered her from the bedroom.

"Who visits this room then, Nathaniel?"

He shook his head. "I've no idea. Go back to your bedroom, Laura; call your maid to help you dress. I'll be in the breakfast room."

Lightheaded, Laura hurried to obey. It was not Nathaniel. But his bitter laugh, so filled with emotion, did little to set her mind at rest.

She dressed in her favorite jade-green gown with the French gilt buttons for added courage. Determined to appear calm, she entered the breakfast room where Rudge stood before Nathaniel.

Rudge bowed. "Your usual breakfast, my lady?"

She doubted she could eat a bite. "A piece of fruit, thank you, Rudge."

When Rudge left them, Nathaniel gazed at her, appreciation in his eyes. "You look very pretty in that shade of green." He poured her a cup of coffee. Strong, the way she liked it.

"I could do with this." Laura sipped the reviving brew, her nerve endings thrumming. "You questioned Rudge?"

"I did." Nathaniel buttered his toast. "He'd given orders for Mina, Amanda's maid, to clear the room and box up its contents. They were to be placed in the attic. But after she left Wolfram, he hadn't checked to see if the work was done. He's very remorseful and will see the room is emptied today."

Laura put down her cup. Rudge had been far too enamored of

Amanda's portrait. Amanda had laughed at him, Cilla had said. "And you believe him?"

Nathaniel shrugged. "I don't see why I shouldn't."

"Might there have been a thief in the room?"

"Rudge will question the staff. We may have a pilferer among them. Perhaps they were disturbed, for nothing appears to have been taken. Anything of great value is in my safe." He rubbed his brow. "Don't worry, Laura, the room will be emptied today. No one need go in there again."

"We could give the maids one of the simpler pieces of jewelry. I'm sure they'd be delighted to have a small broach or a locket."

"An excellent idea. I'll have Rudge see to it."

Nathaniel took a bite of toast as his assessing gaze met hers. Did he believe her? Or did he think she'd dreamed it? She put down her cup. "I went down to the kitchen last night when I couldn't find you. A breeze blew up from the passage that leads to the water."

Nathaniel dropped his toast onto his plate. "Remember your promise, please."

She hadn't promised, and she might well ignore his infuriating order in the future. But she saw little advantage in arguing the point with him now. "I heard someone shut the outside door. Was that you?"

"Yes. I checked on my boat to see if the mooring was secure. A gale was blowing up."

Laura gazed out at the calm, sunny morning. "I didn't hear it."

"The storm didn't amount to much."

"And yet you usually predict the weather so accurately."

He frowned. "I'm touched by your faith in me. But even I can be wrong on occasion."

"Do you know," she said in a conversational tone, aware her words would produce an outburst, "I've learned how to tell when you dissemble."

This gained a reaction, but not the explosive one she'd expected. Nathaniel rose slowly. He looked down at her, an expression in his eyes she'd never seen before. Never wanted to see. Regret.

"The woman I married," he said slowly, "would never have

thought that of me. Let alone have said it."

Laura cringed and looked away from his hurt eyes. She swallowed the bitter taste in her mouth. Why was she the one made to feel in the wrong? "Am I mistaken then?"

Nathaniel paused as Rudge entered with Laura's plate of fruit. Her mouth was as dry as dust, her appetite completely gone.

When the door closed on Rudge, Nathaniel rested his hands on the back of his chair. "I only ask that you do as I say. Am I so very unreasonable?"

She glowered at him. So she was to be the one at fault!

He eased his shoulders with a weary sigh. "I need to escape all this drama. I'm taking the boat out." He tilted his head. "I'd like your company."

She blanched, in no mood to brave the ocean. "No. I…"

He nodded, his eyes bleak. "Very well." He turned and walked to the door.

"Wait, Nathaniel." Her voice trembled. He thought she no longer believed in him. That must have cut deeply into the very heart of a proud man like Nathaniel. And he was wrong. She had every faith in him to protect her, especially in that small boat. She couldn't leave things like this. "I'd like to come with you."

He raised a brow. "You feel safe with me, Laura?"

She swallowed. "Of course I do."

His eyes darkened with emotion. "I shall always endeavor to take care of you. It would be more than my life is worth if anything happened to you."

She gasped. "I've always trusted you to keep me safe."

"It's a perfect day for a sail. We'll leave after your breakfast. You might wish to change your dress. It would be a pity to spoil that one."

The cold wind whipped across the water, churning the waves. If she chose, Laura could reach down and touch the white tips of the gray-green ocean as the swell rolled past them at great speed. The salty air stung her nose. She fumbled in a pocket for a handkerchief, and then abandoned the idea. Despite her caped coat, her legs were cold in the fawn seersucker gown which offered more freedom of movement. What she wouldn't give for Cilla's divided skirt!

Her chilled fingers clutched the yacht's rail again in a slippery grip. Sailing proved both frightening and exhilarating. How easy it would be to topple into that dark, roiling water and sink without a trace. Her gaze returned to the man at the helm, his big, capable hand on the tiller, his dark head turned toward the rocks a frightening few yards to starboard.

Nathaniel had explained the rudiments of sailing, and when his troubled gaze met hers, she desperately wanted to reach out to him and try to bridge the ever-widening gap between them. Didn't he want to know who was in Amanda's bedroom? Or did he think she was being overly dramatic? If he couldn't take her at her word, they would soon lose the genuine passion and regard they shared. A bond which had drawn them together like a strong thread from their first meeting. She would fight to stop that from happening, whatever it took, and yearned for when he would take her to bed without words and make love to her, even though it fell short of what she craved. But not only did he show little desire for her, he remained tightly coiled within himself, his actions brisk and formal when he was forced to touch her.

The foam-crested waves swirled around the boat, and the sea's roar made it impossible for her to make herself heard, even if she could manage the words that might smooth things between them. She watched him in his element with intense admiration. He was a graceful man, and that grace did not desert him on the water. He moved with assurance, raising the sail and yelling at her to avoid the swing of the boom. The noisy gulls followed above in the pale blue sky, perhaps in the hope of a free meal.

The boat tilted, drenching Laura's skirt in salt spray. She gasped as icy water ran down her neck. Oblivious to any discomfort, Nathaniel tacked into the wind, and the boat swung around. They passed the abbey, its ancient beauty stirring within her a sense of foolish pride that this was her home. She craned her neck as it disappeared behind the granite cliffs. She glanced at her husband's handsome profile. He looked her way, his face filled with grim pleasure.

"I love you," she shouted, knowing her words would be torn from her and carried away by the wind.

Nathaniel gave no indication that he'd heard. He stared ahead as they sailed around the rocky headland, past rocks worn razor sharp from the sea's assault. Gravity-defying wildflowers, grasses and seabirds' nests decorated the sheer rock face. Somewhere along these cliffs, Amanda had plunged to her death. The horror of it became so real that Laura shivered.

She could see the roof of Cilla's idyllic cottage; from here, it looked like it was teetering on the edge.

Close to the cliff where the waves beat against the rocks, a dark shape, like a bundle of rags, churned in the water. Laura called out to Nathaniel, but he had seen it too. He swung the tiller and guided the boat closer. The wind caught the sail, driving them back. Cursing, Nathaniel lowered the canvas and picked up the oars. He began to row, pulling the boat through the seething waves. Only a few yards from them, a body rose and fell with the waves to be dashed on the rocks, then drift away again.

"Oh, dear heaven!" Laura put a hand to her mouth with a strangled sob.

Nathaniel brought the boat as close as he could. It was a man, face down, arms outspread. He wore a tan leather jerkin like one she'd seen before.

"Take the tiller, Laura. Careful how you go."

As the boat rocked, Laura moved uneasily toward Nathaniel. She sat and grasped the slick wooden tiller.

Nathaniel placed his big hands over hers with a firm grip. "Like this. Hold it steady."

Nathaniel rowed back to the man. He reached down and grabbed an arm, heaving the man over the side. Any frail hope that he might still be alive dissolved when he fell like a sodden sack of produce into the bottom of the boat. Laura couldn't breathe; it was as though the air had been squeezed from her lungs. She dizzily dragged in huge breaths and tried unsuccessfully to avert her gaze, afraid she'd be sick.

Nathaniel turned the man over, revealing a face reduced to a mass of bloodless flesh, his features torn away by the rocks. His hair, although plastered wet to his head, was bright gold.

"It's Theo Mallory!" she cried.

"Don't look, Laura." Nathaniel pulled a handkerchief from his pocket and laid it over the man's face, then he took the tiller from her and turned the boat for home.

CHAPTER TWENTY

Wet through, Laura stood shivering on the wharf.

"Are you all right, sweetheart?" Nathaniel wrapped his arm around her in a comforting gesture. She wanted to turn her face to his chest and cry, but she steadied herself, nodding dully.

"Go up and change; there's no reason for you to be here." He released her. "It might be a while before Teg brings the constable."

Some hours later, from her window, Laura saw the police constable arrive. She hurried downstairs. Theo Mallory had been positively identified and the body removed to the undertakers in the village. Nathaniel and the constable had gone down to give the bad news to Mrs. Madge.

Laura followed them, wanting to offer the woman comfort. A wail rose from the kitchen.

"Bring Mrs. Madge some brandy, Rudge." Nathaniel took Mrs. Madge's arm and helped her to a stool. "Is there somewhere you can go? You must take time away from Wolfram to recover. As long as it takes."

The tearful maids clustered around, clutching their aprons.

Mrs. Madge seemed of sterner stuff. She shook her head vehemently, saying hard work was the best cure-all for grief. Rising from the stool, she looked vaguely about her and sipped the brandy Rudge had quickly fetched for her.

"I have your dinner party to prepare for," she said in a brisk tone. "You can't do without me."

It was surely inappropriate to hold the dinner now. Laura placed her arm around the distressed woman. "You need not concern yourself with that. The dinner will be postponed until your return."

"Oh no, my lady." Mrs. Madge's eyes were bright with unshed tears. "I'm so looking forward to it. I haven't cooked for a dinner party in such a long time." She turned crimson and glanced from Laura to Nathaniel, no doubt with the thought that the last dinner was prepared for Amanda.

Nathaniel patted her shoulder. "Very well, Mrs. Madge. We shall make the night a triumph."

Mrs. Madge blew her nose. "Thank you, my lord, and now I'd best be getting on with the luncheon preparations."

Neither of them could do justice to Mrs. Madge's efforts at luncheon. When they left the dining room, Nathaniel put a hand on Laura's arm. "Come to my study, sweetheart."

He looked so stern. She followed him inside, her misery like a steel weight.

Nathaniel leaned back against the desk. "The day after the dinner party, I'd like you to leave for Wimbledon. Visit with your parents at home for a while."

"But this is my home," she whispered. He was sending her away. Her breath caught as she fought panic. Was this the end for them?

"Home is where your heart is, Laura. Can you say your heart is here when you accuse me so?"

Laura blinked away tears. She placed her hands on his chest, searching his face. "You're sending me away because we had an argument?"

"No, Laura. Don't think this has anything to do with you and me. It does not." Nathaniel stepped away, but his gaze remained on her as he tugged the bell cord.

Did he expect her to fight him? When he was in this mood, she knew it was useless. She'd been stupid to accuse him of dishonesty when he may well have been trying to protect her. Would she never learn patience? If only he'd allow her to share his worries. But he was right. There was danger here; she could hardly refute it. Not after today.

When Rudge appeared, Nathaniel said, "Bring down Lady Lanyon's trunk from the attic. After the dinner party, she plans to visit her parents for a prolonged stay."

A prolonged stay? Ignoring the satisfied look on Rudge's face as the butler hurried out of the room, Laura turned to her husband.

"Am I to be punished, Nathaniel?" she asked, hoping they might begin to talk.

"For what?" He sighed. "Don't make it any harder, please. I need to deal with this without worrying about you."

"Very well." With a stiff nod, she left the room.

Agnes awaited her in the bedroom. Rudge had wasted no time. Laura's trunk was already there, lying open, awaiting her instructions.

"Leave that for now, please. I shan't be departing for a while yet," Laura said. She still hoped Nathaniel would cool down and change his mind; he needed her now more than ever.

She had to speak to someone or she'd burst. Laura went to tell Cilla the news. She found Cilla working, the strong smell of oil paint lingering in the air. A canvas lay hidden from view beneath its cloth cover.

"You've been working hard," Laura said after she'd explained about Mallory.

"Almost finished," Cilla said. "I find it difficult to believe Theo's dead." She cleaned her hands with a pungent rag. "He was always so pugnacious. That kind seem indestructible."

"Was he rude to you?"

"He knew I disliked the way he behaved around Amanda. But I didn't care what he thought of me."

Laura leaned back against the sofa. "He was disagreeable to everyone I suspect. He was certainly quite rude to me."

"Mallory was arrogant and ambitious. If he saw a way to get

ahead, he'd take it, no matter the consequences. A thoroughly bad type who has gotten his just desserts."

"They don't know what happened to him yet."

"And probably won't." Cilla put the rag down.

"We discovered his body at the base of the cliffs, in a similar spot to where Amanda had been found."

Cilla nodded, her hands in the pockets of her smock. "The tides, I expect."

"Did you see Mallory on Wolfram land? He was staying in the village at The Sail and Anchor."

"No." Cilla raised her brows. "Let the police deal with it, Laura."

"That's difficult though, isn't it? This business affects Nathaniel."

"Mallory probably drank too much in the tavern and wandered around in the dark. It wouldn't be the first time someone's drowned that way."

"Or he leapt to his death because of a broken heart?"

"What a romantic you are." Cilla grinned. "I came across Mallory once in the woods when I was picking wildflowers. Their colors are useful for my work. He had Mina, the maid at Wolfram at the time, up against a tree. Her blouse was open and her skirts hiked up around her waist. It must have pained her, that rough bark rubbing against the delicate skin of her back as he drove into her."

Laura flushed at her blatant description. "Do you think Mallory forced himself on her?"

"No. She was mad about him."

"Was this before he and Amanda...created the rose arbor?"

"I can't remember." She frowned. "What is this about, Laura?"

"I want to understand what happened here," Laura said, frustration causing her voice to tremble. "You don't have the slightest suspicion how Amanda met her death?"

The amusement fled from Cilla's features, rendering her face pinched and rather plain. "No. I thought we were discussing Mallory."

"Mallory told me that Amanda was unhappy here."

"Amanda was a difficult woman to make happy. She wanted too much." She shook her head. "This will be hard on Nathaniel. More fuel to add to the gossip mill."

Laura sucked in a sharp breath. "They can hardly blame him. Why should any of this fall on Nathaniel's shoulders? Mallory had been to the police. He'd told them what he knew. An act of revenge perhaps. Or might he have withheld some guilty person's name and that person killed him to keep him silent?"

"You would make a good detective." Cilla turned toward the door. "I'll make us some tea."

Laura rubbed her arms as she strolled around the small sitting room. There was always so much to distract one here, from a delicate wildflower to a strangely shaped stone. A tiny likeness in an oval frame hung from a blue velvet ribbon on the wall. On closer inspection, the woman resembled Amanda as she was portrayed in Cilla's painting at the abbey.

Struck by a sudden thought, Laura whirled around. She moved quickly to the annex and, with a glance at the kitchen door, lifted the cloth which covered the painting. She gasped. A nude, fair-haired woman lay on a blue velvet chaise. Her expression seductive, she invited the viewer in with a tempting curl of her lovely lips. The position in which she lay reminded Laura of Titian's *Venus of Urbino*. The woman held a posy of flowers in one hand, while the other rested at the top of her thighs hiding her sex. Lying beside her, incongruously, was a blue parasol with a pearl handle, the same umbrella that was in Amanda's portrait. This work was unlike the rest of Cilla's paintings, the fine detail lovingly wrought.

Laura felt as if she'd glimpsed something intimate. Hearing the rattle of the tray, she dropped the cloth and turned to see Cilla staring at her.

Scowling, Cilla placed the tray on the table. "I asked you not to look at my paintings until they were finished, Laura!" She shook her head. "You are so impatient. Why couldn't you wait?"

Laura was surprised by the force of Cilla's reaction. She looked quite bereft. "I'm sorry, I'd forgotten." She wondered if Cilla would ever have shown it to her. "It's Amanda, isn't it?"

Cilla sank onto the sofa. She unloaded the tray. "Amanda was the perfect model. She fascinated me because, inside, she was nothing like she presented to the world." She handed the cup to Laura. "Her beauty mesmerized one. So delicate of feature, so slender a body, and her skin..." She shook her head. "But inside she was as hard as those granite cliffs. I don't believe she was capable of love."

Cilla constantly shocked her. Laura could never be sure what she would say next. "Do you think Amanda broke Nathaniel's heart?"

Cilla shrugged. "How should I know? He doesn't wear his heart on his sleeve."

"I just can't see how Mallory fit into all this. If, as you say, Amanda didn't care for him."

"Amanda was a flirt. She even tried to beguile Pitney, but she got nowhere with him. Mallory was just another of her conquests she used to her advantage. She had him eating out of her hand. I didn't ask her how she went about it."

"But surely Amanda wouldn't have encouraged Mallory. She was carrying Nathaniel's child."

Cilla took a sip of tea. "I wondered if she really wanted to be a mother. She hated the way the pregnancy changed her body and made no secret of the fact."

Amanda might have felt uncomfortable and complained, but that didn't mean she didn't want her baby. Laura wondered if Cilla, so wrapped up in her art and not particularly maternal, might fail to understand a woman's need for a child.

"Have you been lonely? You seem so self-contained."

Cilla studied the painting on the easel. "I'm content to be alone most of the time. People demand too much from you. They're exhausting."

"Amanda's close association with Mallory must have angered Nathaniel."

"Nathaniel's no fool. But he is a man. Amanda would have been able to get around him."

Laura pushed that unpalatable thought away.

"Amanda spoke of employing a nanny and a governess until the child could be sent away to school," Cilla said.

Just like Nathaniel had been, Laura thought with a wrench. "She may well have become more settled and content after the child was born."

"Hmm. I doubt it. But we'll never know."

"Did you accept the coroner's verdict?" Laura asked.

"That she grew dizzy and fell?" She put down her cup. "Seems the most logical. Although when I heard about the smugglers, it occurred to me that she may have stumbled onto something she shouldn't have seen, and they dealt with her. As they may have done with Mallory."

Laura shivered. "Don't they carry out their nefarious deeds at night?"

"She may have angered someone else."

"Not many are given to acts of such violence."

Cilla shook her head. "That's somewhat naïve, Laura," she said dryly. "You can't know what people are capable of."

Laura set down her cup. "I really came to tell you I'm leaving Wolfram after the dinner party. Nathaniel wishes me to stay with my parents until this business is dealt with."

"It will be good for you to get away for a while."

Laura put on her hat. "I must go. He might have need of me."

But for a black chough calling to its mate, the russet, gold and crimson woods were hushed and still, the scent of pine drifting in the air. Leaving the park, Laura approached the abbey. Sunlight sparkled off the pointed arch windows, turning the granite walls a warm apricot. It was so very beautiful here.

It was difficult to be sure of anything Cilla said. The artist's mood changed with alarming speed, and her view of the world was very different than Laura's. But she couldn't ignore what Cilla had said about Amanda. Could there possibly be any truth in it? It robbed her of breath to think Nathaniel had been cuckolded. What did he believe deep in his heart? Whether true or not, beneath the surface of Wolfram there was an undercurrent that poisoned all that was good.

There would likely be an inquest into Mallory's death. Laura didn't want to leave Nathaniel to deal with it alone. But he seemed resolute, and it would not be fair of her to insist on staying when he had enough to worry him.

She had a sudden, desperate need for her aunt's calming presence. Right now, Dora's common sense would be of great help, although she doubted the Tarot would provide the answers to the problems at Wolfram.

Perhaps like her, Nathaniel wished to blot out the gruesome scene they'd witnessed, for she found him busy with paperwork in his study. He looked up and smiled as she entered, the ledgers open on his desk as he totaled rows of figures. He had demanding properties and investments, which despite a secretary, an estate manager and an accountant in London, his personal attention to his affairs was constantly required.

He sat back and smiled. "Was Cilla upset at the news?"

"Not really. She disliked Mallory."

Laura struggled to understand Cilla. She'd thought she'd been a close friend of Amanda's, but they seemed to have had a complicated friendship. Cilla had not been kind about her, but that was her acerbic, sharp-tongued nature. But at times Cilla could be very kind. Laura knew she couldn't repeat any of this to Nathaniel. It wouldn't solve anything and would upset him.

On the open page, she spied the name Gateley Park, one of Nathaniel's estates. He'd mentioned it briefly before. Compared to Wolfram he considered the house to be quite modern, as it was built in the late 18th century.

As she leaned against the desk, he closed the book and turned in his chair to study her. "I'm sorry you had to see that grisly sight this morning. You must have been shocked. I should have given you brandy as well as Mrs. Madge. Are you all right now?"

"Still a bit shaky." She stroked the inlaid leather top on the mahogany desk.

He frowned. "I'd prefer you to send Cilla a note rather than wander around the estate alone." He took her hand. "We had words this morning. I dislike it when we do that."

"As do I, but sometimes something good comes from it. It can clear the air."

He kissed her fingers. "And did it? Clear the air?"

Not entirely, but she wasn't about to start another argument, not after what they'd witnessed and what Cilla had told her. She still reeled from shock at the suggestion the baby wasn't Nathaniel's. It was nonsense. Cilla had a love of the dramatic; that's what made her a good artist. "Have I been unfair?"

"A soul of patience, actually. I've been difficult to live with." He pulled her down onto his lap. "My insistence on you leaving Wolfram has nothing to do with our marriage. Don't think it's because I don't want you here." He stroked her cheek. "You do know that, don't you?"

Laura ran her fingers through his silky dark hair, breathing in his familiar male smell. She took a deep breath. "I suspect you're overly protective like my mother."

He gave a gruff laugh. "I'm like your mother now, am I? That can't be good." He kissed her nose. "Give me time, sweetheart."

He'd never said that before. It gave her hope for the future. She nestled her head against his shoulder, enjoying the comfort and safety his strong arms afforded her. This tenderness, however brief, was what she'd always wanted from him. Frustrated, she wished he wouldn't send her away, but she knew begging him would be useless. "I'll miss you, darling."

"I trust it won't be for too long."

"What is going to happen while I'm gone?"

His arms settled tightly around her waist. "I'm confident we'll find Mallory's killer and round up the rest of the gang. I suspect a member of the staff here at Wolfram."

"Not long after he came here, I heard Mallory talking to one of the grooms down by the seawall when I'd gone for a walk at dusk."

"Who was he?"

"I don't know, but Mallory sounded like he was giving him orders."

"We suspect he was, sweetheart."

"You're convinced Mallory was murdered?"

"The postmortem will confirm my view."

"You promise to be very careful, Nathaniel."

"I will."

"Will you miss me while I'm away?"

"How can you ask that?" His thumb beneath her chin, he lifted her face, and with a deep intake of breath, pressed his mouth to hers. When he drew away, his eyes, which could be a steely gray, were a soft gray-blue like the Wolfram sky after rain. "Not having you here will be a penance."

His kisses usually made her thoughts scatter, but at the word he used, her senses came alert. Did he believe he needed to be punished? For what? "Penance is an odd word."

"The wrong word, perhaps." Nathaniel rose and set her on her feet. "I could have done things differently. But I can still put much to rights given time. I'm keen to do so."

He sounded as if he wished her gone already. She studied the ledger on his desk again. "I'll visit Aunt Dora after I see my parents. Is Gateley Park leased?"

Nathaniel arched his eyebrows. "No." He framed her face with his hands. "What is going on in that head of yours?"

"I'd like to see the property." Could Gateley Park give up secrets about this enigmatic husband of hers?

"Gateley Park was my grandparents' home. My mother grew up there. I haven't been back for a few years."

She gasped. "Why not?"

His expression became shuttered, black lashes lowered. "I've had no reason to."

"Is it in a good state of repair?"

"My man of business assures me it is."

She ignored the warning in his voice and pressed on, determined to have her way with this at least. "It might be pleasant to spend a few days there."

He rubbed his brow. "I've no idea why you would want to visit an empty house."

She smiled. "Perhaps it's more about not wishing to spend too long under my parents' roof."

His mouth twitched. He understood her feelings at least. "The carriage is at your disposal. Will your aunt accompany you? There's only a small village within miles of the property. You'll be thin of company."

"I do hope to persuade Aunt Dora to leave her beloved London."

The furrow in his forehead deepened. "Please urge her to on my behalf." Nathaniel picked up the pen on his desk. "Now, my love, if you'll excuse me, I must get this work done before I ride into the village."

The next morning, Laura rose and breakfasted alone. She'd been pleased when Nathaniel talked frankly, expressing his concerns about the smugglers. None of the house staff were involved he assured her, not wishing her to be nervous in the house.

But they still didn't know who visited Amanda's bedchamber. Laura suspected Rudge, but Nathaniel was caught up working closely with the constable. The head of the smuggling ring who'd orchestrated it all from London had been arrested, and the police were confident they would round up the rest of the gang.

Nathaniel had driven to the police station in Penzance that morning. Not long after he returned, he and Hugh had left to ride over the estate. Laura stiffened with shock when she'd overheard two maids gossiping on the stairs. The carriage had suffered another rock attack on the way home.

As soon as Nathaniel returned, she hurried out to speak to him.

"Just a pebble," he said. "Children most likely." A muscle quivered at his jaw. "Please don't fuss, Laura."

Frustrated, she returned to her work readying two guest chambers for the dinner party, in case the weather turned bad.

She paused from sorting a pile of linen. Why would anyone suspect Nathaniel of these nefarious deeds? It made no sense.

Because he wished her to stay close to the house, Laura occupied herself with the birthday dinner. It proved the perfect distraction from what was going on around her. Mrs. Madge, eager to take her mind off the loss of her son, threw herself into the matter at hand. She proposed several dishes for the menu, determined to try her hand at something new and exotic. She confessed to having discussed the menu with Rudge, but if he contributed anything, it didn't reach Laura's ears. Laura sensed his outrage because she'd chosen the wines. She'd begun to feel it was foolish of her to alienate him by usurping his position and went to broach the matter with him. She found him in the butler's pantry polishing the silver.

"A moment of your time, please, Rudge."

"Of course, my lady."

Rudge followed her to the morning room. He stood before her desk wearing his usual severe expression.

"I would appreciate your opinion of my wine selection." She handed him her list. "I chose my father's favorite wines, but tastes may differ in a warmer climate." She smiled. "And you would be more familiar with the tastes of those here than I."

Rudge scanned the list in his formal manner. "A Rhine wine might be added, my lady."

"Oh, yes, I hadn't thought of it. Excellent suggestion."

Rudge bowed his head.

"If there's anything else you'd like to add, please do."

"I will, my lady. I shall return to the silver, if that is all?"

"Yes, that is all, thank you, Rudge."

Must the man be so obstinate? Nothing had improved between them. Shrugging, she left the house in search of the gardener. It would be a challenge to find suitable floral arrangements for the table decoration now that autumn was upon them. Perhaps some hot house blooms would be in flower.

On the morning of the dinner party, Nathaniel entered Laura's bedchamber as she held up her gown before the mirror. She had hoped to surprise him, but he'd surprised her instead. "Do you approve of my choice?" She turned for him to view the silver-blue satin and chiffon evening gown.

"I like the gown, but it is more suited to our Paris sojourn, perhaps." Nathaniel leaned back against the bedpost. "Something a little simpler for this occasion?"

Pleased to have his interest, Laura laid the gown on the bed and with a smile, sashayed closer to her husband. She placed her hands on his chest. "Do you remember we were to visit Paris this autumn?"

His eyes clouded. "I know. I'm disappointed too, sweetheart. As soon as this business is at an end, we will, I promise."

She gazed up at him. "What if this business is *never* settled?"

He pushed back a lock of her hair and kissed that tender spot below her ear, sending a delightful frisson through her. "It will be," he murmured. "Then I'll come for you. You do understand that your presence distracts me?"

She raised an eyebrow. "I distract you, do I?"

He grinned and chucked her under the chin. "I can't be worried about your safety on top of…everything else."

"Who is watching your back?"

He gently flicked her cheek. "I can look after myself."

She sighed, wishing he would say he couldn't live without her, but she no longer expected such fulsome declarations of love. Somehow his assertion that her absence would be a distraction, or worse, a penance, failed to reassure her. She went to open the armoire. "Something simpler, you say."

He came to her side, surprising her even more. He'd never shown much interest in choosing her clothes. He reached inside. "What about this one?"

"The watered silk?" Laura took the luscious gown from its hanger, red threads glinting among the russet and gold. "It's hardly what I'd call simple."

"It's perfect. You'll look magnificent. Come to my room. I have something for you."

Laura followed him through the open panel. She glanced at the bed they had never shared. It was odd to feel a stranger here.

Nathaniel pulled out a drawer on the rosewood chiffonier and took out a gold-edged leather case. "I've had these cleaned and reset. I brought them back with me from London this last trip."

The parure was of a ruby and diamond necklace, diamond bracelet and earrings, and was absolutely breathtaking.

"Oh, but it's exquisite! She removed the necklace, holding it up to the light to gaze into the fathomless ruby depths. "Why haven't you shown these to me?"

"I wanted to surprise you."

"You've certainly done that." Laura laughed. "Were you waiting until I was well behaved enough to deserve them?"

Nathaniel chuckled. "I'm too impatient to wait that long."

"Oh, you!" Laura pouted at him. "You don't deserve such a good wife."

His smile faded. "No, most likely I don't."

"I was only joking, darling." She threw her arms around his neck and kissed him.

He returned her kiss, pulling her close. "Wear them tonight."

She laughed. "But didn't you just say I shouldn't overdress?"

He grinned at her tease. "You are my wife, Lady Lanyon, and rubies will enhance your natural beauty."

Taking the necklace from her, he clasped the jewels around her throat, his fingers gentle at her nape. He drew her over to the mirror. "See how well they suit you."

When she could draw her eyes away from the dazzling gems, she studied him, amused that he'd chosen her gown to suit them. "I've never worn anything so fine. Mother said I was too young for lavish jewelry."

"With your coloring, you should always wear jewels." He met her gaze in the mirror. "These might have been fashioned with you in mind."

She was confident they were not made for Amanda, for they would not have suited her fair coloring. "Were they your mother's?"

"No. My mother preferred sapphires. These were my grandmother's. She had red hair rather like yours."

"What was her given name?" Laura asked, noticing how his features softened.

"Charlotte. A grand lady," he said in a quiet voice. As if ashamed of his emotion, he undid the clasp and placed the necklace back in the case. "I'll return these to the safe until you are dressed."

CHAPTER TWENTY-ONE

In the evening, Laura came downstairs wearing the low-cut russet silk, the ruby necklace at her throat, diamonds dangling from her ears. Agnes had quite skillfully arranged her hair in loose waves, the front a soft pompadour with small ringlets on her brow.

Nathaniel, handsome in dark broadcloth and crisp linen, came forward to take her arm with a proud and proprietary expression. It pleased her, although she would have preferred to find him blinded by love.

Their guests began to arrive. Mr. Archer, the rail-thin vicar, escorted his wife, Phyllis, her sturdy body clad in purple satin. The quiet spinster sisters, Misses Parthena and Orpha Fairfax, were girlish in white chiffon. Mr. Jack Whitelaw, Nathaniel's rowing chum from Oxford, introduced his wife, Victoria, to her. She was attractive and had a forthright manner, her elegant lavender gown of ribbed silk satin perfect for her fair coloring. Laura immediately warmed to her.

Cilla came in wearing an olive-green dress, a corsage of orchids pinned to her breast with not a speck of paint in evidence. Tall, solemn Hugh Pitney was at Cilla's elbow. Pitney was yet unmarried and attractive. Perhaps he and Cilla might discover something in common, although for the moment, Laura could think of nothing.

"What a beautiful orchid." Laura kissed Cilla's cheek. "It is the same variety as those over by the window."

"His lordship kindly sent them." Cilla nodded at Nathaniel. "You have no need of flowers, Laura; you look like an exotic orchid yourself."

"Thank you, my dear." Laura ushered her guests into the dining room.

She was pleased with her efforts and those of her servants. She would be sure to praise them in the morning. The candles and the crystal chandelier bathed the room in a soft light. The new curtains and chair coverings, made by the upholsterer in Penzance, who was delighted to have the business, were perfect. Brilliant copper beech leaves arranged in Chinese urns added wonderful color.

Earlier, Laura had run a practiced eye over the table, as her mother had taught her. The silverware gleamed. Two rows of glassware for the champagne, sauterne and sherry. A red glass had been added for the Rhine wine, which she had to admit was a nice addition. Silver bowls filled with fresh fruits and dishes of celery, olives and radishes sat on the table.

Mrs. Madge outdid herself with six courses, beginning with shellfish soup, sole in cream sauce, buttered lobster, Cornish hens, ham timbales with cucumber sauce, a soufflé as light as air, and ending with chocolate pudding and pastries. In immaculate black, Rudge expertly poured the wine with his white-gloved hands.

It began as a subdued gathering, with the events of the last week discussed in respectful, hushed voices. But as the evening progressed, the atmosphere lightened. Nathaniel paused to smile at her. He and Jack Whitelaw discussed something about a new diving apparatus at Cherbourg, which allowed a man to go to greater depths in the sea. Laura returned his smile. The dinner proved a success! She had thirsted for such lively company since she'd come here. Thinking of her father, she listened with interest as the conversation turned to the British Army's success over the Boers near Dundee, Natal, where there were heavy casualties. Concern was then expressed for Queen Victoria's health.

Laura drew Mrs. Archer into the conversation, inquiring about her parish duties. The good lady expressed surprise at the spate of babies born in the last few months and how poor Mr. Archer had been hard-pressed to baptize them all.

Noticing how quiet Cilla was, Laura asked her if she'd heard of the latest Albrecht Dürer forgery discovered at a London art gallery.

"Hardly news. There are hundreds, possibly thousands of art forgeries in galleries all over the world," Cilla stated flatly.

After the dessert course, the women left the men to their port and cigars and retired to the salon. While the sisters chatted with the vicar's wife, Victoria leaned toward Laura. "My husband and I were delighted when we heard Nathaniel was to marry again. It would have been a terrible shame if a man such as he was left alone to brood."

Laura took a deep breath, wishing to ask so many questions, which, of course, she could not.

Victoria laid a hand on her arm. "I can see you will be good for him. He has not made the mistake of marrying someone like his first wife. Many men do, you know."

"Not in looks certainly," Laura said. "If her portrait is anything to go by. She was blonde and very beautiful."

Victoria's blue gaze softened. "I don't know you well, my dear, but I can assure you, you are nothing like Amanda in nature either."

"I know very little about her." At least little she could be sure of. Did Victoria mean Laura was not as lively? Amanda would be utterly charming in company, she supposed. Laura looked at Cilla, but she was absorbed in stirring her coffee.

Victoria smiled. "Amanda was pretty and vivacious, but you, I suspect, have a quiet strength."

Cilla rose abruptly to pull back the curtain and gaze out into the darkness. Laura followed, aware of how out of place she seemed here. Had it been foolish of Laura to think that she would enjoy the evening?

"What is it, Cilla?"

"I thought I heard the wind pick up. Perhaps a squall."

"I hope not. Come and sit with me, tell me more about Paris."

Was Cilla enjoying herself? As she sat down again, Laura felt a rush of pity for her friend; she'd hardly said a word at dinner. Perhaps Hugh was not the right sort of man for her. She doubted he was interested in art. When Laura returned to Wolfram, she would cast the net wider to invite men to dinner who would appreciate her. More intimate dinners, where her friend might relax more. She may not wish to marry, but Cilla might enjoy a man's company as much as the next woman.

Before Cilla could speak of Paris, Miss Parthena Fairfax leaned forward. "Don't you agree, Lady Lanyon?"

"I'm sorry, Miss Fairfax. I missed your question."

Miss Parthena repeated her request for Laura's opinion of the vicar's sermon last Sunday. "Wasn't it splendid?"

Laura murmured her agreement. Her memory of the context and thrust of the vicar's argument had quite escaped her.

"My husband does little in the way of formal preparation," added Mrs. Archer.

"Divine inspiration," Miss Orpha said with a sigh.

The vicar's wife nodded, her eyes alight. "Mr. Archer prefers to step up to the pulpit and be fed directly by God."

Laura thought she heard an amused huff from Cilla. She didn't dare look.

The men chose that moment to enter and saved Laura from possible embarrassment. Stimulated by their port and brandies, the men added much-needed stimulation to the conversation. When politics were discussed, Laura absorbed every word with thirsty delight.

A short time later, all the guests departed into the night, the weather having remained fine. Hugh politely escorted Cilla to her cottage.

Laura and Nathaniel stood at the door as the last carriage rattled away. "Did you enjoy your birthday dinner?"

He slipped his arm around her waist. "I did. I must thank Mrs. Madge, especially for the cake. Rather a lot of candles on it, weren't there? But it proved a great diversion. You were a gracious hostess. Your mother would be proud." A corner of his mouth quirked and his eyes twinkled. "If I may say so."

She laughed. "You may." Finding respect in his eyes, her heart warmed. "Shall we have another when I return?"

"We will certainly entertain more often. You look beautiful tonight." He stroked a finger down her cheek and followed it with a kiss.

She held her breath, hoping he'd change his mind about her leaving, but he said nothing more.

"When am I to go?"

He turned away, his face half in shadow. "The day after tomorrow, sweetheart. The best inns have been booked en route, and when you arrive in London, you might like to spend a night or two at the Savoy hotel where we were married."

The honeymoon suite for one? Laura swallowed. "No. I'll go straight to Richmond."

He took her arm, and they climbed the stairs.

"Let's make every minute count," he said in a husky voice. "Hurry and dismiss your maid."

Laura sent Agnes away and quickly finished undressing. Naked and trembling at her boldness, she pushed back her hair as it swung to her waist in tousled waves. Her hand at her throat brushed the ruby necklace. She searched for the spring hidden within the carved molding. The panel slid back. Nathaniel spun around, his shirt in his hands, his broad chest bare. "My God, Laura!" He came swiftly to her. "You're a goddess!"

They would make love in his bed, and he would remember this night long after she was gone from Wolfram. Of that, Laura was determined.

With relief, Nathaniel watched Laura's carriage depart for London. A hollow feeling enveloped him as he whistled to the dogs and walked to the stables. The abbey would seem profoundly empty without her. Before this latest disaster, Wolfram had begun to feel more like the wonderful place it had once been. Praise had been heaped upon his graceful lady wife by those who admired her visits to the poor and her interest in the children's schooling. She was a blessing, the vicar had said.

But it was Nathaniel who was again dogged by suspicion. A deep yearning for closeness had grown within him since Laura entered his life. Was he foolish to hope that when all this was over it might be possible? His father had always said a man should keep a mistress and not allow his emotions to rule him. But hadn't his father failed in his marriage? Nathaniel had never wanted to be like him, but he feared he might be. He sighed. What was he doing mulling over the past when the present and the future required his attention?

There had been distinct rumblings amongst the villagers since Mallory died, and yesterday someone had yelled at him: "Two is one too many for coincidence." A stranger to Wolfram, but there were those here who shared the same opinion. The smugglers might be rounded up, but even when the last of them was brought to justice, the rumors would continue to hound him. He'd never be free.

He shook his head to rid himself of the depressing thoughts. He had work to do if he was to bring Laura home.

CHAPTER TWENTY-TWO

Until the very last moment, Laura hoped Nathaniel would ask her to stay. When he didn't, she gloomily waved goodbye from the carriage window and turned to face the arduous, lonely trip north.

Laura's new lady's maid, Agnes, accompanied her. At the prospect of seeing London for the first time, the maid filled the carriage with excited chatter, which gradually subsided into awed silence as the distance between them and the only place the maid had ever known increased. The constant rain made the trip seem endless, with mist obscuring the view from the window.

The slow journey provided Laura with too much time to contemplate the state of her marriage. Her face heated at the thought of their last night together. Nathaniel was an undeniably passionate lover and a generous man. Nor was he ever unkind to her. But she hated when he clamped down and placed a wall between them, which nothing she did or said could breach.

At Wimbledon, the butler, accompanied by a footman, hurried out as the carriage pulled up. "Lady Lanyon, I trust your trip was pleasant?"

"It was long and tedious, Barker. You're keeping well?"

"I am, thank you, my lady."

Laura entered the house yearning to seek comfort from her

father's quiet strength. Yet she held back when she saw how tired he looked. He seemed to have aged since she left home. The failure of his tilt at prime minister surprised her. She never considered failure where her father was concerned. He'd always triumphed with everything he attempted. She began to doubt her own dreams, which had remained as vigorous as ever.

As soon as she'd changed her dress, she wandered into her father's study to read the London newspapers, searching for any articles on further inroads the suffrage movement might have made. She found nothing to hearten her. "It seems the push for the right to vote has stalled," she said to her father.

He looked up from his desk. "Because of wrong tactics. Men will never be swayed by violence from women."

Her mother entered the study, having been away at a charity luncheon. "Let me look at you, Laura. You're pale. Not increasing, are you?"

Laura sighed wearily. "I don't think so, Mother."

"It won't happen if you and Lanyon spend too much time apart."

"Now is not the time for such talk. Laura is tired after her long journey," her father said sharply, pushing away from his desk. He stood. "Come, let's enjoy a drink before dinner."

It was strange being back in her old home. Laura glanced around the moderately sized drawing room, so different to Wolfram with its rambling corridors, enormous high-ceilinged rooms and wonderful library. There was a certain freedom from convention there, while at the same time, a strong sense of its history.

Later that evening, Laura sat in front of the dressing table mirror in the bedroom where she'd dreamed of a future here in London, before Nathaniel came to change it. Unsettled, she removed the pins from her hair. She ran her fingers through her long locks and picked up her brush. The girl she'd been when she left to be married seemed to have vanished. Laura considered herself her own woman now, and this was no longer her home. The rush of homesickness she suffered was for Nathaniel and Wolfram.

Her mother appeared while Agnes tidied away Laura's clothes. "You may leave us."

After Agnes bobbed a curtsey and left the room, her mother sat on the cream damask chair, her frown reflected in the mirror. "Why are you here?"

"Aren't you glad to see me?"

"That's hardly the point, is it?"

"It's been some time since I saw you and Father. Do I need a better reason?"

"A woman doesn't leave her husband's side but for a *very* good reason."

Laura turned on the stool. "Mother, did you and Father always have separate bedrooms?"

Her mother pursed her lips. "So, that's it."

"I'm sorry. That's what?"

"Trouble in the bedroom."

Laura flushed. "Most definitely not."

Her mother's eyebrows arched. "No? Then what *has* brought you here?"

Laura looked down at the brush in her hands. "Something bad happened at Wolfram. A man was killed. Nathaniel wanted me somewhere safe until the police find the culprit."

"That's the extent of it? I'm relieved it has nothing to do with you and Lanyon."

How like her mother to make light of it. Laura was tempted to say more, but she was too tired.

Her mother rose. "I'm relieved. I pray every Sunday on my knees that you'll have a good marriage. As successful as your father's and mine has been." She came to kiss Laura's cheek. "Good night, my dear."

Laura watched the door close behind her. Her words seemed heartfelt. Perhaps her mother did care more for her than she'd realized. Did her parents have a good marriage? If you scratched beneath the surface, would you find love and fulfillment? Or the lukewarm acceptance and cool compromise she'd often witnessed? Determined her marriage to Nathaniel would be as perfect as she could make it, she rose and went to the bathroom, enjoying a luxury she was determined to introduce to Wolfram without delay.

When Agnes developed a cold, Laura left the maid in Richmond and traveled to the city straight after breakfast. The dew still glistened on the grass when Laura pushed the gate open into the little front garden. Aunt Dora rushed out to hug her with a cry of delight, drawing her inside.

Some new possessions added to the clutter, pen and ink drawings, painted fans, embroidered cushions and poetry books. Laura spied fresh pages of verse on her desk, written in Dora's spidery hand.

"You're in luck, darling girl. I've finished my latest batch of poems. I'm sending it off to my publisher."

Dora held Laura's face in her ink-stained fingers and studied her. "You look peaky."

Laura hugged the soft little body in its drab cotton dress. "I've missed you."

Dora's large eyes widened. "Something's wrong, isn't it, Laura?"

Tears pricked Laura's eyes and she blinked them away. She hadn't planned to bring her tales of woe to her aunt, but she was tired, and that weakened her resolve. She straightened her shoulders. She would try not to indulge herself and worry her aunt. "We can talk later. I'm here to invite you to Hertfordshire."

"What's there to interest you?"

"Gateley Park, one of the Lanyon properties. I plan to spend a few days there."

"Shouldn't you wait for Nathaniel to accompany you?"

"He hasn't visited the estate for ages. But he's happy for me to. Will you come?"

"Well...I don't have much to wear to mix in exalted circles."

"The estate is deep in the country. I suspect that society will be scarce and a trifle dull."

"Then, of course I'll keep you company. And you must tell me all about your new home. You've said little in your letters about Wolfram."

"Have you been consulting your Tarot?"

Dora looked sheepish. "Well, I had to get information from somewhere…"

Laura smiled. "Anything you want to tell me?"

"No." She patted Laura's cheek. "I'm only glad to see you."

Laura hugged her again. "I've missed you."

Dora frowned and drew away. "There *is* something wrong. I knew it; I found The Tower and the Death card again this morning."

Those cards unnerved Laura even though she dismissed the Tarot's abilities to forecast her future. "Ask Sarah to pack your bag; we'll talk in the carriage. Hurry, Barnes is walking the horses."

"Goodness me, you don't give a body much notice, do you?" Aunt Dora rushed to pull the bell.

The trip into Hertfordshire gave them time to talk, but when the carriage swayed, Laura felt too queasy to discuss her life at Wolfram. Instead, she spoke in glowing terms of its wild beauty and talked about Cilla.

"I'm glad you've made a friend." Dora studied an ink stain on her glove. "An artist too, so interesting. But you've told me nothing about the baron."

"Nathaniel is an excellent husband. I have no cause for complaint, but he's distracted by events at Wolfram which he needs to put right."

"I don't like buts." Dora's eyes narrowed. "He is kind to you?"

A bout of nausea rose in Laura's stomach as the carriage rocked. She closed her eyes. "Yes, of course."

"I can see you are not in the mood to talk, so I'll say no more." Dora gazed out the window at the empty, rolling hills passing the carriage. "We've seen nothing but hills, fields and cows for miles. Where on earth are we?"

"The Chiltern Hills. I find the landscape quite pretty."

"I can't argue with that, but we must be near. We've been traveling for hours, and I could do with a cup of tea."

As Dora spoke, the carriage slowed, and they entered a pair of ornate wrought iron gates. Gnarled oaks bordered the lane as they trundled along a gravel driveway where glimpses of the stately mansion appeared through the trees.

Around a bend in the road, the house appeared. The size and magnificence drew a gasp from Aunt Dora, as she took in the impressive balustrade parapet and elegant Baroque ornamentation.

After the carriage stopped on the circular sweep of driveway, the groom jumped down to open their door. He assisted Aunt Dora and Laura from the carriage.

A short man with a flushed face hurried down the front steps, followed by a maid. "I'm Mr. Charleton, Lady Lanyon. His lordship wrote to alert me of your arrival. With such short notice, I do hope you will be comfortable," he said in an anguished tone. "We are not set up for visitors with only a skeleton staff here."

"We are very easy to please, Mr. Charleton." Laura shook his hand. "I'm sure we shall be comfortable. This is my aunt, Miss Lawley. We require little beyond a warm bed and our meals."

"I'm sure we can accomplish that." He hurried down to offer his arm to Dora who made her way slowly up the steps. "How do you do, Miss Lawley? I expect you've had a long and dusty ride from London. I'll have tea brought to the salon."

Laura followed them through the entry into an impressive, well-proportioned room furnished with elaborate Louis XIV furniture, their sensuous curves decorated in gold leaf. China-blue embossed paper lined the walls, the intricately carved white marble fireplace an Adam creation.

After a reviving afternoon tea consisting of sandwiches and feather-light scones with strawberry jam, Laura was taken to her room, which had pretty, rose-patterned wallpaper and windows overlooking an overgrown rose arbor. Exhausted, she sank onto the gilded four-poster's pink satin coverlet to consider the significance of this elegant, neglected house. This was Nathaniel's grandparents' estate. His mother, Lady Olivia, had been born here. More than a little curious about the family history, Laura was keen to discover more.

She grasped the bell pull and rang for a maid to assist her out of her travel-soiled dress, after which she planned to investigate by herself since Dora had grumbled about carriages and rheumatism and went to her bedroom to rest. Tomorrow, Laura would ride through the park, which from her window looked extensive.

The next morning, Laura wandered the gardens with a shawl to protect her from the cool wind. It was a perfect day for riding, with fleecy clouds scudding across the pale blue sky.

She joined her aunt in the breakfast room, where she spooned eggs onto her plate from the sideboard. "Did you sleep well?"

"I found it difficult to get used to the quiet." Dora smiled. "But this morning the birds made such a racket outside my window, it was as noisy as a London street." She eyed Laura's riding outfit. "As you're riding today, I believe I'll spend the day reading. I peeped into the library; there's an impressive collection of books and periodicals there. I must say I'm surprised that Nathaniel has neither leased nor sold this property. The cost of its upkeep must be immense. It's a little sad to see it like this, and odd because the house reminds me of a shrine."

At the buffet, Laura lifted a silver cover and added bacon to her eggs. Dora's use of the word "shrine" reminded her of the flowers placed on Amanda's grave. "A shrine to whom?"

Dora shrugged. "His mother, surely? You know how men are about their mothers."

Laura took her plate to the table. "She died when Nathaniel was a boy. Cilla said he barely knew her."

Her aunt poured her a cup of tea. "He hasn't told you anything about her?"

"No." Laura rubbed her forehead where a headache threatened. "I sensed he didn't want to speak about her."

"There could be different reasons for that. I'm sure you'll find out what you wish to know."

Laura tilted her head. "What makes you think I'm searching for something?" She refused to accept that anything more than mild curiosity had brought her here. Apparently, her aunt thought otherwise.

"That's why we've come, isn't it?" Dora tapped a finger on her Tarot card box on the table beside her. "Perhaps I can help you find out."

Laura smiled, determined to take anything her aunt suggested with a grain of salt.

An hour later, Laura left Dora reading in a deep chair by the library fire and walked to the stables. Mounts for riding were no longer kept there, so she was given the manager's horse, a bow-backed, sluggish animal. She urged it into a trot. The magnificent trees were aflame with autumn color, the parkland overgrown. Dora was right. It was odd to think that no one came here.

A mile or two on, Laura rode through a break in the hedgerow and found herself on a country road. A signpost pointed to Little Gaddesden. A church spire rose above the trees, so the village could not be far away. She urged her bad-tempered horse into a reluctant canter.

Woodlands ringed the quaint village of thatched-roof cottages and lodge houses clustered around a green. Outside the modest gray stone church, Laura dismounted and tethered the horse to an iron railing. The church appeared to be empty. When she knocked at the vicarage, the housekeeper explained that Mr. Maudling was making calls. Hoping to catch him before she left, Laura wandered the churchyard reading the inscriptions on the gravestones. She located Nathaniel's grandparents in their adjacent graves. Searching further, she found Nathaniel's mother's grave. Odd that she was buried here and not at Wolfram. Lady Olivia was only thirty years old when she died. The plain inscription gave no clue as to how she died.

Laura picked a wild briar rose and laid it on the headstone. "I'm sorry we never met. Rest well in heaven."

When the vicar failed to appear, Laura rode back to the house, glad to return her fractious mount to the stables. She found Aunt Dora dozing in the library, still curled up before the fire, her head nodding, her beloved, well-worn Tarot cards on the fruitwood side table. Laura didn't wake her. She crept away and continued her exploration, spending an hour peeking into empty rooms bare of furniture. There were several family portraits hung above the stairs. Nathaniel's mother featured as a babe in her red-haired mother's arms, and later as a pretty child, then again as a beautiful young woman dressed in a full-sleeved blue gown, her fair hair in tight ringlets.

Olivia's death while Nathaniel was away at school must have affected him deeply. Her delicate feminine beauty reminded Laura of Amanda. As Victoria had said, men did sometimes marry women who looked like their mothers. Laura was so very different, and not only in looks. In every conceivable way, she suspected.

She joined her aunt for luncheon in the dining room. While she was out riding, a neighbor had called to leave his card and a request for them to join him for afternoon tea.

"Mr. Burrows is an elderly gentleman whose lands adjoin Gateley Park on its southern border," Mr. Charleton informed them.

"How kind. I'll certainly call on him," Laura said. "If you'd like to come, Aunt, we'll take Nathaniel's carriage and give the horses an airing."

Dora nodded. "I wouldn't miss it."

Mr. Burrows' home lay several miles away, closer to Berkhamstead. The white-haired gentleman's estate was smaller than Gateley Park, his home in the square, Dutch style.

"I couldn't contain my excitement," he said, as he led them into the drawing room, walking with the aid of a cane. "Neighbors at Gateley Park again, despite being a brief visit. It's some years since a member of the family has come here."

Mr. Burrows offered Laura a plate of biscuits. "And Lord Lanyon, is he in good health? I did wonder."

Laura assured him that Nathaniel was in excellent health but his principal estate and the House of Lords demanded much of his attention. She took a bite of the almond-flavored biscuit and regretted it. It was too sweet. Her stomach churned so much these days. She was sure it was the uncertainty of her future and her constant worry about Nathaniel's safety. Did he miss her as much as she did him? When would he write and ask her to come home?

As she sipped her tea, she couched her questions tactfully, hoping that since he was older than Nathaniel's mother, Mr. Burrows might remember her.

"Lady Olivia was a fine-looking young lady, if a bit flighty." He began to fill his pipe. "I hope you won't mind if I smoke?"

"Not at all, Mr. Burrows," Laura said, although her stomach roiled. "My father enjoys a cigar or a pipe."

"I'm not one to speak ill of the dead," he said and drew on the stem. "But I suspect as a girl Lady Olivia worried her parents, for they arranged a union with the baron when she was just out of the schoolroom. She returned here years later very ill." He stroked his white moustache. "She died far too young."

"Was the baron here with her?" Dora asked.

"I don't believe he was." Mr. Burrows clamped his teeth on his pipe with a disapproving frown. "But I don't listen to gossip."

The conversation then turned to matters pertaining to the county and the village.

Laura opened the window as the carriage returned them to Gateley Park and drew in lungfuls of fresh air which failed to make her feel much better.

"I wonder how we can discover more about the scandal," Dora said.

Laura felt both nauseated and perturbed in equal measures. "What makes you think there was a scandal?"

"Of course there was a scandal. Where there's smoke, there's fire, and gossip follows, although often nasty and with little respect for the truth."

"What about idle gossip, which can come from nothing at all?" Although curious about Nathaniel's mother, Laura disliked delving into family scandals that Nathaniel had not wished to tell her. She could only hope that one day he would be able to speak of it.

"You should take the opportunity to learn the truth, you know," Dora said. "It's not wrong to want to know exactly what you're dealing with."

Laura drew in a breath, afraid she'd stumble on something shocking that she would find hard to keep from him. She followed her aunt into the library.

"We shall see what mysteries *l'art de tirer les cartes* can reveal to us. Let us consult the oracles." Dora's supple fingers spread her Tarot cards over the table.

Although reluctant, Laura couldn't resist sitting down to watch her aunt. The placing of each card was heavy with importance as Dora laid them out in their familiar configuration.

When Dora looked at her, she reminded her of a bright-eyed sparrow. "I have asked a question."

Laura leaned her arms on the fruitwood table. "What question would that be?"

"It concerns your future. Let's see what evolves," her aunt said, annoyingly mysterious. The Queen of Cups appeared upside down. "Reversed!"

"Which means?" Laura asked impatiently.

"Even reversed, the Queen of Cups is a good outcome; it just means that you must be patient. Stay focused on the loving side of your personality. True, deep love for others encompasses understanding that those you love are on their own timelines. Don't push. Good things come to those who wait."

Laura bent her head and studied her hands. "Surely I have…"

"Hush. Look, Laura." Dora tapped the cards. "There are other matters at hand."

Laura stared. The Queen of Cups was covered by The Devil. And the King of Pentacles sat in judgment over her. On the right side was the Page of Cups, below her the Knight of Wands, and on the left The Fool.

"Who might the Page of Cups be?" Laura asked.

"I believe it is Nathaniel as a boy, when something happened that still deeply affects him." Dora pointed to the last card. "The outcome card is Death, as we already know."

"Death?" Laura asked anxiously, caught up despite herself. "Whose?"

"It could be Nathaniel's mother or his first wife. Both have had a marked effect on his life."

"I'm not enjoying this. What about this one, The Tower?"

"I wasn't going to mention The Tower. It means profound change and possible danger."

"Danger?" Laura cried. "Who's in danger?"

"Placed as it is, it could possibly be Nathaniel."

"Oh no." Laura slapped her hands to her cheeks as the blood ran cold in her veins.

Dora patted her shoulder. "I said possible danger. He is not hurt or dead."

"Please put the cards away." Laura swallowed a feeling of dread and pushed back her chair. "I don't believe in the Tarot."

Dora obliged. "We shall have to discover more ourselves. In my humble opinion, your life won't be as good as it should be until we discover what lies in the past. It greatly affects the present and the future."

"Dear Aunt Dora," Laura kissed her aunt's soft cheek, "I wish you wouldn't talk like a proverb. It gives me goosebumps."

CHAPTER TWENTY-THREE

The next few days passed slowly. There was little to do beyond reading, and riding the stubborn mare was more of a chore than a delight. After Dora's disturbing Tarot reading, Laura grew more anxious and impatient for word from Nathaniel. She rode to the village post office and sent him a telegram: *Darling, I long for word from you. Please tell me you're all right. Your loving wife, Laura.*

She rode back to the house. A colorful drift of leaves covered the ground beneath the trees, as autumn's beauty faded into winter. Aunt Dora was in the library, surrounded by tomes of poetry.

"Sit down, dear girl," Dora said with a vague smile. "Find something to read to pass the time."

Laura bit her lip. "Very well, but I have no intention of spending winter here."

"No. Of course not," Dora said. "Winter is some weeks away."

Somehow that did not offer Laura any sense of comfort. Why had Nathaniel not contacted her? She thought again of Dora's Tarot cards.

Desperate for something to do, Laura began an unfinished linen sampler she'd found in a workbox, the birds and flowers yet to do. Because of her impatient nature, she found sewing tedious, and it did not quell her anxiety about Nathaniel, although it did keep her hands busy. Gold, green, black, magenta, dark brown and copper silks decorated the meandering border entwined with the family initials. There was an autumnal scene at its center, beautifully stitched, an elegantly dressed lady in blue standing among trees, a house and a church in the background.

Two days later, the embroidery had failed to soothe Laura's mind, and after hours of work, with all the flowers completed but the birds yet to do, she threw the sampler down. She roamed the patterned carpet from one end of the room to the other, turning with a swish of her gown.

"My goodness. You're like an African lion I saw at the London zoo," Aunt Dora observed.

Laura sank onto the sofa beside her. "I can't help fearing something's wrong at Wolfram. I haven't received a reply to my telegram."

Dora cast her a guilty glance. "But you sent it only two days ago."

"Telegrams are supposed to be quick."

"I've worried you." Dora looked upset. "I consulted my cards again this morning. I didn't find anything to concern you in the reading."

"If I could only hear from him. The telegram might not have been delivered. I'll ride to the post office and inquire."

"Very well. Perhaps the fresh air will do you good."

On the way to the post office, Laura called in at the vicarage. Her growing curiosity banished any reservation concerning Nathaniel's mother. Dora would approve. This time the vicar was at home. He smoothed his thinning gray hair and apologized for not calling on her. There had been an epidemic of whooping cough in the village environs, which had claimed several small lives.

"How sad. Is there anything I can do?" Laura asked.

"Thank you, my lady. I believe we are at the end of it, God willing."

"That is good news at least." Laura hesitated, aware her request was badly timed and would likely sound odd. "My husband's mother,

Olivia, is buried here. I am curious about her. Did you know her?"

"Not well. Her ladyship had married when I came here. I met her at the end of her life. She suffered greatly, poor lady. And her baby, who was born too early, did not survive, of course."

"I'm sorry to hear that she suffered," Laura said, fighting to mask her shock.

He stroked his chin. "His lordship's grandparents were good people. They took their daughter in and cared for her until she died. Many would not have done so."

"I believe they were." To admit she knew so little would be an insult to Nathaniel and might become known in the village. The villagers had already shown considerable interest in her, the men removing their hats and bowing, the women bobbing a greeting in the street.

"Is your stay here a long one, Lady Lanyon? The church ladies' committee has expressed a wish to meet you."

"Only a few more days, Mr. Maudling. But I should be delighted to receive the ladies. Shall we make it afternoon tea tomorrow at two?"

He smiled. "They will be most gratified. I shall relay your message. Is there some other way in which I might be of help?"

"Thank you, Mr. Maudling, but no." The sky beyond the window had grown dark and threatening. "I'd best hurry. It appears to be about to rain."

There was no reply awaiting her at the post office. Riding back to the house, the dark clouds fulfilled their promise and opened with a deluge. When Laura arrived home, her habit was soaked through, and she ran straight up to her bedroom to change.

When she came down again, she found her aunt in her usual chair in the library. "This is a cold house, Laura."

"I'm sorry you're cold. Are you miserable here? I gave instructions only to light fires in rooms we use."

When she told her aunt the news, Dora nodded sagely. "The question I asked about Nathaniel's mother revealed much suffering."

Laura sneezed.

"Come closer to the fire, child. You should not have been out riding in this weather. You might have caught a chill."

Laura took a chair by the fire, sighing as warmth spread through her cold limbs. "Why would Nathaniel's father cast his wife out?"

Dora tilted her head. "The baby wasn't his?"

"That's the logical explanation, but if not his, then I wonder whose it was. It still would have been Nathaniel's brother or sister." She sighed. "How could his father be sure? He might have been wrong."

"Don't be naïve, darling girl. Of course he would have known. Some men might turn a blind eye and bring the child up as their own, once an heir had been produced. Apparently, he wasn't one of them."

A smile tugged the corner of Laura's mouth. What would her spinster aunt know of such things? Her smile faded at the thought of the woman whose life was mapped out in the paintings in the gallery. Her death had denied Nathaniel a happy childhood. Laura's head began to throb, and lights danced before her eyes. "I think I'll lie down for a while."

Dora's eyes widened. "Lie down in the daytime? I do hope you haven't caught a chill." She sat up. "Might you be pregnant?"

"This seems very much like a cold. I've not been sleeping well of late."

"You have been disturbed by something or other since you arrived from Cornwall," Dora scolded.

Laura climbed the stairs, her legs leaden. It was probably only worry about Nathaniel. What could have prevented him from answering her telegram?

The storm had battered Wolfram for four days, flooding the roads and cutting off Wolfram Village from Penzance. The gale-force winds uprooted an old oak on the village green. Horizontal rain pelted anyone who had the courage or the necessity to leave their homes. In oilskins, Nathaniel worked beside Hugh and the farm workers, tying down sheeting to cover bales of hay and shepherding livestock into the shelter of barns and stables. They returned to the abbey for a hot meal to find a man from the village with terrible news: a ship had foundered on the rocks.

Snatching up his telescope from the study, Nathaniel raced up into the tower with Hugh behind him. Leaning over the stone parapet, he located the three-masted vessel in danger of breaking up, battered ruthlessly by the mountainous waves.

"There are men still on board," Nathaniel yelled above the roar of the wind and sea. He wiped the end of his telescope. "They're trying to launch a rowing boat. They'll never succeed. We'll have to get out there. Are you up for it?"

"I'll say."

"Ask for volunteers in the village," Nathaniel called as they ran back down the winding stairs. "Find a fisherman prepared to take his boat out."

Hugh gave a grim nod. "I'll see you at the wharf."

Nathaniel thanked God for Hugh. He was a fine man and a great asset to Wolfram. Since Mallory's death, he feared he'd leave for a more attractive position that a man of his capabilities would have no difficulty finding, but so far, he had stayed. Nathaniel had been tempted to confess his fears concerning Amanda to Hugh, things which he'd never told another soul, but in the end, he thought better of it.

At the dock, two men joined them on the small fishing boat. They headed out to the foundering ship. The precipitous waves were filled with floating boxes, ropes and debris, while the men still on board the sinking vessel struggled to stack the rowboat lashed to the side with their goods.

"What the devil? They'll go down. Greedy to the end," Nathaniel cried, his words caught by the roar and flung away. A man's body floated by them. Nathaniel reached down to grab him, but he disappeared beneath the surging waves.

Hugh shook his head. "He's gone."

They reached the boat as, with a thunderous crack, a mast fell across the deck, pinning a man beneath it.

"I'll go and get him," Nathaniel shouted.

"No, milord! It's too dangerous," Hugh yelled.

"Tie a rope around me. Give me plenty of slack."

The last of the crew clambered over the side into their rowboat, which rode perilously low in the water.

Nathaniel peeled off his slicker. "Get those men on board before their rowboat goes under."

He dove into the swirling waters, a sturdy rope tied around his waist. A wave broke over his head, sending him rushing toward the bottom. Lungs bursting, he kicked his way to the surface and was immediately swept away, as the men gave him slack on the rope. Another wave hit him, slamming a floating bucket into his shoulder. It took every ounce of his strength to keep his head above water as he swam to the stricken ship. The waves dragged him toward the prow and banged him against the side. He grabbed a dangling rope and heaved himself slowly aboard, lashed by the waves.

As he fought to gain his feet, the ship gave a groan, and the bow dipped into the sea. The waves broke over the deck, flooding the timber beneath Nathaniel's feet. He held on as the wind howled around him. The bow rose again, sending him sliding over the tilting, slippery planks. He reached the man, who still lived, wedged beneath the mast. The boat shuddered and another mast fell, missing Nathaniel by a foot. The sudden jerk caused the mast to roll off the man's legs. Salt spray stung Nathaniel's eyes, threatening to blind him. He swiped at them with his forearm, then hauled the injured man to the side, diving overboard with him, as the ship, with another mighty groan, slid beneath the sea.

THE BARON'S WIFE

CHAPTER TWENTY-FOUR

With a grunt of effort, Nathaniel held the injured man afloat as Hugh and the fishermen dragged the fellow on board. In the rough swell, Nathaniel hung on, his strength failing as he waited for his turn to be pulled aboard. He had come close to death before; it wasn't a new experience, but this time had special significance. This could be a second chance for his marriage and his life. The smugglers were finished; after this, they couldn't start their business again. And as his life and his past mistakes swept before his eyes, he vowed he would make Laura happy.

A huge wave broke over him, sending him spinning away from the boat. The rope snapped. Nathaniel, salty brine filling his throat, sank into the depths. Thoughts of becoming another victim of Davy Jones' Locker made him kick violently.

When he resurfaced gasping for air, the fishing boat had drifted farther away. Finding himself closer to an outcrop of rocks within sight of the shore, Nathaniel fought to keep his head above water and swam toward them, aided by the strong tide. It would take all of his boyhood skills to climb high enough up the green-tinged granite slopes to rest before striking out again. If he couldn't rest, in his exhausted state, he knew he would never make it.

Laura slept deeply on and off for what seemed like weeks. Whenever she opened her eyes, she saw her worried aunt beside the bed. Her limbs ached and her head pounded.

When the drowsiness left her, she pushed herself up on the pillows, surprised at how weak she'd become.

"You've been sick for three days," Dora said. "I was tempted to send for your mother."

Laura eyed her with a frown. "I hope you didn't."

"No. There was some concern that you might have contracted whooping cough." Dora hovered over her with a bowl of broth, waiting to feed her. "I'm so relieved you're back with us."

"I can manage, thank you." The beef soup was tasty, but she had little appetite. She put down the spoon and dabbed her mouth with the napkin. "I'm sorry I worried you. Has a telegram come?"

Dora smiled. "Yesterday." She took the telegram from her pocket.

Laura anxiously read it. "Nathaniel's well, thank God. He says he's been busy working with the police. He makes no mention of my coming home." And no word that he loved or missed her.

"You can't expect much from a telegram," Dora said soothingly. "At least he's all right."

He was all right. With a deep, gratifying sigh, Laura threw back the bedclothes. "I shall get up today."

Dora frowned. "Are you sure you should?"

"I'm much better. Send the maid in, will you please?"

An hour later, upon entering the library, Laura caught sight of Dora tucking papers under a cushion. Her aunt looked up with a guilty expression.

"What have you there, Aunt Dora?"

Dora retrieved a bundle of letters and handed them to her. "I decided to wait until you were stronger before I showed you these." She shrugged. "While you were sick, I searched the attics."

"You went up to the attics? It seems I can't leave you alone for a minute before you busy yourself with something you ought not."

Laura's fascinated gaze settled on the letters, spotted with age and tied up with a faded blue ribbon. She held out her hands, and her aunt deposited the bundle into them. "I suppose you've been frightfully bored."

"*Au contraire*. I am never bored in my own company. But I haven't read them," Dora said with quiet dignity.

Laura sat and patted her aunt's knee. "I'm sorry. I'm a bit bad tempered. But certainly curious. Shall we read these together?"

Dora's eyes brightened. "I'll ring for tea."

As they nibbled mustard and cress sandwiches and drank their tea, Laura opened each letter, smoothing out the fragile paper.

"They are love letters to Nathaniel's mother, Olivia, from someone who signs himself, *Your loving protector*."

"He did little to protect her at the end," Dora said wryly.

Laura folded them. "I'm not going to read them."

Dora looked disappointed. "Oh, why not?"

"I know they appeal to the poet in you, Dora, but I'm... Wait a moment." Laura examined a plain white envelope. "This one is from Nathaniel's father, Lord Lanyon."

Dora moved closer. "What does it say?"

Laura read quickly. "It's as we feared. He refuses to acknowledge the child as his." She read down. "He accuses Olivia of debasing herself and the Lanyon name with the steward at Wolfram. He writes that she broke his heart, and that he will never set eyes on her again." Tears blurred Laura's vision. "How sad."

"Men!" Dora huffed.

Laura folded the letter, added it to the rest and retied the blue ribbon. "Although he was a boy, Nathaniel must have heard something of this. It would have been a bitter, lonely time for him."

"Will you tell him you know?"

"I cannot." Laura handed the letters to Dora. "You must return these to where you found them."

"But surely this needs to be discussed between you."

"I hope it will be someday. Right now, it's enough to know."

Laura now understood some of what made Nathaniel behave

the way he did. No wonder he found trust and intimacy difficult, especially after the rumors concerning Amanda and Mallory. He was more open with his dogs and horses than with Laura.

"The rumors about Nathaniel's first wife and her affair with the gardener is like history repeating itself," Dora said. "It would be doubly hard for him."

"Yes, even if they weren't true. Poor Nathaniel. So much sadness in his life."

Dora raised her brows. "How do you know they weren't true?"

"Cilla didn't believe it."

"How could she be sure?"

Laura pulled the shawl closer around her shoulders. "She was Amanda's friend and confidant."

"But might Amanda have lied to her?"

"Dora, do stop this. It is not going to help anyone."

"What do you intend to do?"

Laura stood. "We shall return to London tomorrow."

"I forgot to tell you. The ladies from the church committee called to see you while you were ill."

"Oh, dear, I did invite them. I'll write and apologize, donate to the church fête. Really, Dora, this house should be lived in by someone who can involve themselves in village affairs. I shall ask Nathaniel to sell it."

"I quite agree. Before we do," Dora said, "I want to show you something else I found in one of the larger bedchambers while you were sleeping."

Laura followed her cryptic aunt up the stairs. They entered an airy bedchamber. "There!" Dora said triumphantly.

During her inspection of the house, Laura hadn't entered this room. It smelled musty, and the furniture was covered in dust sheets. A portrait in a gilt frame hung on the far wall. A lady with a calm, attractive face sat with a small dog perched on her knee, dressed in the fashion of the last century. Painted by a well-known artist, the folds of her rose-patterned damask gown were so cleverly wrought they looked almost real. Her auburn hair was arranged in ringlets at her nape. She had a strong face, with a long nose, a generous mouth and a whimsical expression in her eyes.

"I think I would have liked her," Laura said.

"There's something about her which reminds me of you, not in looks, but in spirit," Dora said.

"She looks more serene than I," Laura said with a laugh. She suspected Dora was becoming overly sentimental. She gazed fondly at her aunt. Had she worried her terribly? "Nathaniel told me Olivia's mother had red hair. There are other paintings of Lady Charlotte here, but nothing quite this detailed." Laura studied the woman's face for features like her grandson's. She found it in the brow and high cheekbones. She touched the painted canvas as if she might connect with the woman who died so long ago. "Nathaniel was fond of her."

Dora's eyes shone. "There you are then."

"She took care of her daughter until she passed away, despite the scandal."

"Yes, I can see compassion and intelligence in her eyes."

"If Nathaniel thinks I'm like her in some way, I must endeavor to live up to her."

"Darling girl." Dora put her arm around Laura's shoulders and gave her a hug. "You already have."

CHAPTER TWENTY-FIVE

After the fresh, clear skies of Cornwall, London had lost a good deal of its charm for Laura. The dirty streets were crowded with coal smoke and yellow fog fouling the air.

She had chosen to stay with Dora rather than come under her mother's scrutiny again, but that proved a mistake. Dora's small townhouse was inundated with visitors. They crowded into her rooms and talked about nothing other than literature and art. Normally, Laura would have been delighted, and she wondered what had gotten into her. It was not like her to seek the peace of her bedroom when stimulating conversation was on offer. Her patience had worn thin as she waited for word from Nathaniel. She was tired and still not fully recovered from the chill. She yearned to go home to where she could hear the birds and see straight to the horizon with the smell of the briny sea on the wind. She decided not to wait much longer. If she hadn't heard from him, she would leave within a few days.

When the last of a group of enthusiasts left, Laura suggested she and her aunt take the air. There'd been a thunderstorm earlier, but the rain had since stopped. They left the house intent on visiting the British Museum. Gray clouds still hovered low over the rooftops when they emerged from Tottenham Court Road Tube Station and hurried down Great Russell Street. When it began to rain again, they stopped to put up their umbrellas. An omnibus raced by, sending a wave of water onto the pavement and drowning Laura's boots. Annoyed, she lowered her umbrella and bent down to inspect them.

"I say, do be careful with that thing."

From beneath the ruffled fringe of her umbrella, Laura saw a pair of male legs dressed in brown tweed.

"I am sorry," she said, raising her umbrella over her head.

"Laura?" Behind his glasses, Howard Farmer, her friend from university, stood before her. His hazel eyes crinkled at the corners. He removed his hat, and she noted how prosperous he'd become, his clothes good quality, his muttonchops trimmed. "How good to see you again, Laura. Lady Lanyon," he said with a bow. "I beg your pardon."

"It's Laura, please. It is good to see you again."

He eyed her carefully. "How are you?"

"In good health, thank you. Do you still attend women's suffrage meetings?"

"But of course."

"I would love to hear of the latest developments."

Howard was a pacifist, who believed in the rights of men and women to vote. He'd taken part in a rally alongside her and the other women from the university.

"You remember meeting the suffragist, Millicent Fawcett? She has cut ties with the Pankhurst sisters, as she believes their militant behavior will set women's right to vote back for years. Millicent plans to sail to South Africa with other women to inspect the horrendous concentration camps where the Boer soldiers have been interned. She sees that as giving women responsibility in wartime and a revival of interest in women's suffrage."

"I'm inclined to agree with her." Laura remembered their heated arguments about the war. "And I'm glad to see you haven't joined the army. I confess to having lost some of my imperialistic zeal."

He shook his head. "I had a change of heart and tried to enlist but was rejected on medical grounds."

"I hope it's nothing serious?"

He smiled, pushing back the spectacles on his nose with a finger. "Poor eyesight."

"How brave of you to try." She was pleased he was doing well.

A noisy humph drew Laura's attention to her neglected relative. In her desire for knowledge, she'd quite forgotten her. "Oh, how remiss of me. You must meet my aunt, Miss Lawley. Dora, I'd like to introduce Professor Farmer."

"Delighted." Howard shook Dora's hand, as Laura explained how they knew one another.

"Howard is now a lecturer at the London University," Laura added.

"What do you teach, Professor Farmer?" Dora asked.

"The Classics."

Laura sighed inwardly as Dora's eyes brightened. "You must come to my Thursday soirée. I promise you will meet some interesting people, Professor."

Howard raised a sandy eyebrow and met Laura's gaze. He was waiting for her to sanction it. "Yes, please do come," she said. She could hardly say otherwise.

The rain grew heavier. Dora gave him her address, and they said hasty goodbyes. Howard strode off in the opposite direction, while Laura and her aunt approached the steps leading to the museum.

Laura shook her umbrella in the foyer. The last time she'd seen Howard was the day he'd come to her home to play tennis. She'd been embarrassed when her parents made their disapproval of him evident. "I would prefer him not to come."

"I don't see why. He's an interesting man. You must have a lot in common."

"We did, once."

Laura had to admit she would like to learn more about his new position. As long as he didn't ask too many questions about her.

On Thursday, guests packed into Dora's rooms for her soirée. The parlor was filled with the mingled odors of wet woolens, human sweat, coal fire and pipe smoke.

Conversation became a dull roar in Laura's ears and her head spun. "Heavens." She put a hand to her forehead. "Whatever is the matter with me?"

The maid opened the door to yet another visitor. As Howard Farmer walked into the room, his gaze settled on Laura. He nodded to her with a smile and made his way over to greet Dora.

Moments later, looking concerned, he came to where Laura stood, her hand on the back of a chair. "You look very pale. Are you well, Laura?"

Laura smiled wanly. "It's a bit airless in here." Black spots danced before her eyes. "I'm afraid…" she murmured, as darkness closed over her.

When she opened her eyes, she was in Howard's arms, the rough wool of his coat against her cheek.

Dora tutted behind them as he carried her into the front hall. "You need fresh air."

"Please put me down."

Howard set her on her feet but still held her, his arm around her waist to support her as she tried to gain her balance.

The maid rushed to answer the doorbell. On the doorstep, Nathaniel looked up from removing his gloves. Within the confines of Howard's arms, Laura gazed into her husband's eyes, which were as cold as the granite walls of Wolfram.

Laura moved her head restlessly on the pillow. Across from her, too far away for comfort, Nathaniel sprawled in a chair. His eyes were no longer like stone; they now held a dangerous light. "Dora told me you've been ill."

She smiled, her pulse beating fast at the sight of him. "I was faint earlier, but I'm much recovered. Just a slight headache."

"Then you can tell me who that man is who so thoughtfully assisted you."

"Dora invited How…Professor Farmer." She rubbed her brow.

"We ran into him on the way to the museum—"

"He is an acquaintance of yours?" Nathaniel's voice was icily polite.

"We met at Cambridge. He wasn't a professor then."

He gave her a dark look. "You've met him socially since?"

Laura chewed her lip. "Only once. We played tennis at my home. Before I met you."

His dark eyebrows rose. "That is all?"

Although never alone, she and Howard had spent a lot of time together at Cambridge. She wasn't about to add fuel to a smoldering fire and held out her arms. "I don't believe you've kissed me."

Nathaniel still frowned but rubbed a finger over his bottom lip. Did she detect a slight lessening of his resistance?

"Has this man ever kissed you?"

"What a question." Laura remembered Howard's defiant goodbye kiss in the breakfast room at Grisewood Hall before he left to catch the train. To admit it now would be disastrous. "Don't you trust me?"

Thankfully, Nathaniel didn't pursue the question of a kiss. "You've not seen him again until now?"

"Only the time he climbed into my window at Wolfram and ravished me. Really, Nathaniel." Laura twitched a fold of her skirt to cover her legs. The sight of him always made her breath catch. Her gaze wandered over him, admiring the way the light from the window shone on his thick, coal-black hair. "Please, darling, you're making my headache worse." Not feeling up to a dramatic scene, relief threaded through her when he rose and came to the bed. He held himself away from her, longing in his eyes.

"I've missed you." His voice sounded strained.

Laura understood that was a huge concession for him to make. She was reminded of the young boy who had suffered the loss of his mother at a tender age. Visualizing him, long legs like a young colt, his mother dead and his father vengeful and grief-stricken, filled her with love and compassion and a need to have his arms around her.

"I have missed you too, darling. Every minute."

She coiled her arms around his neck and drew his lips down to hers, delighting in his closeness, his familiar smell, his masculine strength. "Have you come to take me home?" she asked breathlessly when he drew away.

"Yes." He held her chin in his hand, his concerned gaze roaming her face, a slight frown on his brow. "You look tired, Laura. What has made you faint?"

"I caught a chill at Gateley Park, but I'm fine now. I can't wait to go back to Cornwall."

A warmer light sparked in his eyes. "You have missed Wolfram?"

"Most dreadfully. It's my home. But not as much as I've missed you."

He bent and kissed her again, a scorching kiss that made her body hot with yearning.

Nathaniel lay down beside her and pulled her against him, his hand sliding down over her bottom.

"Nathaniel!" Laura flicked an anxious glance at the door. "Dora's bedroom is next door. The house is full of guests; anyone might come in."

He rolled her over on top of him and murmured into the hollow of her shoulder. "Dora has too much sense. Just let me hold you." He kissed the tender spot on her throat below her ear. "I want you so much."

"I want you too," she whispered, filled with a burning need for him. It had been a torturously long time without him. But voices erupted out in the hall, and there was no key in the lock. Nathaniel's hand slipped under her skirt and stroked her leg. She'd almost reached the point where she would throw caution to the wind. Her skin tingled at his touch. She gasped when she felt him hard against her thigh.

He took her mouth again, deepening the kiss until they both gasped. She pulled away with an eye on the door. "Nathaniel—"

"Hush. Or someone may well come in."

Laura giggled. "We can't—"

Nathaniel reached under her dress and eased down her

bloomers. With another quick glance at the door, she slipped out of them.

Tucking her underwear beneath the pillow, he rolled off the bed and held out his hand to her. "Come here."

Laura stood. "Where on earth…?"

He led her to an upholstered chair set in an alcove. Sitting down, he gathered up her skirts and pulled her onto his lap. In the long mirror hanging on the opposite wall, from the waist up they looked like a marriage portrait of a well-dressed couple. She held her breath as he guided himself inside her.

"Oh, yes, darling, yes…" She put her hand to her mouth to quiet herself as his hands cradled her bottom beneath her gown and moved her against him. He groaned softly, his lips against her neck as he thrust into her. Their panting breaths filled the room.

"You don't want that Farmer chap, do you?" he demanded fiercely.

"No! I chose you," Laura gasped, as her body clenched, and heat radiated to her aching nipples. She teetered on the edge of glorious oblivion. "Because I love you, Nathaniel. I think I did from the day I met you."

"Is that true?" He sounded incredulous.

She moaned softly. "Why would you doubt it?"

Laura was lost as his hands on her brought her to climax. Nathaniel held her tight against him and groaned.

As their breathing slowed, she turned within his arms to look into his face. His dark eyelashes masked his expression. Would the wall come down between them again?

Dora's voice sounded on the staircase. Laura jumped off his lap. "I want to know what's been happening while I've been away. Everything!"

Nathaniel rose too. He smoothed back his hair and straightened his clothes. "I will tell you. But later, sweetheart. Order the maid to pack your things. I'll wait downstairs."

As Nathaniel closed the door behind him, Laura touched her burning face and marveled at his audacity, as she hurried to retrieve her bloomers. He was such an exciting, unpredictable man. She peered into the mirror at her flushed face. Her headache had gone. He had not said he loved her, but he had missed her. And when he looked at her as if nothing in the world could satisfy him but her, she knew she must do as Dora's Tarot had suggested and be patient.

When she came downstairs, Howard sprang up from a chair by the door. "Laura! I was concerned. Are you all right?"

Aware that Nathaniel must be talking to Dora, Laura took Howard's outstretched hand in her gloved one. "I am, and I apologize for such dramatics, Howard. Thank you for assisting me."

Howard searched her face. "You are happy in your new life?"

"What business is it of yours whether my wife is happy or not?" Nathaniel stood at the sitting room door, eyes narrowed. "Release her hand." He took a step forward.

Nathaniel looked like a dangerous animal ready to spring. Alarmed, Laura pulled her hand from Howard's.

"I beg your pardon, my lord," Howard said stiffly. "But Lady Lanyon and I have been good friends for some years."

"I will answer the question," Laura said in a calm tone. "I am very happy, Howard, and I apologize for alarming you."

The look of fury on her husband's face was unreasonable. She would have been angry had she not understood what caused his irrational jealousy. How many years would it take before he could trust her completely?

Howard took his hat and coat from the maid. He nodded to Laura and ignored Nathaniel. "I trust that is so."

"It was good to see you again, Howard," Laura said. "Congratulations on your new appointment."

"Thank you, Laura. Good day to you both."

After the door closed behind Howard, Laura placed a hand on Nathaniel's chest. His heart pounded beneath her palm. "You must learn to trust me. If you don't, our life together will suffer."

He raised her chin to look deep into her eyes. "Then don't throw suitors like Howard Farmer in my way."

"I didn't plan to. I told you, Aunt Dora invited him."

"Very well, let that be the end of it." He nodded, but his seeming indifference didn't fool her.

"As mine and Howard's paths are unlikely to cross again, it will be."

Laura waved from the carriage window at Dora, who saw them off after promising to visit them soon. On the way to Wimbledon, Laura turned to him, unable to suppress the impatience in her voice. "Now tell me what has happened while I've been away."

"We had a violent storm. Raged for days. Cut the phone lines, so I didn't get your telegram for some days. It was necessary to rescue the crew of a ship that foundered on the rocks. A three-masted vessel—"

"I've seen that ship," Laura interrupted. "It sailed around the point on the day I rode to the cove. Theo Mallory was there."

Nathaniel stared at her. "You didn't tell me you met Mallory on that day."

Laura had purposely not told him, knowing he would gaze at her in the way he did now. "I thought Hugh would have told you. He had followed me." She raised her eyebrows. "On your orders, I believe?"

Nathaniel's mouth firmed. "Tell me exactly what happened."

Laura described how Mallory had emerged from behind a rocky outcrop.

"Did he make advances to you?"

"Don't you think I would have told you if he had?"

Nathaniel's eyes narrowed. "Go on."

Laura sighed. "He'd left when I saw the ship. It came from the same direction as he did, sailing quite close to shore. Do you think Mallory might have been—?"

"What did you talk about?"

"Nothing of note." She was not about to repeat Mallory's nasty accusation, and sought to distract him. "We spoke for a moment and then he left, and I rode back to Wolfram with Hugh. After I watched a seal...I haven't told you about the seal! But that is for later. I want to hear more about the ship."

He smiled. Our fishing boat reached the ship as it began to break up on the rocks."

"You went out in the storm?" Laura cried, horrified.

"Hush. We found the crew loading boxes into a rowing boat. The rest of the cargo floated on the waves, some of which washed up on shore. We were lucky to get the men safely on board the boat with few casualties. When we later examined their cargo, it matched that we found stored in an empty cottage. With a bit of persuasion, the men talked. The under groom from Wolfram, Throsby, and two men who helped bring the contraband in from across the Channel have been jailed."

"Is the ship still on the rocks?"

Nathaniel shook his head. "It sank to the bottom minutes afterward."

She eyed him. He was not telling her the entire story. She shivered and held his hand to her cheek. Unnerved, she remembered Dora's Tarot reading. "I'm glad I didn't know about it."

"I told you, sweetheart," Nathaniel laughed. "I know those waters."

She shook her head. "The poets put it perfectly: man is weak against the might of nature."

He kissed her cheek. "Perhaps your mother is right about you reading too much. It was a storm. And as you see, I'm here to tell the tale."

"You would use my mother's words against me?" She tried not to smile. She was determined to hear it all and not be distracted by his charm.

"I wouldn't dare." Nathaniel's eyes flared, and his teasing smile made him irresistible.

She giggled. "Please continue."

"The inquest into Theo Mallory's death is to be held in a few days, and there will be those who will not want the truth to come to light. Those whose relatives are involved in the smuggling will remain tight-lipped."

A shiver ran down Laura's spine when she thought of Mallory, his face disfigured and bloodied, floating in the waves at the bottom of the cliff. She nestled against her husband as the carriage clattered along the avenue toward her parents' house.

"There's more isn't there, Nathaniel?"

He put his arm around her. "I've always believed Amanda was murdered. Perhaps she saw something she shouldn't, and the villains pushed her off the cliff. I just don't know. Two years after she died and with Mallory and the smugglers gone, I considered it safe to marry again. The very day after I brought you home to Wolfram, I saw that ship and realized it wasn't over; that cutthroats and smugglers were still using this coast for their nefarious purposes. And then Mallory returned."

Suppressing a shudder, Laura gazed up at him. "And that is why you went out every night?"

"It's not a lie that I'm a poor sleeper. I took the boat out sometimes. I sailed close to the shore seeing if I could spot any activity either in the grounds or in the caves, but I never saw anything untoward." He sighed. "But now that Mallory's dead, and the smugglers' ship gone to the bottom of the sea, it's safe to bring you home." He lifted her chin with the heel of his hand. "You *do* want to come home to Wolfram?"

Some unexpressed thought lurked in his eyes; something he wasn't prepared to tell her, but he'd revealed so much, it would wait for a better time. "Yes, my love."

She still didn't know how big a piece of his heart Amanda still laid claim to, but Laura pushed the thought away with the knowledge that he wanted her.

CHAPTER TWENTY-SIX

Laura collected Agnes and said goodbye to her parents. Five days after they departed London, they arrived back in Wolfram, having stayed at inns along the way, enjoying being together, discussing their future and engaging in nights filled with passion.

The sun set earlier now. To Laura, under a golden moon, the village appeared almost magical. Whitewashed cottages climbed the hill, milky-white windows aglow with candlelight; lamplight threw flickering shadows over the waterfront, with the arc of sky above a deep indigo tumbled with stars. Across the water, the solid granite walls of the abbey rose from the dark gardens.

Laura was already metaphorically rolling up her sleeves, keen to resume her visits to the church, the school, the neediest villagers and the tenant farmers.

"A hunter's moon," Nathaniel observed. "They'll have a good catch."

Laura smiled. She drew in a deep breath of the familiar salty air laden with fresh, fishy odors. She was home.

The sea caressed the granite banks of the causeway as the carriage crossed. At the stables, the dogs erupted through the door with joyful barking. Laura left Nathaniel to greet them and to speak to the groom. She entered the house, gazing at everything anew. Even Rudge, standing impassively at the door, appeared a little less implacable.

Realizing she was hungry, Laura hurried to change for dinner. "Did you enjoy the trip, Agnes?"

The maid's eyes were like saucers. "Never knew a city to be so big, milady! I prefer Wolfram. I'd get lost up in those parts!"

She laughed as Agnes shook out the green silk taffeta. But after slipping the dress on Laura, the maid struggled with the buttons. "It seems a little snug, my lady."

"Can you tighten the corset laces?"

Agnes tugged at the strings on Laura's corset.

"Oh, stop. I can't breathe. This dress has never fitted me well. That might be why I seldom wear it. I'll wear the gray, Agnes."

She'd been aware of the corset pinching. Was she putting on weight? Her pulse picked up as she began to count. What with the trip and the illness, had she lost track? She couldn't be. Her last monthly courses were just before she left for London. But might she have fallen pregnant on the last night she and Nathaniel were together? Laura stilled. A baby? She clasped her hands together as hope and joy spread through her, her first thought to run to Nathaniel. She spun away from the mirror. She couldn't disappoint him. She must be sure.

"Milady?" As Agnes held up the dress, Laura made the decision not to tell him until she was certain. But how perfect a homecoming it would be. She hugged the thought to her with a smile.

That evening when they lay together, Nathaniel was tender, as if he already suspected she might be with child. But of course, he couldn't know. When she woke in the morning, he slept beside her, his arm resting over her waist.

Thrilled to find him there, she raised herself up on an elbow. "Good morning, darling."

"Good morning, my sweet." A smile lifted the corners of his mouth, and his gray eyes smoldered. He reached for her. "Mmm. You smell delicious, all warm and rumpled. What have I been missing?"

She cradled his face and kissed him, hopeful of having crossed some invisible barrier and put past hurts behind them.

Later, walking through the park, Laura breathed in the cold, salt-laden air with relish. The dogs had joined her and rooted about in the deep drifts of papery leaves.

Reaching Cilla's gate, Laura ordered the dogs home. Obedient, they turned and ran off as she knocked.

Cilla opened the door dressed in her painter's smock. "Laura! You're home. I've been busy. I plan to have these ready for my exhibition."

A testament to her hard work was stacked along the walls: canvases bursting with an explosion of bright color in a freer style, which Laura had never seen from her before.

"They're extraordinary." Laura turned to Cilla and laughed. "You have a daub of violet paint on your nose."

Cilla smiled and rubbed at it. "Look at you, you are positively blooming."

Laura flushed, remembering what had recently taken place in her bedchamber. When she and Nathaniel had tarried over breakfast, she'd told him more about her trip. She decided not to mention the letters Dora found, afraid it would destroy the peace and happiness of the morning, but she fully intended to draw him out concerning his grandmother and the neglected estate when the time was right. But right now, she enjoyed that he was happy. His prized mare was in foal. Laura considered burgeoning life in the stables to be apt. She resisted hugging her stomach and prayed she was with child.

Cilla eyed her. "Where have you gone off to, Laura?"

"I'm sorry." Laura smiled. "I was woolgathering." She wandered along the paintings, each one more striking than the last. "I'd like to buy one of these."

"I don't think they're suitable for Wolfram."

It occurred to Laura that Cilla would want to show them all in London. "If not all are sold, of course."

"I could paint your portrait?"

Laura thought of the magnificent one of Amanda that had once hung over the fireplace. "No. You're too busy."

"I'll find time. It would make a nice present for Nathaniel." She frowned. "He will employ one of the renowned portrait painters to paint you both when his heir arrives."

Cilla looked so disgruntled that Laura rushed to reassure her. "I know he would love a portrait of me painted by you. If you do have time, I would love it too!"

The more she thought about it, the more the idea appealed. The temptation to hang a portrait in the library to rival Amanda's both chastened and amused her.

"I've finished up here, so why don't we begin?"

Laura widened her eyes. "Now?"

"Why not? The light is still good."

"Very well. Where would you like me to sit?"

Cilla took her arm. "Over by the window." She studied Laura with a practiced eye. "Your moss green dress is good, if a little plain. We need a touch of color." She went to her bureau, opened a drawer and returned with a coral necklace she fastened around Laura's neck.

As Cilla set up her canvas and prepared her palette, Laura glanced in the mirror. She touched the rough, irregular-shaped beads set in gold. They were exactly like the necklace she'd seen in Amanda's room. "This is pretty. Where did you buy it?"

Cilla turned to look. She frowned. "I can't remember. A London market most likely."

"I've never seen you wear them."

"I don't wear much jewelry." Cilla began to sketch on the canvas with a sure hand. "I bought them for the color." She bent her head over her palette, mixing paint. "I admired the coral necklace Amanda used to wear."

After half an hour of sitting, Laura began to fidget, and Cilla put down her brush. "That's enough for today." She carefully arranged a cloth over the painting, ruining any chance of Laura seeing it.

Laura stretched. "I hoped to see what you've done. But I shan't break your rule again."

Cilla smiled, shaking her head. "You've been very patient. May I offer you some tea?"

"Thank you, but it's grown late. I should go home."

"Tomorrow then? Once I have the composition right, I work fast. I'll have this finished in no time."

Laura smiled. "Tomorrow then." She envisaged her portrait hanging above the fireplace, somehow making Wolfram feel even more like home to her.

The next afternoon, after sitting for Cilla again, Laura joined Nathaniel in the village. The inquest into Theo Mallory's death was about to begin. She had insisted she come and held his hand as he pushed through the people crowding around the doorway of the town hall in Penzance. She slid onto a wooden bench beside Cilla. The other seats were soon filled. The rest jostled to find a place or stood at the back of the room. The atmosphere was heavy with expectation, the murmuring hum rising in volume.

With a bang of the coroner's gavel, the voices dropped away. The post mortem was read out. Mallory had died from several severe blows to the head and face from a blunt object. He was dead before he hit the water. A collective gasp traveled around the room.

It had not been an accident, nor had he taken his own life. Someone had killed him. Laura gazed around at the faces, as shocked whispers filled the hall. Many stared at Nathaniel. He held himself erect on the seat beside her, his stony profile as grim as she'd ever seen him.

Mrs. Madge, Mallory's mother, took the stand dressed in a black gown. She pushed back her shoulders and raised her chin. "My son returned to Wolfram to put a stop to those who've discredited the family name." She stared around the room, her eyes defiant.

Florrie Havers, who was well known to the sailors around the dock and the inns, came to her feet. "Pity you didn't ask him where he got 'is money. Theo gave me a bottle of port and some tobacco for a tumble, 'e did." She laughed, a hand on her wide hip. "But I would have done it for nothing."

Mrs. Madge moved faster than Laura would have thought her capable. She was across the room and had a good grasp of Florrie's hair before anyone could stop her. The hall erupted with people shouting, as the two women were pulled apart. Mrs. Madge still clutched Florrie's curly hairpiece in her hand as they led her away.

A man dragged Florrie screaming and cursing out the door. The low rumble ceased as the room settled down again, everyone leaning forward expectantly.

The facts emerged. A witness, fisherman Bill Murphy, told how he'd seen Mallory with Will Throsby, the under groom from the abbey. Heads swiveled to look at Nathaniel, as Murphy described how on the night Theo disappeared Bill was returning a mended fishing net to his boat. He saw the two men arguing heatedly near the seawall.

Throsby was then brought into the room from his jail cell where he'd languished on a charge of smuggling. His face was pinched and he fidgeted, turning his hat around in his hand. Under hard questioning, he broke down and confessed he'd been told to kill Mallory. If he hadn't done it, he'd be the one lying dead. He'd hit Mallory with an oar several times, then pushed his body into the water. When asked to explain why, he grew angry. "Mallory lied. Swore to us that 'e and Lady Amanda would protect us should anything go wrong. They were thick as thieves. And then 'e gave us up to the police."

There was an uproar in the room. The gavel came down several times before it quieted again.

"Who gave you the order to kill Mallory?" the coroner asked.

"I don't know 'is name," Will said. "Never saw 'im before. Came from up north. Said if I didn't do it, me Ma and little sister would be tossed into the sea." He sniffed and wiped his nose with the back of his hand.

"Did your employer, Lord Lanyon, know of this?" The coroner asked.

"'Is lordship knew naught about any of it. We used 'is land is all. While 'e was gone to London." Will pointed at Nathaniel. "I feel bad about that, Yer Lordship. You was always good to me."

"Then why in God's name didn't he come to me for help?" Nathaniel murmured with a sad shake of his head.

Once the coroner had given his verdict of murder, set a trial date and banged his gavel, the hall exploded in noisy debate as everyone filed outside.

Nathaniel escorted Laura to the waiting carriage. "I have to speak to the constable. If you don't want to wait, I'll send the carriage home."

"Of course I'll wait. I'd like to come with you."

"Perhaps you should hear this." He took her arm and walked toward the police station.

She smiled, pleased to see the strain gone from his face. "Do you think this will be the end of it?"

"Lord, I hope so."

She listened as Nathaniel discussed the findings with the constable. Mallory had been involved in the first smuggling operation up to his neck. He'd signed his death warrant when he came back to Wolfram and tried to muscle his way into this one. And he'd intended to blackmail Nathaniel, spread it about that Amanda's baby was his. He'd boasted about it when drunk in the tavern two days before his death.

"By then no one believed Mallory's lies," the constable said. "Roe at The Sail and Anchor threatened to beat Mallory to a pulp if he said another word about it. Threw him out on his ear."

Laura was shocked into silence. She placed a protective hand on her stomach. The constable was right: Mallory had been revealed for the scoundrel he was. His word meant nothing. But what did Nathaniel believe?

Laura glanced up at him as they walked back to the carriage, his big hand clasping hers. Surely now they could get on with their lives. The thought warmed her. The nausea she had suffered a month ago was gone, and she felt amazingly well. Once the doctor confirmed her pregnancy, she could confidently tell Nathaniel her news. A baby would bring them closer and help to banish the sadness that had clung to Wolfram like a dark cloud. But even as she thought it, a shiver raced down her spine. Would they ever know how and why Amanda died?

CHAPTER TWENTY-SEVEN

Something woke Laura. Finding Nathaniel gone from the bed, she propped herself up on her elbows. The last few days, he'd remained with her until morning. Moonlight swept through the gap in the curtains and cast a silvery glow into the far corner of the room. She watched, transfixed, as the light appeared to take shape. Did she imagine the force that seemed to gather in the room? Strange that she wasn't afraid.

"What do you want?" The shape shifted and formed the vague outline of a woman. "Is it you, Amanda?" Laura whispered.

Silence.

Laura gripped the bedcover, unable to move, fighting to penetrate the gloom. A breeze stirred the curtains, and the ray of moonlight shifted. This was ridiculous. She found the matches, and with trembling fingers, lit a candle. The bedroom looked the same as it always did. Her imagination was getting the better of her. She raised the candle to check the time on the mantel clock. It was almost two. Nathaniel had no reason to search the grounds now that the smugglers were gone. Where was he? Surely he hadn't returned to his cold, lonely bed in the chamber next door. Was he working in his study? Really, he needed his sleep.

Perhaps he was just restless and didn't wish to disturb her. She had to believe he would welcome her company. She slipped from her bed and donned her dressing gown and slippers. The open panel revealed an empty room, the bed smoothly made.

Disheartened, she stepped out into the hall. A light flickered beneath Amanda's bedroom door. Laura almost gasped aloud. So, he was there. The muscles of her legs seemed rigid as she forced herself to walk to the door, determined to confront him. Her fear of facing his obsession with his first wife almost choked her. Rudge had had Amanda's bedchamber emptied of all possessions; what drew Nathaniel to the room? Did Amanda still have his heart?

Gearing herself up for an awful scene, Laura slowly opened the door.

Apart from the furniture, the room was bare of its showy paraphernalia. A candle stub burned low on the mantel, its feeble glow a small circle of light. A man in dark clothes bent over in the shadows, his back to her. She heard a strangled sob.

Was it Nathaniel? Distressed, Laura slammed the door shut, and with quick steps, somehow made it back to her room. She collapsed on the bed in tears. As she wiped her eyes, she thought about what she'd seen. His sobs seemed wrong. Had she jumped to a hasty conclusion? She ignored the urging of her rational mind to remain in bed until morning and snatched up a candle, determined to face whoever was in that room.

This time, when she turned the doorknob with trembling fingers, only the acrid tang and trail of smoke from the extinguished candle wafted about the empty space. She retreated to the corridor where the huge tapestry stirred in a cold draft and rubbed at the goosebumps on her arms. He must have heard her shut Amanda's door. She peeked into Nathaniel's bedchamber to make sure he hadn't returned. Empty.

Her fierce need for the truth roiled in her stomach, washing away any sense of fear. She gave up an attempt at stealth. After opening all the doors along the corridor to empty rooms, she descended the staircase. Through the long window, moonlight threw shifting shadows over the great hall below. The massive fluted stone columns were wide enough to hide a man. Laura feared an intruder would reach out and grab her as she hurried past. It was irrational. No one could break into Wolfram at night; Nathaniel had assured her everything was always locked up. Her throat turned ash-dry, which no amount of swallowing could moisten. It was deathly still and cold as she hurried along the corridor.

Nathaniel's study was empty. On closer inspection, the whole floor lay in darkness and was silent as a tomb. Only the whoosh of the waves beating endlessly against the seawall and the screech of a barn owl broke the silence.

Her candle sputtering, Laura continued down to the kitchen, praying to find Nathaniel enjoying a second helping of Mrs. Madge's apricot tart. But that room too was empty, the stove unlit. Gleaming copper pots and pans hung from their hooks above the scrubbed table. A lingering smell of lemon oil and coal mixed with something sweet and freshly baked filled the air. The scullery and the servants' hall beyond were so dark as to seem impenetrable.

Laura's knees threatened to fail her as she faced the fact that Nathaniel was not in the house. Her mind skittered, failing to find a viable reason. There was no squall, no lightning nor thunder to draw him outside. And no smugglers.

She was about to return to the main floor when a creak made her pause. A cool draft caressed her cheek like a ghostly hand. She knew from whence it came: the cellar stairs. Would Nathaniel be down there? Aware of the precious life she believed she carried, Laura negotiated the stone steps with care, passing the entrance to the wine cellar. The chill breeze grew stronger, encircling her. She shivered and clutched the banister with stiff, cold fingers.

Trying to control her noisy breath, she continued down past shadowy doorways, which led into the cavernous storerooms that had once been part of the vaulted cloisters of the abbey. The stone ceiling pressed down, and a drip of water echoed like the steady beat of a drum. Her candle fluttered alarmingly in the damp current of air. Why hadn't she stopped to light a lantern? Gripping the rail, she prayed her candle would stay alight. She couldn't face the thought of climbing back up in the dark.

At the bottom, the outer door stood open, framing an expanse of clear, star-studded sky. Laura hurried forward and emerged into the stiff sea breeze. She was a few steps from the water's edge, where the moon danced over the water. To the right of her, tall shrubs formed alarming shapes, blacker than the sky. The sloop rocked gently at the wharf. Nathaniel was not out on the water. How foolish to think he would be.

Laura's skin crawled and the hair on the back of her neck shivered. She should not have come! As she retreated to the doorway, a dark figure exploded out of the bushes and ran at her. Laura had no time to evade the forceful shove, strengthened by the momentum of their mad dash. Hands struck at her, punching her in the chest. Losing her breath, she careened backwards. The candle sailed off into the darkness as she fought to gain her balance. Her heels hit the seawall and over she went, arms flailing. The icy water sucked her under, her body rigid with shock. In her heart-stopping panic, she sank into the dark depths of the sea.

She had never learned to swim. Now for her baby's sake, she fought to live. Using her bare feet, her slippers gone, she kicked her way to the surface and burst into the air with a cry, swallowing salt water. With a desperate cough, she spat out briny water and took quick breaths to fill her lungs before she sank again. When her thrashing arms and feet brought her up once more, she gasped as she bobbed around. She cried out, but her voice was lost in the ocean's roar.

Laura had managed to stay afloat for several minutes when she realized the pull of the tide had caught her and was sweeping her away from land. Horror, cold and fear blocked all thoughts but one. What if the tide carried her around the point to be dashed to her death on the rocks? Would they find her floating at the base of the cliff like Mallory and Amanda?

She spat out seawater and yelled. But her faint calls for help hardly made a sound, as she watched the solid lines of the abbey highlighted against the moonlit sky retreat. Thrashing her arms and legs,

Laura quickly tired. Would she die never learning why anyone would want to kill her? Who had been in that room? She should have stayed, confronted them. Her chest constricted with small, abrupt spasms as the cold froze her core. Her legs cramped painfully, and she strained to keep them moving, hampered by her hair blinding her and her clothing plastered against her skin.

Laura had no concept of time; everything slowed down. She slipped beneath the surface again. The idea that it would be easy to let go and drift to one's death began to appeal. Her baby! Forcing her legs to work, she fought her way up. She broke the surface and dragged air into her laboring lungs. Resignation stung at her more than the salt in her eyes. It was hopeless to fight. She might keep herself afloat for a while longer, but she couldn't swim to shore.

Her fragile strength ebbed away, and her limbs faltered in their struggle to keep her head above water. Her mind wandered as she came to accept her fate. She would drift until she sank one last time. She forced open her stinging eyes. Over the swell of the waves, a blur of lights shone directly ahead. Trying to make out if it was a ship or land, she bumped hard against something beneath the water. The solid mass grazed her side, the flash of pain rousing her.

She clung to the pitted stone against the pull of the tide as her mind cleared. Supported, energy surged back into her limbs. Was it the rocks beneath the cliff? Laura raised her head but saw nothing except the starlit sky above her. She could not be below the cliff, for there was a row of lamplight to her right. The village! She clung to a fragile, desperate hope.

The causeway.

With the last of her energy, Laura clawed at the stone, breaking nails and scoring flesh from her fingers as she pushed her way up. Her knees and toes scraped across its rocky, shell-encrusted edge, her frozen body barely registering pain. She heaved herself over the top and onto the roadway with a weak cry, then crouched on her knees. She swayed on the edge as wavelets spilled over the causeway and threatened to drag her back into the inky sea. Was the tide ebbing or flowing? She wished she'd tried to understand such things. The sea might claim her again before she could reach land. Fear brought her to her feet. As she fought the pull of the water swirling around her thighs, Laura couldn't gauge the width or direction of the causeway. Any moment she might step off back into the ocean again.

Fixing her gaze on the abbey tower highlighted by moonlight, she waded forward. Each step was painful, and it was useless to try to hurry. It seemed an age before she felt hard-packed earth beneath her feet, and as she climbed further, the water vanished like magic. She collapsed to her knees with painful sobs. Several minutes passed as she crouched there too exhausted to move.

Annoyed with herself, Laura pushed to her feet, then bent to pull away the ripped shreds of fine silk and lawn clinging to her legs, which threatened to trip her. She stumbled forward. A refrain kept repeating in her mind. Who wanted her dead? Then another frightening thought. Were they still near?

Deep shudders shook her as she staggered along, guided by the dark shapes of trees bordering the road. The salt stung her scratched, bloody legs and feet. A faint glow appeared somewhere along the lane. As she drew closer, she fought to make sense of the shadows and jerked with fear at the muffled sounds, which now reached her.

Laura rounded a corner of the stables where a lantern's glow lit her way across the black cobbles. She tottered into the warm stables, which smelled of horse, hay and leather and offered a return to normalcy. She swayed on her feet. A lantern hung from a beam, shining down on a groaning horse. The animal lay on its side with two men bent over it, their voices low. Then Nathaniel chuckled as the white sac containing the foal emerged from its mother. The dogs leapt up and rushed to Laura, almost knocking her over.

"Nathaniel," Laura whispered, her throat too painful and raw to speak.

Nathaniel spun around. His eyes widened. "Mother of…" He ran to catch her as her knees gave way. Strong arms caught her up and held her against his chest. Safe.

"You'll get wet," she stuttered, relief warming her cold body but failing to quell her shudders.

"What the devil...Laura, what happened?"

He laid her in the hay in the empty stall next to where the groom dealt with the new foal. Nathaniel shrugged out of his coat, and as he slipped her arms into it, she looked down to see that she was almost naked. Her legs were bare and a breast was exposed through her ripped nightclothes.

"Laura, for God's sake, tell me," he pleaded, his eyes incredulous, his voice ragged.

Laura swallowed; her throat felt like she'd eaten broken glass. She grimaced. "Someone pushed me into the sea."

"Who? Why?" He shook his head slowly.

"I don't know," Laura said, annoyed. She only wanted to lie down somewhere soft and warm and sleep.

Nathaniel turned to the groom. "I'll leave you to manage here."

The groom's alarmed gaze was fixed on Laura. "Of course, milord."

"Good man."

Nathaniel hefted Laura into his arms and strode to the house. She shivered uncontrollably as she rested her head against his shoulder. He put her down to unlock the front door, holding her upright with one arm. Then with her in his arms, he climbed the stairs.

"Your prized mare has a foal; you should go back."

He frowned, his gaze roaming her face. "Is *that* what you think of me?"

In her chamber, Nathaniel placed her gently on the bed. He peeled her out of his coat and threw it onto a chair. "These wet things must come off."

He stripped her naked and grabbed a towel, then rubbed her skin vigorously, careful to avoid the cuts and deep scratches. The friction made her skin glow. Her head fell back on the pillow, and she closed her eyes.

Nathaniel examined her body, moving her about with gentle hands. "Nothing worse than cuts and scratches." He tucked a blanket around her. "Wake up, Laura. You can sleep after you tell me how this happened."

She gazed at his lean, worried face. "I went down the cellar stairs to look for you. The door was open. When I left the house, someone pushed me into the water."

"Oh, my love. I've been so afraid…" He gathered her to him and kissed her gently. His warm mouth breathed life into her. "But why go down there, for God's sake?"

She must tell him about the man in the room. She would in a minute. With a sob, she wiped away the tears that coursed down her cheeks. "The tide took me to the causeway. I had to climb over it."

"Good God. My brave love." Nathaniel pulled a handkerchief from his pocket and wiped her tears. "Those cuts must be cleaned and dressed. I'll help you into a dry nightgown and send for the doctor."

"Is that necessary? Can't it wait until tomorrow? I just want to sleep, Nathaniel."

"Yes, it is necessary. Oyster cuts can be nasty. Tomorrow then." Nathaniel opened a drawer and returned to tug a fresh nightgown over her head. His deft fingers tied the bows at the neck. Going to the panel, he disappeared into his room. Minutes later, he returned with a tumbler of brandy and supported her shoulders with his arm. "What made you look for me, Laura?"

"Something woke me."

Laura took a deep sip and choked. The fiery liquid burned its way down her sore throat, warming her frozen insides. After another sip, she gave him back the glass and rested her head on the pillow. More hot tears traced a path down her cheeks; she didn't seem able to stop them. She began to talk, her explanation sounding garbled even to her ears, while Nathaniel held her hands.

"You found a man in Amanda's room weeping?"

She nodded, fighting sleep.

His concerned eyes darkened with hurt. "And you thought that man was me?"

A sob rose in her throat. "Don't chastise me, Nathaniel. I can't fight with you now."

"Chastise you? What sort of brute do you think me?" He chafed her hands between his large, warm ones. "It's my fault." He shook his head. *"All my fault.* I thought with Mallory gone this was over. It isn't."

Confused, Laura frowned. "But who was in that room?"

"Someone who can get into this house. I will find him, Laura, and when I do…"

"It must be Rudge. He was obsessed with Amanda. He dislikes me."

"But Rudge isn't here. I gave him the night off. I saw him leave, and once the tide rose over the causeway he couldn't have come back."

"Not even by boat?"

"Rudge in a boat? He's from up country. He isn't happy on the water."

"You can't be sure of that." She put a hand to his cheek. "Who was the man who attacked me then? Who was weeping in that room?"

"I don't know, sweetheart."

She studied him. Was he telling her everything? "And why would anyone want to kill me?"

"It makes no sense. To get at me, I suppose." Rising from the bed, he pulled the bell. "I believed after Amanda died that I shouldn't marry again. But Mallory had been gone two years, and I wanted you with me." His breath caught. "I love you, Laura. I didn't believe I could love anyone like this again. I was miserable without you. I can't do it again."

"That's just as well because I'm not leaving without you." She stroked his cheek, his declaration bringing intense joy.

Despair haunted his eyes. "I was certain that Mallory had killed Amanda. I suspected they were having an affair, although she denied it. I didn't want to face it. I shut down, buried myself in my work. Then after Amanda died, the police couldn't find anything to link him to the smugglers or Amanda's death. Then he left Wolfram. I sensed we weren't done with him. His mother was here, and I feared he would come back one day.

"Once I brought you to Wolfram, I realized I needed to keep track of Mallory. Roe at The Sail and Anchor found someone for me. And then Mallory turned up. I tried to have him put behind bars, but he was a slippery fish. He'd thought by giving the police a few names, he could disappear again. He outwitted himself, however. His arrogance was his downfall. I thought it was over when he died." He cradled her head in his hands and kissed her. "Oh, my love, I might have lost you."

Her breath caught. "You do love me then."

"Love you? More than my life. I did try not to get too close, Laura. I didn't think I had it in me to love like this. I've been so very wrong."

"Did Amanda hurt you so dreadfully?"

"At first perhaps. But Amanda merely confirmed my belief that women were never to be trusted."

"You thought I was seeing Howard behind your back."

"I've had to learn to trust again, Laura. And for a while I didn't think I could." He trailed the back of his fingers down her cheek. "Jealousy is a terrible thing, sweetheart."

"I know. I've suffered from it myself."

His eyes widened. "You have? When?"

"Cilla."

Nathaniel huffed out a sigh. "Now that is ridiculous. Cilla, my sweet, doesn't like men that way."

"But she had a lover when she lived in Paris."

"Another woman. When she came here she was close to killing herself; that's why I gave her the cottage."

"That never occurred to me." She frowned. "Why didn't you tell me?"

"I didn't feel it was my place to." He kissed her fingers. "I thought she should tell you. And what does it matter?"

"People should be free to love whomever they choose, though I personally couldn't imagine loving anyone but a man."

"Any man?"

She smiled. "One man in particular."

He examined her cut fingers, turning over her hand to kiss the palm. "But you didn't get a prize with me. I've fought demons for most of my life." He smiled wryly. "My father told me to run my marriage like a business and find a mistress. I've never given a thought to a mistress since the day I met you." He shook his head. "Madness to think I could keep you at arm's length. It was impossible, almost from the very first. I didn't have a hope."

"So, you went sailing at night to escape me?"

"When all this is over..." He frowned. "You're to come with me next time. We'll take a bottle of wine and a couple of Mrs. Madge's pasties and throw a line over the side in the moonlight. I've brought a catch home for the table many times.

"You tore down my defenses, Laura. You're the best part of me. I am nothing without you."

"*My love.*" Laura drew his face down to hers and kissed him. She told him about the letters Dora had found at Gateley Park. "I didn't read them, but there was one from your father that made me understand just what you had been through."

Pain darkened his eyes. "It was a bad union. My father was a reserved man, and my mother wanted everything from life."

She threaded her fingers through his. "It made me cry. You must have been lost and hurt, my darling, and very much alone."

"Not alone. My grandmother came to the school every visiting day. She brought me treats and told me I was loved. She was a wonderful woman." He shook his head. "I thought I saw that special quality in you the first time I set eyes on you. You have a big heart, Laura. You care for others. And you've made me a better man. I thank God you came into my life."

She inhaled deeply. "There's something else I must..." As she spoke, her stomach felt strange, and she suffered a surge of fear for her baby. So tiny and new, would the babe survive the trauma?

A knock came at the door. "Come," Nathaniel called.

Agnes entered sleepily, her hair in a long plait down her back. "You rang, milady?"

"Bring hot water, salve and bandages," Nathaniel ordered. "Your mistress has hurt herself."

Agnes' mouth fell open.

"Don't just stand there, girl," Nathaniel snapped.

Agnes rushed from the room.

"What were you going to tell me?"

Laura's lids drooped. "It can wait until later. I'm so very tired." The ominous heaviness she felt low in her stomach made her afraid to tell him. She couldn't bear to disappoint him now.

He pulled the blanket up around her shoulders. "Rest, my love. When Agnes returns, I'll leave you. I must check the house and grounds. I won't be long."

"Please be careful, Nathaniel."

He looked grim. "My hunting rifle's in the study. I'll load it." He turned to the maid, who had just returned. "Stay until I come back, Agnes. Lock the door and don't answer it to anyone but me."

Agnes gaped at him. "Yes, milord."

Laura sipped the brandy while the maid bound up her cuts. A little woozy, she drifted off to sleep. She dreamt that Nathaniel had been hurt. Waking with a start, she found he'd returned and sent the maid away. She still trembled with shock.

"Stay with me," she begged, holding out her arms.

"No one was lurking about the grounds. I won't leave you again tonight. Sleep, my love."

He stretched out beside her and gathered her into his arms. She coiled up against his reassuringly strong body and fell into an exhausted sleep.

CHAPTER TWENTY-EIGHT

When the doctor came the following morning, he confirmed Laura's pregnancy. "Do you think I'll keep my baby?" Laura asked him in a desperate whisper.

"Difficult to tell," the doctor said. "I would advise you to remain in bed for at least two or three days to be on the safe side. We'll know more after that. Shall I congratulate Lord Lanyon?"

"Not until we're sure, Doctor Owens."

Laura lay back on the pillows. If her mother knew of this, she'd demand her to return to London and have the best doctor from the Royal College of Physicians attend her. And she didn't trust Nathaniel not to agree with her mother. Just a few days and then she would tell him.

Cilla came to inquire after Laura when she failed to keep their appointment for the sitting. She didn't tell Nathaniel about the portrait, for which Laura was grateful; she wanted to see the painting first. It might not be flattering, and the glowing portrait of Amanda was a constant reminder of Nathaniel's first wife, whose incomparable beauty must have once ensnared him, if not at the end of her life. It was as if Cilla had poured all her love into that portrait. Love? The thought gave Laura pause. Might Cilla have been in love with Amanda? But Cilla had spoken so bluntly of her faults, Laura doubted it could be so.

After two days in bed, which bored her to distraction, the worrying sensation in her stomach eased. When she rose the following morning, apart from her cuts and scratches, she felt extremely well.

Nathaniel had not left her side during the night, his rifle propped close by the bed. Yesterday, the constable questioned her, but she could tell him nothing helpful.

"Let's go over it again," Nathaniel said, as they ate in the breakfast room. He smiled. "Judging by your appetite, you seem to have recovered from your ordeal."

Laura put down her knife and fork. She'd eaten two eggs and a pile of bacon and nibbled at a piece of toast and jam. "I saw a man in dark clothes sobbing."

"Try and think now, anything you might remember."

She took a sip of tea and returned her cup to its saucer. "He was turned away from me, and the room was in shadow. I smelled something odd though."

Nathaniel leaned closer. "What exactly? A lingering perfume, tobacco, a man's body odor, tallow? We use beeswax here."

Laura's mind swirled like a London fog. "I'm sure there was tallow, but that's not it." She frowned and rubbed her forehead. "Something that shouldn't have been there."

"Don't worry about it now, darling." Nathaniel placed his hand over hers and gave it a squeeze.

"It will come to me eventually. I have a good memory." Laura took a last bite of toast and eyed the fruit bowl as she considered a banana. "I'm so hungry. I can't understand it. Maybe it's shock."

"It probably is." Nathaniel's eyebrows rose when Laura gave into temptation and reached for the fruit.

"It's a treat to find a banana here. I do love them so." She peeled back the skin and then took a bite, enjoying the smooth, sweet taste. "I do wish I could remember at least something to help you."

Nathaniel looked pensive. "Don't concern yourself with it now. It may come to you later."

Rudge came in to replenish the tea, and they lapsed into

silence. Laura studied Rudge as he fussed around the sideboard, narrow-shouldered in his dark suit. He was a slightly built man. She remembered how he spoke of Amanda when he showed Laura the painting. She'd laughed at him, Cilla had said. Had he been obsessed with Amanda? Enough to want to kill her, as well as the woman he considered a usurper?

The butler exited the room. "How did Rudge get on with Amanda?"

"Very well. She had him eating out of her hand."

"He was in love with her," Laura said.

"He admired her. But love?"

"It was obvious in the worshipful way he handled her portrait." She shuddered. "He stroked the frame as if it was her flesh."

Nathaniel's mouth tightened. "That's possible, I suppose, but, darling, are you sure you aren't..."

"Rudge has *never* liked me."

"I can't believe anyone would dislike you. And as I've said, Rudge was not here that night."

"You can't be sure of that."

"Why would he want to hurt you?"

"He has never once smiled at me since I came here. And he has offered no sympathy after my near-drowning." She narrowed her eyes. "He must know I saw him in Amanda's bedroom. He might have murdered Amanda too."

"Now you really are being fanciful. He loved Amanda, yet he killed her?"

"Haven't you heard of a crime of passion?"

Nathaniel sighed. "I can understand your nervousness." He raked his fingers through his hair. "Rudge could not have killed Amanda."

"How can you be sure?"

"I find it very difficult to believe Rudge would hurt you, even if he could have returned to the abbey during the night. He would have had to come by boat. I'll question him and make inquiries of the fishermen. In the meantime, best not to spend time alone in his company."

Nathaniel watched her choose an apple from the bowl on the table, and his anxious expression became tinged with gentle amusement. "Don't you think you've had enough breakfast, my dear?"

"Thank you, yes. I'll take this with me to eat while I write my correspondence."

He slipped his arm around her waist and chuckled. "That tiny waist of yours will become but a beautiful memory."

She raised an eyebrow. "And if it does, will you still love me?"

"Every splendid extra inch of you." He dropped a kiss on her lips.

She paused, yearning to tell Nathaniel her news. But she couldn't risk him sending her to her mother until she gave birth. Right now, her bargaining abilities would be useless against Nathaniel's need to protect her and the baby. And hopefully, the malicious person who'd attacked her would soon be found. Nathaniel would discover she was right about Rudge. She shivered and wished him gone from Wolfram today. But as Nathaniel remained convinced of his innocence, that was unlikely.

They strolled to the stables. The usual stable smells greeted them at the door, along with the moist heat of a new birth.

"Mr. Pitney has asked if he might see you. He is in the office, my lord," the young stable boy said, ducking his head respectfully to Laura.

"Tell him I'll be but a moment."

In the stall, the young foal wobbled unsteadily on its four white feet. "She's beautiful," Laura said. "What will you call her?"

"I thought I'd name her after you."

"Could you call her after my twin sister, Eliza?"

He smiled. "Eliza Girl it is then."

A hand on his shoulder, Laura kissed his cheek. "Perfect."

"Laura, I don't believe I've introduced you to my new groom, Cadan Hammett."

"Milady."

Cadan had a pleasant, open face. Nathaniel had told her he was married with a child. Embarrassed, Laura hoped she didn't flush, aware of how much of her the man had seen when she'd stumbled into the stables half-clothed.

Nathaniel was drawn into a discussion with the groom about the welfare of the new foal.

"I'll leave you to your work while I visit Cilla," Laura said.

"Wait just a moment. I'll come with you."

She did not want to risk him seeing the portrait. "But it's daylight and only over the hill. What if I take the dogs with me?"

Nathaniel frowned. "No, Laura. Wait for me. I'll be finished with Pitney in a little while."

"Could Cadan escort me then?"

"You are impatient, Madam! Escort Lady Lanyon, Cadan."

"Yes, milord."

"Take the dogs; they need exercise." Nathaniel whistled. Orsino and Sebastian pricked up their ears and loped over to mill around them. "They are well trained and fond of you. Ask anything of them, and they will obey."

"Come, Orsino, Sebastian."

Laura walked into the park with the groom trailing a respectful distance behind. A breeze rustled through the dead leaves, scattering them over the lawn. A gardener raked them into piles and burned them. Smoke coiled up into the air to be grabbed and whisked away by the wind. She'd barely noticed the change in the weather and still wore a light cloak over her walking dress. The seasons advanced more slowly here and were milder than northern climes. The dogs frolicked around her. Orsino ferreted out a red squirrel and chased it up a tree. After a bout of frenzied barking, the dog gave up and ran back to join them.

As the roar of the sea greeted her, Laura shivered and kept her distance from the cliffs, shrugging away her fear of some unknown assailant wanting her dead. Was Nathaniel's confidence in Rudge misplaced? She called the dogs to heel at the cottage. With a wave, Cadan left her.

The door opened before Laura reached it. "My dear," Cilla took her hands, "I'm so relieved to find you well. I was horrified when I heard what had happened. What an extraordinary business. Do you have any idea who the devil it was?"

Rudge's name hovered on her tongue. "No idea at all, I'm afraid."

Laura ordered the dogs to sit at the front door. She followed Cilla into the cottage. The smell of oil paint made her slightly nauseous. She'd taken an aversion to certain smells recently, while they'd never bothered her before.

"Perhaps they mistook me for someone else, although it's utterly terrifying. Especially after Amanda's unsolved death." She settled on the chair, trying to push away the terror that remained with her.

"No recollection at all?" Cilla went to her easel.

"Nothing useful."

"Why don't you ask Nathaniel to take you away for a holiday?"

Laura frowned. "I don't see how that would help."

"Well, it makes sense if you're in danger."

Laura crossed her arms. "I'm not leaving Wolfram again."

"Your portrait is almost finished," Cilla said with a conciliatory smile.

"You don't still need me to pose for you?"

"Once I have the sketch down, I work quickly. My memory for details is excellent. One more sitting tomorrow will do it."

"When do you leave?"

"The London exhibition opens next week."

"How exciting. Are you prepared? Nervous?"

Cilla bit her lip. "Prepared and nervous."

Laura fell silent as Cilla worked. She didn't feel comfortable in this room. It seemed airless, despite an open window. An hour later, they stopped for tea.

"Let's have it outside," Laura suggested.

The creeper over the loggia had shed its leaves, and the sun flooded down on them. Laura removed her hat and lifted her face to the warmth.

"You'll freckle," Cilla said.

"I never have."

"Amanda had to be careful." Cilla stirred her tea. "She had that milk-white skin of a blonde; she was never without her hat and her umbrella. Took that frilly pastel blue parasol everywhere with her." Her laugh had a bitter edge. "She was quite aware that the blue matched her eyes."

"Didn't I see a similar parasol in the painting you just finished? The one I peeked at on the easel?"

"Yes. I painted it from memory, as it was never found. Lost in the sea, most likely."

"She had the parasol with her when she disappeared?"

"Yes."

Laura glanced across the sea. Today, a channel of dark purple dissected the blue-gray water. She remembered the chill of the water and how terrified she'd been when the tide swept her away from land. She took a deep sip of hot tea to banish the block of cold fear. Would they never be at peace here?

"What time of day did Amanda go missing?"

"She posed for me on that day. It was about two o'clock when she left. No one saw her after that."

"Where else might she have gone?"

"To visit Mallory. She couldn't stay away from him."

"There was some suggestion at the inquest that she had an affair."

Cilla stood so swiftly she knocked the table and spilled the tea. She peered into the teapot. "More hot water, I think."

When she returned, Laura repeated her question. "Is that what she told you?"

Pouring water into the pot, Cilla spilled some onto her hand. "Ouch!" She sucked a finger. "Amanda needed validation of people's undying love. But she didn't enjoy the physical side of things. She would have charmed Mallory; perhaps she did visit him that day for another bout of his cringing devotion."

Laura took a sip of tea. "Then why would he kill her?"

"Who knows?" Cilla shrugged. "Love can drive a person mad."

"But she was with child."

"That wouldn't prevent Amanda from flirting."

"But her condition should have stopped Mallory from pursuing her."

Cilla's eyebrows rose. "This is beyond your comprehension, isn't it? Such a sheltered life you've led."

"I suppose I do expect people to act decently," Laura said coolly. She put down her cup. "Nathaniel didn't want me to stay long. I've tried to keep the portrait from him, so I'd better go."

Cilla pushed back her chair. "It might be best. I'm not good company today."

Laura flinched at her expression. Cilla's fierce reaction seemed unexpected. Her eyes glittered with fury. "Whatever is the matter?"

Cilla shrugged and began to stack the cups onto a tray. "Talking about Amanda affects me. She treated people badly, especially Nathaniel. Working alone will calm me."

"I'll let myself out."

Laura walked through the house to the front door, troubled by Cilla's obvious dismissal. Had the mention of their different upbringings upset her? It was true that her life had been easier than Cilla's, but she didn't feel she should apologize for it.

"I'm sorry, Laura." Cilla followed her and placed a hand on her arm. She smiled. "Come tomorrow. I'll finish the portrait."

"The last sitting?" Laura asked with a rush of relief.

"Yes. A short one."

"Good. Tomorrow then."

Outside on the step, the faithful dogs bounded to their feet. She bent and patted both of their satiny heads. "Good dogs. Let's go home."

Cilla did feel a great deal for Amanda, although she wasn't blind to her faults. Laura wondered if it had been a romantic love or a close friendship. Laura continued through the park. Cilla might not have entirely approved of Amanda, but she still suffered a terrible loss. The dogs suddenly took off as Nathaniel appeared through the trees.

"I would have preferred you wait for me," he said when he reached her. He placed an arm around her shoulders, his expression grave. She hated that he worried about her.

Laura laid her head against his chest.

"Are you all right?"

"Yes. It's just that I love you so."

"And I love you. But that's a good thing, isn't it?"

He grinned and tipped her chin to kiss her. Laura wrapped her arms around his neck. Whatever had happened, she couldn't tamp down the burst of rapture at his simple declaration so freely given.

Nathaniel whistled to Orsino who sniffed the bushes a few yards away. "I'm for a good dinner and a brandy by the library fire."

"Me too. A good dinner anyway." Laura smiled up at him. "Do you know I haven't a clue where Rudge's accommodation is in the house? Does he reside with the other servants on the floor above ours?"

"Yes, but he's not in the same wing as the maids."

"It would be easy for him to slip down the back stairs to Amanda's room, wouldn't it?"

Nathaniel frowned. "I have questioned him, Laura. He was staying with a friend in the village. He has provided me with a name."

"She might lie for him."

"What makes you think it's a woman?"

"Isn't it?"

"No, it's Fred Peterson and a few others. They meet to play cards."

"And he spent the night there?"

"No. He crossed not long after you did. Once the tide was out."

Laura paused and turned to him. "I know you don't like to talk about when Amanda died..." She paused at his bleak expression. "Do you remember where everyone was that day?"

"Of course I remember!" he snapped. "Do you think I'd forget?"

Would he ever be free of her? "I'm sorry if this upsets you." To her dismay her voice broke slightly. "But where was Rudge that afternoon?"

"You're not going to let this go, are you?" Nathaniel passed a tired hand across his brow. "Amanda disappeared sometime in the afternoon." He thought for a moment. "I was working in my study;

Rudge had been away on an errand in the village."

"Do you remember what the errand was?"

He sighed. "Something personal, I believe."

"Rudge often goes to the village, doesn't he? I remember he was absent the day I arrived here."

"I'm not his jailor, Laura. He has time off. If he wishes to spend it purchasing something or meeting a friend, it's fine with me, as long as the standard of his work meets with my approval. And it always does."

"I think you should ask him where he was."

"After all this time? He gave his explanation at the inquest. And he was seen in the village, returning to the house later to perform his duties."

"So, he could have..."

"So could I, for that matter," he said sharply. "Have you ever thought of that?"

"Not for a second. Don't be ridiculous, Nathaniel."

He stared down at her, his eyes hard. "You've heard the rumors." A muscle twitched at the corner of his mouth. "You could hardly have avoided them. There are some who still suspect me even now."

"But I am not one of them!"

"I can't blame them," he said in a grim tone.

Fear scudded through her. "What do you mean?"

He glanced away. "It was common knowledge Amanda and I weren't happy. We quarreled often. We fought on that day. She said the baby wasn't mine. I was eaten up with jealousy when she rushed out of the house. I should have gone after her."

He shook his head. "The Bible says a man's pride shall bring him low. I expected Amanda to come straight back, apologize for telling such a dreadful lie, but in my heart I knew it was true. But she was pregnant and still deserving of my protection. I am not my father, and I refused to act like him. Amanda would have been disgraced as my mother was. Mallory would not have cared a damn for her. I went after her, but I couldn't find her. I never saw her again." He raised his troubled gaze to Laura. "I expected her to be with Cilla; they were good friends. She'd been there but disappeared some hours later…" His voice faltered. "Did she go to Mallory? Quarrel with him? Did he kill her, or had she gotten involved in the smuggling and they did away with her?" He rubbed his eyes, and when he dropped his hands, his gaze swung away from hers. "I'll never know the answer to that now."

Laura grasped the lapel of his jacket and forced him to look at her. "I know you would never have been deliberately cruel, Nathaniel."

"I wish I'd been more patient with her." He ran his hand through his hair. "Her taunts brought out the worst in me. She was wild, restless, preferred city life and was never happy here. It was expedient to blame Mallory, I suppose. But if I'd been the kind of husband she wanted…"

"We will find out the truth." She squeezed his arm, aware it was unlikely after all this time. They had reached the lane and the first of the stone cottages. She stopped at the gate. "This was Mallory's cottage, wasn't it? Can we go inside?"

Nathaniel stared at her. "It's empty. I'm about to have it fixed up for Cadan and his family."

"It isn't empty of furniture. I've seen inside. Come and look." They walked up the weed-strewn path. A pile of dead leaves gathered at the front door. The wooden lintel was swollen with damp, and the door creaked as Nathaniel forced it open.

"This needs some carpentry. There's a lot to do to make it habitable."

The narrow hall smelled rank with mold, and cobwebs swung from the ceiling in the draft. Covered in brown cloth, the sofa was still in the tiny parlor. The acrid odor of ashes in the fireplace mingled with the smell of candle smoke. A candlestick sat on the mantel, a matchbox beside it.

Nathaniel squatted before the fire. He stirred the ashes with a stick. "This fire's been recently lit."

Laura rested her hand on his shoulder. "Yes, I can smell it." She wrinkled her nose. "And something else." She turned away with a moue of distaste. "Let's see upstairs."

The low-ceilinged bedchamber was musty, the support beams

thick with dust. Logs and kindling were stacked in the fireplace. Two wine glasses perched on a small table by the bed. The bed was made up with sheets, a blanket and two pillows.

"This is from the abbey," Laura said. "The linens don't appear to be damp. They haven't been on the bed very long. Someone has slept here recently, certainly since Mallory left."

Nathaniel glanced distastefully at the bed. "That pungent odor is the smell of sex. Lovers have used this room."

"This cottage has been used for assignations," Laura said.

"So it would seem."

"It would have to be the staff."

He took her arm. "Let's go. The place unnerves me."

Laura smiled. "You don't approve of your servants enjoying a romantic tryst?"

"What they do on their own time is entirely their business." He slipped an arm around her waist and drew her along with him. "But not here. We must uphold certain standards. Especially now."

They left the cottage, and Nathaniel called the dogs to heel. "I need to know who it is."

"There's sure to be a way we can find out. If someone was to—"

"You will have nothing to do with this."

Laura sighed. "What do you plan to do?"

"What I don't intend to do is leave you alone at night. I'll have someone trustworthy watch this place."

"Who?"

"Ben Teg."

"Ben is the perfect choice. He's been at Wolfram all his life, hasn't he?"

"Yes. He's a good lad."

At dinner that evening, Laura couldn't prevent her gaze from straying to Rudge as she ate her dessert. His impassive manner belied his sharp scrutiny of the servants. He was too self-contained, too much the loner. It was unhealthy. Would he give vent to his repressed feelings in some way? Was it possible he exploded into violence when Amanda spurned him? Anything seemed possible. A strong aversion to the man closed Laura's throat, and she pushed her plate away. Nathaniel seemed convinced Rudge was not capable of such a crime, but she wished the butler gone from their lives. Nathaniel must let him go.

Laura's corset clutched her ribs despite Agnes having laced it loosely. In another few months, she would have to have some new gowns made. Rudge hurried to pull back her chair with his spotless, white-gloved hands. His distinctive pomade smelled heavier tonight, making her stomach clench.

The next morning, Laura came down to find Nathaniel closeted in his study with Ben Teg. Moments later, he followed her into the breakfast room. He smiled at her as Rudge began to serve him.

"What did you learn from Teg? Did something happen last night?" Laura hissed when Rudge left the room.

Nathaniel glanced over his shoulder. "Not here. After breakfast."

She waited impatiently for Nathaniel to finish his ham and eggs. He toyed for an age with his coffee, reading the newspaper.

Laura banged down her cup. She folded her napkin. Moments passed, and she almost burst with curiosity. "I believe your cup is empty, my lord."

He gazed at her with heavy-lidded amusement. "You'll spoil your digestion if you eat so fast."

"Never mind my digestion. Come to the study."

He folded his paper and rose leisurely. "Very well."

Nathaniel shut the study door, and Laura stood waiting, her arms folded.

He leaned back against the desk. "Ben took up his post behind the oak tree in the lane. At midnight or thereabouts, two people entered the cottage."

"Who? Who were they?"

Nathaniel raised his eyebrows. "Old Rudge, for one."

She gasped. "Rudge? Surely not. And who else?"

"Sophie, the barmaid from The Sail and Anchor."

Laura widened her eyes. "No!"

"Yes."

Laura put her hand to her mouth. "I don't believe it."

"They remained until close to dawn."

"Well, I must say I'm shocked." And surprised to find her opinion of the butler as a moody loner mourning Amanda had been wrong.

Nathaniel sighed. "It would be amusing, I grant you, if things at Wolfram were not so dire."

"You will question Rudge?"

He raked both hands through his hair. "I'm afraid I must."

"I wish I could be there."

"Well, you can't."

Laura gathered up her skirts. "Then I shall go and see Cilla."

"Not until I'm free to take you."

"Oh, Nathaniel. We women need to talk freely. Without a man's presence."

He raised his brows. "What on earth about?"

"Women's concerns. It was all right yesterday, was it not?"

"I need to talk to Rudge. As soon as I can, I'll replace him."

Relief flooded through her. "Well, that's the best news I've heard in a while!"

"Teg will escort you. Take the dogs again. Remain with Cilla until I come for you."

"Your wish is my command, sire." She sashayed past him.

Nathaniel spanked her bottom.

Secretly delighted that her husband was unbending a little more each day, Laura spun around with a look of fake shock. "Nathaniel!"

"Then you shouldn't wiggle your hips like that, my dear." He pulled her onto his lap, taking her mouth in a passionate kiss.

Laura's breath caught. Her response to his nearness remained as swift and heated as ever. "After last night, husband, I believe you to be greedy."

Nathaniel laughed and released her. "Off with you then before Rudge finds us making love on this desk."

"As if he can talk." It troubled her though. If it wasn't Rudge who attacked her, then who was it?

CHAPTER TWENTY-NINE

Teg left Laura at the cottage gate. Cilla watched him walk away. "Nathaniel is taking no chances with you, I see. We'll finish today. I'm very pleased with your portrait; I believe it's one of my best."

"That's wonderful." Laura couldn't wait to see it, but she would wait until Cilla was ready to show her. Her mood seemed to have improved since yesterday, and Laura didn't want to stir the waters. She settled into her chair. "How long will you be away?"

Busy with her paints, Cilla frowned. "I don't intend to return to Wolfram."

"Never?"

Cilla blended blue and green with a dab of yellow paint on her palette. "My time here is over. After the exhibition, I'm returning to France."

Laura didn't feel as sorry as she'd thought she would at the news. Cilla's mercurial moods made friendship difficult. "Paris seems the perfect place for you to work."

"And live the kind of life I choose without being frowned upon and treated like a leper." She shrugged. "I'm confident I can put my sad past there behind me. Write a new chapter."

How difficult it must be for Cilla. "You may meet someone who you could love, who will love you."

Cilla halted, brush in the air; she gazed out the window at the scudding clouds. "I don't believe in love."

"You had a lover in Paris once, did you not? Might you rekindle that relationship?"

Cilla began to paint wild brush strokes onto the canvas. "She died." Her voice sounded oddly implacable.

"I'm sorry."

"Are you?" Cilla gazed at her with raised brows. "You would find my problems difficult to understand."

"I do hope you'll find happiness, Cilla." Laura flushed, fearing they were about to enter dangerous territory again. She shifted on her chair, wanting this over so she could return to the abbey.

Cilla became quiet as she worked steadily.

Half an hour passed and Laura found it increasingly difficult to keep still. Cilla wiped her brush. "It's finished."

"It is?" Laura could hardly contain her eagerness and jumped up. "May I see it?"

Cilla stepped back. "Yes. It just needs varnish."

Laura studied it. She understood in a flash how Cilla's moods played out on the canvas. The calm, settled look in the eyes of her subject contrasted greatly with the wildness of the background. She'd placed Laura beneath the loggia in her green gown. Behind her, the cliff seemed fearfully close. She might be about to step off into space. Gulls wheeled across an unsettled sky with thunderclouds gathering over the horizon. There were slashes of violent, thick paint on the background, which might have been done by a different artist from the one who painted Laura so exquisitely: the pearl combs in her burnished hair, her soft, creamy skin tones, the delicate lacework on her collar and cuffs and the coral necklace.

Laura could not hang this work above the fireplace. Not where they would see it every day. It was an extraordinary painting, but it was also disturbing.

"It's a very fine work," Laura said soberly. "You are a talented artist, Cilla."

Cilla unscrewed the lid on a bottle of varnish and painted a section. "I'll have to wait until the paint dries before I apply the rest of the varnish. You think it a good likeness?"

"It's clever; I do see something of myself here."

"I'm rather proud of how well the eyes turned out."

Laura bent closer. "Are my eyes really so green?"

"I would hardly embellish them. You must know they are."

It was like an accusation. Laura straightened. The painting repelled her and made her feel ungrateful. "You've flattered me, Cilla, thank you."

"I merely paint what I see."

Laura watched Cilla clean her brushes. She studied the painting again. Rendered in oils, Laura sat, hands folded, while chaos appeared to rage around her. It was in the threatening sky, the wild trees and the turbulent sea. She was like the calm center of a storm. Laura took a deep breath. She supposed that was how Cilla saw Laura's life.

Cilla screwed the lid back on the bottle. She glanced out the window. "It looks like rain."

"I'd best get the dogs back to the stables. I didn't bring an umbrella."

"I'll lend you one." Cilla went to a cupboard and opened the door. She reached in and pulled out a mannish black umbrella.

Laura saw a flash of blue. She peered closer, then grabbed onto the sofa back as her legs wobbled. A pastel-blue parasol stood in a corner of the cupboard. A dainty thing, so unlike anything Cilla would have bought for herself. It had a pearl handle exactly like the one in Amanda's painting. Laura exhaled a ragged, sharp breath as she recalled the smell in Amanda's room, the memory of which had been gnawing at her. It was the smell of varnish.

Cilla swung around, eyes wide. "You are far too sharp, Laura. You shouldn't meddle."

Laura stepped back. "That can't be Amanda's."

Reaching into the cupboard, Cilla took the parasol out. She twirled it in her hand. "Pretty thing." She opened and closed it. "Oh, I shouldn't have done that." She laughed. "It means bad luck, doesn't it?"

Not wanting to believe what she feared, Laura swallowed a knot of dread. "You found it?"

"I've always had it."

"Then why say it was lost in the sea?"

Cilla dropped the umbrella and went to the table that held her paints. "Now, why do you think?"

Laura's voice sounded raspy to her ears. "You killed her?" She couldn't take it in. "You killed Amanda? I thought you loved her."

Cilla turned, her hazel eyes stony. "You've never loved anyone to the point of madness?"

"I love Nathaniel. I would die for him."

"But if he made love to another woman, would you want to kill him?"

"*No.*" Laura tried to breathe, the air stagnant like heat in her lungs. Her head spun, and she grew fearful she might faint. "I could never kill a living soul."

"*Passionless!*" Cilla's gaze darted around the room.

Laura wanted to bolt from the cottage; she seemed rooted to the spot as she leaned back against the sofa, clutching the rough fabric in her curled fingers. "But why, Cilla?"

"You wouldn't understand what it's like to love and hate in equal measure." Cilla shrugged. "When I told Amanda I loved her, she laughed at me. The way we once laughed at Mallory and Rudge and her other conquests. While I enjoyed participating in her games, I did not like being the subject of them."

"What games?"

"She tested every man she met and had no respect for any of them. When Nathaniel was away in London, she slept with both Rudge and Mallory. She used to compare them. She was out of control. The only man she respected was Nathaniel. She never spoke badly of him. Perhaps she knew I wouldn't have been party to it."

"She must have loved Nathaniel."

"She never loved anyone," Cilla spat. "But Nathaniel is one of the few I trust. I did him a favor killing Amanda. But he cares for you, and I regret hurting him." Cilla shook her head at Laura as if she was a child who couldn't learn her lesson. "I told you, Amanda was incapable of love. But she knew on which side her bread was buttered. Nathaniel wanted a child, so she was prepared to oblige him. And she didn't care whose it was."

Laura edged toward the door where the dogs waited.

"No, you don't!" Cilla leapt forward and grabbed Laura's hair, twisting her fingers in it, scattering combs.

"Let go of me!" Laura winced and tried to pull away. With horror, she saw the small knife Cilla held. She must have snatched it from her paint box. Laura felt the sharp edge at her throat and stilled in fear.

"I'm sorry, Laura. I really like you, but I can't let you live to tell your little tale. You are going to disappear in the same way your predecessor did, my dear. A tidy end, I feel."

Laura's throat blocked. She swallowed desperately. Her heartbeat thudded in her ears. "Let me go. They'll know it was you. Leave Cornwall. I'll say nothing. You can get away."

Cilla hissed in her ear. "Out the back door. I could slit your throat, but it would make a terrible mess, which I won't be able to explain away."

Laura's blood turned to ice. Her fight to stay alive in the sea had weakened her more than she realized. Robbed of her usual strength, Cilla's grip felt like a strong man's. Laura wished she could think, but fear for her baby clouded her mind. Nathaniel! He couldn't go through this again.

"How did Amanda die?" Desperate, Laura tried to distract Cilla as she propelled Laura out the back door of the cottage.

"I asked her to pose nude for me after the baby came." Cilla drew in a sharp breath and tightened her grip on Laura. "She sneered at me. Told me I was lewd. That I fancied women because no man wanted me." She made a guttural sound low in her throat. "I walked with Amanda to the end of the lane; it was almost dusk. She remembered she'd forgotten her parasol, and because she tired easily, I told her to walk on, while I went to fetch it. I was halfway home when I realized both of us couldn't remain at Wolfram. She didn't deserve to live; she had so little regard for me. I stalked her from behind the trees until she walked by the cliff."

Cilla looked at Laura blindly, as if she gazed inward. "She rubbed the small of her back as she stared out to sea."

The tender image of a pregnant woman filled Laura with compassion. Fear for her own baby tore at her heart. "If you tell me she stumbled and fell, we'll say no more about it!"

"Nice try, Laura. Do you think I'm stupid?" Cilla held Laura's long hair in a brutal grip, while she stroked the edge of the knife over Laura's throat, as if it was Amanda's throat laid bare. "Killing her was easy after Simone."

Her hair felt as if it was being ripped from her skull. Laura bit down on a scream and forced herself to sound calm. "Simone?"

"My French lover. She fell to her death down a flight of stairs."

"You killed her too?" Laura's voice choked over the words.

"Simone deserved it." Cilla sounded unmoved by her devastating pronouncement.

Laura had to keep Cilla talking. "Why?"

"She cheated on me with a man."

"Let me go, Cilla. We can talk about this."

Cilla merely tugged harder and dragged Laura off her feet. They moved beneath the loggia. With the sharp edge of the knife nudging her throat, Laura was afraid to fight her. "It was you in Amanda's bedchamber," she gasped. "Dressed as a man."

"Amanda often invited me to her room in the early days. She gave me a key and showed me the secret passage. I wore a man's clothes then too. Amanda thought it was amusing."

"Where is the secret passage?"

"Has Nathaniel not shown you?" She clucked her tongue. "It lies behind the large tapestry in the upper corridor near your bedchamber. Steps lead down to one of the storerooms near the sea door. When Nathaniel was away, I slipped inside often. I couldn't stay away even after all her things were gone."

"Those coral beads were hers."

"She owed me." Cilla pushed Laura along the path toward the

cliff edge. "I doubted anyone would notice a small thing of little value. But you're smart, Laura. Too smart for your own good."

"You wanted something to remember Amanda by. Once she was dead, you had nothing."

Cilla growled like a wounded animal. "Shut up."

"You tried to drown me."

"I didn't plan to kill you," Cilla said, her matter-of-fact tone oddly pitiless. "But you saw me in Amanda's bedchamber."

"It was dark. I didn't know it was you."

"No. When no one came to accuse me after you turned up safe and sound, I knew I was in the clear. You fool! I was going away. I wouldn't have tried to hurt you again. But now I must." She dug the knife in, and a sharp pain stung Laura's throat. Warm blood trickled down her neck beneath her collar. "How *did* you survive the sea? You told me you couldn't swim. I was amazed."

Laura swallowed. "The tide washed me onto the causeway."

"The tide won't help you this time."

"Cilla!" Laura cried. "You won't get away with it. Nathaniel knows I'm here."

"I'll tell him it was an accident. Why would he suspect me? We are friends, and I have a perfect reason to leave Wolfram. I'll be gone in a matter of days."

The sheer drop was only a few feet away. It was now or never. The prick of the knife had brought Laura to life. Cilla would not be dissuaded. She was intent on carrying out her awful threat. At the prospect of a grim death like Amanda's, Laura's determination to stay alive hammered at her. She wanted her baby. She wanted her life with Nathaniel. What would become of him if he lost her too? She gathered the last of her strength and shoved away from Cilla. The effort brought Laura to her knees. Cilla bent over her and struggled to regain her grip.

"Orsino! Sebastian!" Laura yelled.

The dogs bounded around the corner of the cottage. Cilla laughed and shook her head. "Useless animals. Nathaniel chose them for their looks. As he chose his wives."

Looming over Laura, she raised the bloody knife.

With a growl, Sebastian ran at Cilla. The dog leapt up and struck her on the chest. Cilla went reeling. Sebastian showed his teeth, ready to spring again.

"Get away, you stupid animal." Cilla slashed at the dog but missed. The knife flew out of her hand and soared through the air. She stepped back, all her concentration focused on catching it.

Laura watched in horror as the grassy cliff edge gave way beneath Cilla's feet. For one long moment, she teetered there, disbelief registering on her face, her hands grasping at air. Then with a shrill cry, she was gone.

"Oh my God," Laura cried.

Sobbing, she touched the cut on her throat, her fingers coming away sticky. The dogs whined, unsettled by the smell of blood, and milled around her.

"Good dogs!"

Laura climbed shakily to her feet. Pushing her hair out of her eyes, she edged as close as she dared. The white-crested waves pounded the base of the cliff and surged in a cloud of spray, eddying around the jagged rocks. She searched the deep green water for some sign of Cilla, but there was nothing. Worried that the dogs might get too close to the edge, she stumbled away, calling them to heel.

Laura stumbled from Cilla's garden, as the pain at the back of her throat turned to racking sobs. Still disturbed, the dogs danced around her, tripping her up as she lurched along. She fought to compose herself and could only think of Nathaniel. She needed him to hold her close.

Fearing she would faint, it took her ages to reach the house. Nathaniel was with Rudge in his study. He looked up from his desk and paled. She put a hand to her throat and found it drenched with blood. Her collar was soaked.

Nathaniel shoved away from his chair and ran to her. "Rudge, get the doctor and send for the constable."

She gazed into his grim face. "Cilla…"

"Don't talk, Laura." He pulled her into his arms.

CHAPTER THIRTY

After Doctor Owens had assured Nathaniel that Laura was fine, and he'd seen the doctor out, Nathaniel returned to her. There was such relief in his face that her tears blurred her vision. Shadows crept into the room. Beyond the window, dusk had fallen. Laura watched Nathaniel smartly pull the curtains, as if to put an end to the horror. He lit candles around the room and then came to sit on the bed.

"Don't worry so." Laura straightened a lock of his hair as he leaned over her. "You were right, darling. The dogs did protect me."

"Dear God!" He rubbed a hand over his face. "It never occurred to me. I knew Cilla was eccentric, as artists can be, but murder…" His voice shook, his eyes troubled. "She killed Amanda."

"I believe she was quite mad."

Nathaniel looked so exhausted that she caught her breath. "I brought her here, like a cuckoo in the nest, and she repaid me by killing Amanda and the baby." He took a deep, shuddering breath. "She almost killed you. If she had…"

"But she didn't. And it's over."

She had gasped out the whole story as they waited for the doctor. He'd immediately sent Hugh to the police to help organize the retrieval of Cilla's body.

Laura needed to be positive and strong. *For the three of them.* She stroked back his hair. "Darling, the pall hovering over Wolfram has gone. We can look positively toward the future."

He bowed his head, his shoulders shaking.

A wave of fierce protectiveness consumed her. The past would not destroy their happiness. She had the means to right all wrongs. "I asked the doctor not to tell you, but he's confirmed that I'm pregnant, and there's no sign of any damage done."

"Laura!" Nathaniel raised his head, his gray eyes alight with hope.

She smiled. "Yes, my darling."

He searched her eyes. "How much I have wanted this."

"You guessed?"

His grin pulled at her heart. "No. But I did allow myself to hope when you seemed to be eating for two."

"Despite everything, I'm in surprisingly good health. This baby wants to be born."

Nathaniel held her hand in his warm one. "Perhaps the good Lord has taken pity on me."

"So He should. You've suffered enough."

He entwined his fingers with hers and gripped her hand tightly as if she was about to float away. "If Cilla hadn't died, I might have dealt with her myself."

"Hush."

"Oh, I can hate with great ferocity, I've recently discovered." He stroked her hair back from her brow. "As well as love very deeply. But you're right. We must look toward the future."

"While we're discussing the future, there are three things I'd like to address."

He smiled. "Anything, my love."

"Can we have the secret passage in the corridor bricked up? I think I've had enough excitement for a lifetime."

He kissed her palm. "I will have it done immediately."

"I would like to have some say in the choosing of the new butler and the housekeeper."

"Let's make it a mutual decision about the butler, shall we? You may certainly choose the housekeeper. You'll have the house in tiptop order in no time."

"And won't Mother be pleased." Laura chuckled. "She will insist on a visit once she hears I'm increasing."

He arched a dark eyebrow. "You'll invite her?"

"Oh yes. It will give me great pleasure to gain her approval at last."

Nathaniel laughed. "You're a dutiful daughter at heart, Laura."

Laura screwed up her nose. "It seems I am."

He tilted his head. "You mentioned another request?"

Laura gazed into her husband's smiling eyes. "Next time you go to parliament, I wish to go to London with you."

He raised a brow. "Why do I suspect you have a reason?"

"My father writes of the setbacks women fighting for equal rights have suffered. While I don't intend to join Emmeline Pankhurst and her sisters, I'd like to become involved in the movement again."

"Next you'll be wanting a political career."

She studied him. "Would you mind if I did?"

"Do you know, Laura, I don't think I would." He laughed. "I'll even purchase a house in London. We must celebrate." He pulled the cord. "Perhaps not sherry. Would you like some tea?"

"Oh yes, please."

"I need to tell the staff that you're well. Mrs. Madge is very worried."

Alone in her chamber, a fragile light shone into the room. Tonight, Laura was sure it was only moonlight and not some ethereal manifestation dancing along the wall.

But just in case, she said softly, "Rest in peace, Amanda."